"Damn it, C[...]"

Nick said, pain las[...] not going to hurt you."

"You already have."

"Don't you think I know that? If I could change that, I would. But I can't. All I can do is try to make it up to you in any way you'll let me."

"Nothing will change the way I feel about you, Nick. No matter what you do."

"Maybe not, but I'm not leaving until this thing with Joe, Jr., is settled. Whether you like it or not, I'm trying to save the kid's butt."

"Like you saved Joe's?" Cory regretted the words as soon as she said them, but it was too late.

Not even a muscle moved in Nick's face, but his eyes were alive with some savage emotion. "What do you want from me, Cory?" he demanded in a low, seething voice. "Do you want me to eat my gun because I let Joe down? Would that make you happy?"

Dear Reader,

As usual, this month's Silhouette Intimate Moments lineup is a strong one, but there are two books that deserve special mention. First off, Nora Roberts completes her exciting "Calhoun Women" series with *Suzanna's Surrender,* the story of the fourth Calhoun sister and her successful search for love. You won't want to miss this book; Nora Roberts fans all around the world are eagerly collecting this new series from an author whose name is synonymous with the best reading in romance fiction today.

Another author of note is Judith Duncan. Her name may already be familiar to some of you, in which case you know that *A Risk Worth Taking,* her debut for Intimate Moments, promises reading pleasure well beyond the ordinary. For those of you who aren't familiar with her previous work, let me say only that the power of her writing and the depth of the emotions she captures on paper will astound you. This is a book that will haunt your memory long after you've turned the last page.

But I can't let these two special events keep me from drawing your attention to the other two books we're offering this month. Paula Detmer Riggs is an award-winner and a veteran of the bestseller lists, and *Silent Impact* is a perfect example of the deeply emotional style that is her hallmark. And let Marilyn Tracy introduce you to two characters who truly are *Too Good to Forget.* Memory—or the lack of it—can play strange tricks; in this case, those tricks lead to marriage!

In coming months, look for more of your favorite authors— Emilie Richards, Marilyn Pappano, Kathleen Eagle and Heather Graham Pozzessere—to name only a few—writing more of your favorite books.

Enjoy!

Leslie Wainger
Senior Editor and Editorial Coordinator

PAULA DETMER RIGGS

Silent Impact

SILHOUETTE·INTIMATE·MOMENTS®

Published by Silhouette Books   New York

America's Publisher of Contemporary Romance

SILHOUETTE BOOKS
300 East 42nd St., New York, N.Y. 10017

SILENT IMPACT

ISBN: 0-373-07398-4

First Silhouette Books printing September 1991

Printed in the U.S.A.

PAULA DETMER RIGGS

discovers material for her writing in her varied life experiences. During her first five years of marriage to a naval officer, she lived in nineteen different locations on the West Coast, gaining familiarity with places as diverse as San Diego and Seattle. While working at a historical site in San Diego she wrote, directed and narrated fashion shows and became fascinated with the early history of California.

She writes romances because "I think we all need an escape from the high-tech pressures that face us every day, and I believe in happy endings. Isn't that why we keep trying, in spite of all the roadblocks and disappointments along the way?"

For Daddy, with love.

Chapter 1

"Oh my God," Cory Kingston whispered into her silent kitchen. Through the hundred-year-old glass in the back door she saw the wavering silhouette of a large man in the blue uniform of the Ojai Police Department.

Four years ago another policeman in a different uniform had appeared at the door to tell her that her husband, Los Angeles Police Detective Joseph Kingston, had just been killed, three nine-millimeter slugs in his chest.

Her hand shook as she unbolted the door and swung it open. It was a few minutes past six-thirty in the morning, and her three children were still sleeping upstairs.

Cory herself had only just stumbled out of bed. Her flaxen hair was a mass of sleep-tumbled curls, and her eyelids still felt heavy. Behind her, the big white elephant Victorian she loved was eerily silent.

A haze hung over the lawn like a shroud. A cold October wind blew against her face, shivering her skin. She swallowed hard and attempted a polite smile. "May I help you with something, Officer?" she asked.

"Mrs. Kingston? Corinne Kingston?" The officer had cold eyes and a watchful manner. His name tag read T.

Blount. The badge pinned above his heart was very much like Joe's shield, the one that had been buried with him.

"Yes, I'm Corinne Kingston. Is this about the alarm at the Sunshine School? Did the squirrels set it off again?"

"No, ma'am, I'm not here about an alarm." He glanced past her into the kitchen. "Uh, is your husband available, ma'am?"

"My husband is dead. Maybe I can answer your questions?"

Blount shifted uneasily. "Uh, yes, ma'am. I'm looking for Joseph Dominic Kingston. I believe he's your son?"

"Joey? Why on earth would you want to see Joey?"

"Is he here, ma'am?"

"Of course he's here. He's upstairs. Asleep. His alarm won't go off for another half hour." And then he would sneak another five minutes under the covers. Even at sixteen, her first-born, like her, hated mornings.

"Would you wake him up, please?" Under the professional politeness, Cory heard an implied threat. *Cooperate or else, lady.*

Her back straightened, and her stubborn chin rose. The sense of kinship she'd felt for Joe's brother officer disappeared. Between honey-blond lashes, her gray-green eyes began to smolder. "Perhaps you'd better tell me what you want him for first." Her tone was polite, with just a hint of challenge deepening the naturally husky timbre.

The officer's face hardened, and his hesitant manner vanished. "He's wanted for questioning."

"Questioning? About what?"

"An incident at the high school, ma'am. Is he here?"

"What kind of incident?" Cory persisted.

"Breaking and entering, and assault."

Cory drew a violent breath. "*Assault!* On whom?"

"On a John Doe sleeping on the high school grounds. We have reason to believe your son was one of four boys who trashed the principal's office last night before they beat up the old guy."

"Beat up? How badly?" Cory had trouble saying the words. She had trouble even thinking them.

"The kids got lucky. The victim's pretty disoriented, but the doc thinks he'll live. Otherwise, the charge would be murder."

"*Murder?*" Cory groped for the doorknob. This has to be a bad dream, she told herself. It has to be. "Joey's never even been in a fistfight with another kid," she said, her throat suddenly pinching tight.

Blount appeared unimpressed. "Yes, ma'am. Would you show me his room, please?"

Instinct told her to slam the door in the man's face. To protect Joey at all costs. But what good would that do? Blount would only get a search warrant and come back. Besides, it was better to settle this right now or she would drive herself and Joey crazy, worrying.

Quaking inside, she stepped back and indicated that he could enter. Blount lumbered past her, reeking of tobacco and sweat.

Silently she closed the door and tried to gather her wits. When Joe had been alive, she'd been used to large, blunt-faced men gathering in her kitchen. But those men had been friends. This man suspected her son of a terrible crime.

No, she thought. It's not possible. Joey was a good kid. A bit rebellious at the moment, but that was his age. All the books said so.

"I'm sure this can easily be cleared up, Officer. Joey was at the movies last night. He told me all about the picture when he got home. It was one of those gory ones the kids love."

"What time did he get in?" Even as he spoke, Blount was giving the homey kitchen a quick professional sweep.

"A little before ten," she said, her voice stiff and without its usual lilt. "He's very good about keeping his curfew."

"Did you notice anything unusual about him?" Without giving her a chance to answer, he advanced further into the kitchen. His foot hit one of four-year-old Timmy's trucks, sending it skittering across the floor to crash into the pine cabinet.

"Sorry," he muttered. "Got a kid into trucks myself."

Nerves jangling, Cory nodded. The scent of fresh-brewed coffee that filled the kitchen, so enticing a few moments ago, was making her sick.

"Wait here, please. I'll get Joey for you."

"If you don't mind, I'll come with you."

Because it wasn't really a question, Cory didn't bother to answer. Acutely aware of the burly man following two paces behind, she led the way down the hall and up the wide staircase to the second floor landing. There were four rooms opening off the central hall, two on each side. A large bathroom occupied the space at one end.

Joey's room was across from the master suite. His door was closed. *Enter at your own peril* was hand-painted in white on a sheet of red paper cut in the shape of a stop sign.

Cory knocked softly, then eased open the door. "Joey? Wake up, hon—" Her words ended in a gasp of surprise. The bed was still made. The room was empty.

Blount gave the room a quick but thorough search, looking under the bed before opening the closet door. A mishmash of teenage clothing was jammed into the space. The jumbled contents of the shelf above the rod threatened to tumble forward. The floor was covered with a heap of smelly sneakers, scuffed baseball cleats and dirty jeans.

"He's not here." Blount hung an accusation on his words.

Cory went cold. Her face felt frozen. Her body seemed to go numb from the inside out.

"But...but he was sitting right there studying when I kissed him good-night at eleven." She gestured toward the desk under the window. Books and papers were strewn haphazardly over the dusty surface. A half-eaten sandwich rested on an open notebook. A paper cup from a burger joint balanced precariously on the windowsill.

Blount's gaze made another circuit of the room, as though he'd decided he'd missed something. "Can you think of any place he mighta gone to?"

Cory thought about Joey's friends. None of their mothers allowed sleep-overs on school nights. "I can't imagine—wait a minute. The TV! Sometimes he falls asleep watching music videos in the den. I should have thought of that right away.''

She whirled around and was out of the room before the officer could react. Hearing him behind her, she raced down the stairs two at a time, her bare feet slapping the runner, her fingers sliding along the polished rosewood bannister.

When she reached the foyer she turned right, skidding on the hardwood floor. The door to the den was closed. She took a deep breath, then threw it open.

''Joey?'' she called as she rushed into the book-lined room. Silence greeted her. The TV screen was blank. Joey wasn't there.

Cory made it to the worn brown couch and sank onto the sagging cushions before her knees failed her. Her hands were clammy, and her heart seemed to be pushing against her throat.

''Any idea where the kid might go?'' Blount asked from the doorway.

Cory shook her head. Her mouth was suddenly filled with cotton. ''He's never done this before. I don't know where.... Maybe Skip's house.''

Blount drew a small notebook from his back pocket and slipped the stub of a pencil from the coiled binding. Without looking at her, he flipped to a blank page, then said, ''Skip who?''

''Skip Barnhart. He's Joey's best friend.''

''Address?''

''Uh, I don't know exactly. I mean, I've dropped Joey off there a hundred times, but I've never noticed the number. It's at the corner of Via Jacaranda and Palm. Pink stucco. You can't miss it.''

Blount scribbled in his book. ''Anyone else? Relatives? Grandparents.''

''No, not really. We moved here from L.A. four years ago, after my husband's death. The therapist thought it would be better for the children to start over, without a lot of bad memories.''

''How about someone in the city? A former neighbor, a friend of the family?''

In her mind Cory saw a dark, lean face dominated by brooding tobacco brown eyes and an off-center, wickedly seductive grin. Dominic Donatelli, known as Nick to his friends—and he had many—had been Joe's partner and Joey's godfather. He'd also been the best man at her wedding. And her first love.

"No. . . there's no one."

Eyes narrowed, Blount's gaze slid to the desk and a large color photograph of two men in LAPD blue, their arms thrown over each other's shoulders. Both were grinning at the camera.

"One of them your husband?" Cory heard the subtle difference in his voice and saw it in his face. Suddenly she was no longer the enemy.

"Yes, the blonde. This was taken shortly before he and . . . his partner made detective."

Seeing Joe's blue eyes twinkling up at her, she could almost hear his laughter booming in the way she'd loved. Nick's image was slightly blurred, as though he'd moved a split-second before the shutter closed. But then, Nick was always restless, too restless to be tied down to a wife and family. At forty-two, he was still a bachelor.

Blount's face creased in concentration. "Why do I know these guys?"

"Maybe you remember seeing it on the news when my husband was shot? He was with the Hollywood division."

Recognition flickered for a moment in the man's pale irises. His manner warmed slightly. "Yeah, sure. Now I remember. The perp was just a kid, thirteen, fourteen, something like that, and already a junkie."

"He had just turned thirteen."

Joe had died a hero, buried with full honors by the department. The mayor himself had given the eulogy. But that knowledge didn't help her when one of her children woke in the night, crying for the daddy who would never come home again.

"Perp was killed, too, right?"

"Yes. Joe's partner shot him." She inhaled slowly, trying to handle the flood of memories Blount's questions had released. Joe's waxy face looking cold and lifeless in the coffin. The children's crying. Nick's haunted, grief-stricken eyes. The images were burned into her brain like bloody etchings on stone.

She had never hated before. That kind of violent emotion was foreign to the sheltered world of the only daughter of two scholarly professors, but she hated Nick Donatelli with a passion that shook her. Maybe that poor strung-out teenage robber had physically pulled the trigger four years ago, but in every way that mattered, Nick had been the one who'd really killed Joe.

The officer shifted his weight, his gaze sliding from hers to inspect the toes of his heavy shoes. "I'm sorry, ma'am, about your husband," he said when his eyes returned to her upturned face.

Cory acknowledged his awkward sympathy with a smile that felt forced. "Is there anything else, Officer? I don't know why Joey's not here, but I know there's a logical reason. I believe in my son. I know he wouldn't do the things you described, and I intend to prove it."

Blount put away his book, then gave her a sympathetic look. "If your son is innocent, Mrs. Kingston, he's not helping himself by running away. Sooner or later we'll find him, and if he resists arrest, he might get hurt bad."

Cory shuddered. According the Ojai PD, Joey was now a fugitive, no better than a common criminal. The thought made her sick to her stomach. She glanced up to find that Blount had moved closer, his homely face registering concern.

"Mrs. Kingston, are you all right? Is there someone I can call for you?"

"Thank you, but I'm fine," she said with a shaky smile. "I just need some time alone."

"Sure thing, ma'am. I understand."

Head high, she walked with him to the back door and watched until the black and white squad car pulled out of the driveway.

As soon as he was out of sight, she closed the door and slumped against it, her thoughts racing. No matter what, she couldn't let Blount or anyone else take her son to jail. Unspeakable things happened to young men in custody, especially slender blond boys like Joey.

"I can't let that happen," she whispered, beginning to shake. "I have to do something." But what?

Think logically, Cory, she ordered. What would Joe have done?

Get a lawyer. Wasn't that what he said everyone did as soon as a cop showed up at the door? "That's it. I'll call Theo," she muttered with a quick glance at the phone.

Theo Kennedy was the only attorney she knew in Ojai. She'd gone to him for help in setting up her private preschool right after she'd relocated to the area.

Okay, that's the first thing, she thought, forcing steel into her backbone. Call Theo and do what he says. After that, what?

Joey. She had to find Joey before the police did. And then . . . then she would do whatever she had to do to protect her son. Cory bit her lip, her expression becoming fierce. No one was going to hurt her baby ever again. No one.

Detective Sergeant Dominic Donatelli swung his vintage Corvette into the space beneath his beachfront apartment and slid from the leather seat, careful to keep his head still as he slammed the door and headed up the steps. Pain zigzagged through his skull with each step, echoed in his gut by a churning nausea.

The apartment complex was still wrapped in eerie post-dawn silence. The drapes were drawn at every window. Security lights still burned.

Somewhere to the east the sun was shining, but the curving Santa Monica coastline was socked in. Autumn was starting out gloomy and gray, just like his mood.

At least he'd busted the bastard, he thought grimly as he shoved open the wrought iron gate and walked with slow steps across the empty courtyard.

It had taken him three weeks of unpaid overtime and a lot of lost sleep, but a sleaze-bag vice lord and pimp named Ramon Vegas Morena was now locked in a smelly, crowded holding cell in Central Booking, charged with a long list of unsavory felonies, including assault with intent to kill on a policeman.

This time Nick had gotten lucky. The slug from Morena's .357 Magnum had only creased his temple. The sickening throb would stop in a day or two, the police surgeon had assured him. In the meantime, he was on recuperative leave for the next week.

Lord knew, he needed it. His eyes had the bleary look of a man coming off a week-old drunk, and his olive skin was unnaturally pale. As for his temper, it was hair-trigger and unpredictable. Even the watch commander had given him a wide berth when he'd brought Morena in.

Stifling a yawn, Nick collected three days of mail from his box, then headed for his corner apartment. He was in such a fog that he didn't realize someone had called his name until he looked up and saw Herb Newcomb, the *L.A. Tribune* reporter assigned to the police beat, leaning against the wall next to his front door.

They'd met at Joe's funeral. Newcomb had been a cub reporter then, trying to score a promotion. He'd brought his camera, even though the *Tribune* had sent its own photographer.

He'd used a telephoto lens. Nick hadn't seen him. A stark black and white photo of Nick's grief-racked face, tears glistening on his cheeks, had appeared on the front page the next day above the caption, *Hero or Coward? Donatelli Faces Police Review Board in Questionable Death of Partner.*

Nick had been exonerated, but not before he'd endured months of silent scorn from his fellow officers. Since then, Newcomb had carefully kept his distance—until now.

As soon as he caught Nick's eyes, he straightened to his full height, bringing the two men eye to eye. "Hey, man, you look wasted as hell," Newcomb drawled, his linebacker bulk blocking Nick's way. Their eyes clashed, Newcomb's a dissipated gray, Nick's flinty brown.

"You're in my way," Nick said without inflection. Newcomb's eyes narrowed, giving him the look of a bull about to charge. Nick's expression didn't change.

He's bluffing, Newcomb thought, until he saw the empty coldness in those black-as-death pupils. A cold feeling, like a heavy tread on a grave, passed through him. Newcomb took a step backward but managed not to flinch.

"My sources say you took Morena down by yourself this morning—just like in the movies. My sources also say it's a miracle you're not laid out on a slab in the morgue."

Nick flicked a disgusted look at the reporter's phony smile and wondered which one of the guys on the night shift was in Newcomb's pay. If he ever found out, he promised himself, he'd make sure that particular leak was plugged but good.

"You heard wrong."

Nick fished in his pocket for his key. His throat was raw from the cigars he'd smoked and the coffee he'd swigged to keep himself awake during the long night hours waiting for Morena to return home. The last thing he needed was a verbal sparring match with a self-serving reporter.

Newcomb glanced pointedly at the large patch of gauze half-hidden by the tumble of thick black hair over Nick's forehead. "You run into a door, that it?"

"Must have," Nick said with a shrug before fitting his key in the lock. Before he could open the door, Newcomb stopped him with a hand on his forearm.

"Give me an exclusive and I'll make them forget all about what happened with Kingston."

Nerves honed to a razor edge, Nick stared down at the hamlike fingers clutching his arm. "You're about to lose that hand," he said, his gaze flicking from Newcomb's hand to the reporter's face.

Newcomb dropped his hand but held his ground. "See anything of Kingston's widow these days? Corinne, wasn't it? Rumor has it she was your girl before Kingston took her away from you. Classy lady, as I remember, and damn sexy. Probably has half the bird dogs in the department sniffing her trail these days."

Nick's face went deadly still. His big fist grabbed a handful of Newcomb's shirt. With just the strength in his arm and shoulder, Nick jerked the burly man to his toes and held him there.

"Corinne Kingston is off-limits, slick," he ground out in a frigid voice. "One more word and you'll be eating through a straw."

Newcomb's ferret eyes narrowed. "You lay a hand on me and I'll crucify you, Donatelli."

"Try it."

"Don't think I can't. We both know you froze in that liquor store heist. Hung over was the story I heard. Affected your judgment. Or was it your reflexes? Either way, Kingston bought it because of you."

Nick pictured his fist slamming into the man's face. But he would hate himself for hurting a man just because he was right. With a vicious curse, he withdrew his hand, and Newcomb staggered, catching himself with a hand against the wall.

"Write your story, Newcomb. I don't give a damn what anyone thinks about me, especially you."

The reporter's mouth twisted. "Guilt does strange things to a man, doesn't it? Especially a cop with an attitude. Makes him take chances no sane man would take." He shoved his Dodgers cap to the back of his head and leaned against the wall, a smirk on his face. "How many medals have you gotten in the last four years? Three, isn't it? One for each bullet you've taken? But they don't help, do they? You still hurt, don't you, Donatelli?"

Rage still pounding in his head, Nick jerked open the door. "Remember what I said, Newcomb. If I hear you've been talking about Cory Kingston, I'll kill you." He went inside and closed the door, leaving the reporter standing outside.

Seconds later Nick heard the ringing clang of the gate and let his tired shoulders slump against the door. God, would it never end? Four years, and he was still paying.

The hell of it was, much as he hated Newcomb, the man had him pegged dead-on. He *was* trying to prove something—to his fellow officers, to his superiors and, most of all, to himself.

He'd blown it, and Joe had died.

Every damned day since that morning, he'd carried the guilt inside him, eating at him, tormenting him. Sleep could blunt it for a few hours. Playing a fast game of volleyball on the beach sometimes took the edge off for a while, but the guilt was always there, burning like lye in his gut.

He'd known men to eat their gun because of guilt. Others had turned to the bottle or drugs. But not Nick Donatelli. Oh no. Not for him, the coward's way out. Hell no, he'd just buried himself in the job.

It had worked, hadn't it? Sure it had.

Everyone knew that Nick Donatelli closed more rough cases than anyone in the whole damned department. Yeah, he was one tough guy, all right. Didn't he have the scars on his body and the citations in his service jacket to prove it?

No one messed with Nick Donatelli these days. Word on the street said he was a cop with a death wish. And everyone knew a guy like that wasn't afraid of God himself.

With a muttered curse, he pushed himself away from the door. He needed a shower and something to fill his rumbling belly before he headed for bed.

After being shut up for three days, his place reeked of stale air and dust. The three rooms and a bath were dark as a tomb. Stifling a yawn, he started to open the drapes, then froze, his ear cocked toward a muffled cough coming from his bedroom at the end of the hall.

Even as he drew his service revolver from the holster snugged against his left side, his mind was running through the possibilities.

A burglar? Some creep out for revenge? The list of cons who wanted Nick Donatelli dead was a long one.

Eyes narrowed against the gloom, he began moving cautiously along the narrow hall, his back hugging the wall, his Smith & Wesson .38 pointed toward the ceiling.

A few feet from the open bedroom door he stopped, standing statue still, mentally picturing the layout of his bedroom. If the guy had any smarts at all, he would be waiting in the bathroom to the right.

As he took a lungful of air and slowly let it out again, a deadly calm came over him. He went in fast and low, arms extended in proper firing position, his narrowed gaze sweeping the room.

A flash of color to the left caught his eye. His finger tightened on the trigger as he spun toward the movement. *"Don't move!"* he shouted.

The man sprawled across the bed bolted upright, a split second from death. "Don't shoot, Uncle Nick," he pleaded. "It's me. Joey."

Chapter 2

Nick froze, his gun still aimed directly at his godson's chest.

"Joey?" he whispered. But instead of Joey's face, he saw another face, younger, pale eyes crazed above a Saturday night special.

"Uncle Nick? Hey, you're not going to pass out, are you? Uncle Nick?"

Nick's stomach twisted. White noise roared in his ears, and adrenaline flooded his system. Sweat broke out on his forehead. He couldn't breathe.

Time telescoped backward until he was standing in a seedy all-night liquor store in West Hollywood.

He was in front, as usual. But Joe saw the kid's gun first, rising above the counter.

"Watch it, Nicky. He's gonna shoot!"

A beat too late, Nick folded into a crouch and drew. Shots exploded. His. The kid's. So many shots he couldn't count them.

Joe screamed, his hands clawing at his chest, blood pouring from a huge hole. So much blood—on the floor, on his shirt, on Nick's hands as he struggled to staunch the obscene flow.

In the distance Nick heard the wail of a siren and silently urged them to hurry, even as he cursed God and himself, even as he begged God to spare Joe's life.

Joe's hand clutched his arm, his strength nearly gone. "Promise me...take care...Cory...kids. Promise, Nicky." Blood bubbled from his mouth, and his breath was a mere rasp.

Nick had never been so scared. "I promise," he choked out. "But you can't die. I won't let you. You've got a new baby coming, remember?"

"Name...Timothy," Joe managed to gasp out before the severed aorta pumped the last of the blood from his body.

"No! Damn it, no!" Nick shouted, cradling Joe's lifeless body against his. Blood soaked his sweatshirt, his hands, his face, mingling with hot tears of anguish.

"I'm so sorry, partner," he cried brokenly. "God, I'm sorry. It's my fault, all my fault."

Seconds later, when the paramedics came rushing in, they took one look at the suffering in his eyes and were convinced that he, too, had received a mortal wound.

"Uncle Nick? Should I call someone? I didn't mean to scare you."

Gradually, his focus changing from blurred to razor-sharp, Nick became aware of the boy on the bed. Terror had frozen his too-pale features into a mask. His green eyes were fixed on the barrel of Nick's .38.

Nick drew a long breath, exhaling slowly, cleansing his lungs. Gradually the shaking stopped, and the images faded. Still raw inside, he holstered his weapon and wiped the dampness from his face with icy fingers. It had been months since he'd had a flashback like that one. God help him, he didn't want another one soon.

"For God's sake, Joey," he ground out when he could make his throat work again. "How the hell did you get in here?"

The shock slowly ebbed from the boy's eyes. Splotchy color returned to his face. "I told the manager you were expecting me, and she let me in. I fell asleep, waiting for you."

Nick shrugged out of his jacket and tossed it on the bed. In the way of all experienced investigators, he sized up the boy without seeming to. Scared, he thought. And something else. Defiant, perhaps. But why?

Four years had passed since he'd seen the kid. He was more man than boy now, with his father's wide shoulders and long legs. But the torn jeans and sloppy T-shirt reminded Nick of the rambunctious kid who used to pester him for horseback rides whenever he'd stopped by the Kingston house at the end of watch. But Joey was no longer a boy, and Nick was no longer welcome in Cory's house.

"Just like that?" he asked. "She didn't ask for an ID?"

"Oh, well, yeah, sure," Joey said in a tumble of words. "I mean, at first she was real careful, you know, asking me for my name and my ID and all, but as soon as she saw that old picture of... of me and you and Mom and Dad I keep in my wallet, she got real friendly like. She's a neat old lady."

"That *neat old lady* nearly got you killed."

Joey dropped his gaze to the rumpled bedspread. "I guess it was dumb, not lettin' you know I was comin', but I was afraid you would tell me not to."

"Why would I do that?"

The boy shrugged. "You know, 'cause of Dad and all," he mumbled, his pale, tired face turning pink to his ragged hairline.

He had inherited his mother's hair, thick and glossy and the color of champagne. But Cory's hair was always smooth and perfectly groomed. Joey's looked unkempt and dirty. The skull and crossbones earring didn't help, either, Nick realized, and then wondered what Cory thought of her son's new image.

"Does your mother know where you are?"

Joey's face closed up. "Not exactly."

"Yes or no?"

"No."

"Damn it, Joey. You know better than that."

Nick walked to the phone by the bed and lifted the receiver. "What's the number?"

"Don't call Mom, Uncle Nick," Joey begged in a ragged voice. "Not yet."

"Why not?"

Joey's shoulders slumped. "I'm in bad trouble." His voice cracked into silence, and his Adam's apple bobbed three times before he could find his voice again. "Mom... Mom will kill me when she finds out."

A problem at school, Nick decided, replacing the receiver. A prank of some kind. Or truancy.

He knew all about that kind of trouble. When he'd been Joey's age, they'd called him a hood. The so-called good kids had shunned him. The jocks had been scared to cross him. His teachers, too.

His old man had used a belt on him when he'd ditched school, for all the good it had done. His teachers considered it a miracle that he'd got his diploma. Some considered it a miracle he'd still been alive to graduate.

"What kind of trouble, son?" he asked, forcing himself to concentrate.

Joey lowered his gaze and stared down at the floor, seemingly fascinated by the pattern on the carpet that he was tracing with the scuffed toe of his sneaker.

"There's these guys from school, see, and they asked me to go to the movies with 'em last night. Only, 'stead of that, they ended up at the school with this bottle of booze one of 'em boosted from his dad's liquor cabinet." He stopped and looked up at Nick, a muscle in his cheek spasming.

"You got wasted?"

"Yeah, did we ever!" Joey grinned. Nick didn't.

"What happened?" Afraid he would pass out if he sat down, Nick leaned against the wall and tried to ignore the exhaustion hammering at his brain.

Joey cleared his throat, then continued, his voice taking on a defensive edge. "One of the guys had this idea to have some fun. You know, spray things on the wall by the principal's office, dumb juvenile stuff like that."

Nick raised his eyebrows. Even that small movement hurt, reminding him that a high-velocity slug had plowed a long slice in his skin.

The adrenaline rush was fading, leaving him drained and short-tempered. He needed a hot bath and cool sheets. He wanted a drink.

"Only you got caught? Is that it?"

Joey began to prowl the room, eyes taking in the sparse furnishings and bachelor clutter. When he saw an old soft-ball mitt lying on top of a jumble of sweats and skivvies on the room's only chair, he stopped to run his fingers over the oiled leather. For an instant Nick thought the kid was going to cry.

"Joey?"

"How's the team doing without Dad?" the boy asked in a muffled voice, his fingers stroking the glove.

"Not so good." Nick felt the back of his neck tighten. Instinct told him he wasn't going to like the rest of Joey's story.

"Mom says I'm a natural athlete, just like him."

"He was good."

"But you're better. Even Mom says so. Or she used to, anyway."

Joey angled a look in Nick's direction. "She'll be furious because I came here. She said you're not our uncle any-more and not to call you that."

Nick bit down so hard the pain in his head exploded into agony. Son of a bitch, he didn't need this right now.

"Guess we ought to talk about that sometime."

"Guess so, but not now, okay?"

Silence settled like the morning mist. The neighborhood was beginning to stir. In an hour the streets would be clogged with beach traffic, and the beach itself would be bustling with tourists, people he didn't know, people who didn't give a damn about a lonely cop who prowled the beach at all hours because he couldn't sleep.

Fighting a need to lash out, at himself, at Fate, at this kid's mother, he leaned against the windowsill and con-fronted the boy head-on.

"Lay it out for me, Joey. What's got you so scared?"

Joey gnawed on his lip before saying in a subdued tone, "Promise you won't tell Mom."

"No promises. Talk."

Looking slightly green, Joey began to do just that. "There was this guy sleeping under the bleachers on the football field. We musta woke him up, 'cause he comes charging out at us, yelling crazy things, swinging this broken wine bottle. Toby...uh, hit him. In self-defense, I swear it."

Nick looked down at his boots. There was a splotch of blood on one toe. His blood, this time. He shuddered, his gut twisting. Sweat broke out on his palms, and he wiped them on his jeans.

"Is the man dead?" he asked, keeping his gaze on Joey's face.

Panic leaped in the boy's eyes. "I don't know," he said in a low voice. "We got the hell outta there, but someone musta called the cops, 'cause we saw patrol cars and an ambulance when we cruised by a few minutes later. You know, to check things out and all." He fell silent, his gaze darting around the room as though searching for an escape.

It's not that easy, kid, Nick thought. You can run, but the memories go with you. "Have you talked to any of the other guys since last night?"

Joey shook his head. "As soon as Mom was asleep, I cut out and snagged the first ride I tried for." He stared out the window for a long, silent moment, then said raggedly, "I never want to see those guys again, Uncle Nick. I swear!"

Nick dragged in a lungful of air, expelling it slowly. "You got one thing figured, Joey. From what you've told me, I'd say you're definitely in trouble. The thing is, what are you going to do about it?"

Joey whipped his head toward Nick. "Me? What can I do?"

"Tell your mother the truth, for one thing."

Joey shook his head. "Huh-uh. No way. She'll ground me for the rest of my life."

"So you intend to lie to her?"

Joey looked startled. "Well, no, not exactly."

"What *do* you intend to do?"

"Uh, I thought I could just hang out here for a while. You know, sort of veg with you until everything blows over—if that's okay with you."

Letting Joey see his irritation, he said sternly, "Assault and battery doesn't blow over. If that old guy dies, you and your drinking buddies could be tried as adults. Public opinion is forcing prosecutors to clamp down on gang violence these days."

Joey's expression turned sullen. "It was just for fun. You know, like that time you stole some rich old guy's Cadillac when you were fourteen."

Nick felt heat rise to his face. "How'd you know about that?" he asked sharply.

Joey hesitated, then said in a low voice, "I heard Mom and Dad arguing something terrible one night about you, about the chances you took. She said you were going to get him and you both killed one day, all because you had this big chip on your shoulder on account of your past." He eyed Nick cautiously. When Nick remained silent, he continued. "So I asked Dad, and he told me."

Nick scowled. Knowing Joe, he must have had a good reason for breaking a confidence, but Nick sure as hell didn't know what it could have been.

"Did your Dad also tell you I spent a year in reform school because of that little escapade?" he asked in a clear, cold voice.

Joey's hopeful look faded. "No."

"Well, I did. And I'm not proud of it."

Joey looked curious. "Dad said you were running with this gang in East L.A. before you went into the Army and got sent to Nam, but 'cause of the killing and all, you got your priorities straightened out, and that's why you were a good cop."

He'd had his priorities straightened out, all right, but it wasn't the war that had done it. At least, not directly. After his third arrest the judge had given him a choice. Enlist, or do another stretch inside. And this time, because he'd turned eighteen, it would be in the state prison.

A year later, a battle-hardened veteran at nineteen, he'd come home with a chest covered with ribbons, and the judge had sealed his criminal record. Outside of his family, only Joe and Cory knew the truth about his past. And now Joey.

"Is that why you came to me? Because you thought I would understand?"

Joey nodded. "I knew Mom would make me go to the police and tell on my friends."

"What did you think I'd do?"

Joey fidgeted, but his eyes remained defiant. "I know the way things work. All you have to do is call someone in Ojai and ask 'em to forget about me. You always said, cops take care of their own."

"Not by breaking the law they don't."

Nick noticed the dark circles under Joey's eyes. Cory's eyes. Even now, he sometimes jerked awake in the night, haunted by those eyes.

He crossed to the closet and shoved it open. Moving stiffly because of the throbbing in his head, he tugged his shirt over his head and tossed it into the corner. The sudden movement sent dizziness shooting through him, and he slammed his hand against the wall to keep from going down.

"Uncle Nick? God, you look like you're going to puke."

Nick thought that was the least of his worries. "Stand back. I just might."

Joey laughed nervously. "What happened to your head? Did you get yourself into another fight in a bar?"

Even the kid knew about his reputation. "No."

He snatched a shirt from a hanger, then rummaged in his dresser for socks and underwear.

"Are you going somewhere?" the boy asked, watching him and looking more and more concerned.

"Yeah, to take a shower."

"Now?"

"Yeah, now. I haven't been out of these clothes for three days. My head hurts, and I'm not real pleased with you, son, so don't give me any trouble."

"Maybe I should go," Joey grumbled, his gaze darting to the door.

"Go where?"

Joey shrugged one shoulder. "Don't know."

Nick reached out and pulled him into a clumsy hug. "Stay. We'll talk."

"I guess." Joey didn't look happy at the prospect of more talk.

"You hungry?" Nick asked as an afterthought.

Joey nodded, a half-grown kid trying not to show how scared he was.

"All I got is leftover pizza. Probably green by now, though."

"Pepperoni?"

"What else?"

"Killer!" Relief lightened the boy's expression until he looked younger than his years.

Nick remembered the countless nights in the past when he'd shown up on Joe and Cory's doorstep, laden with pizza and his own six-pack of beer.

Joey and Jennifer had invariably talked him into a game of Monopoly. Just as invariably, because she'd been afraid he would kill himself on the freeway going home, Cory had bullied him into spending the night on the couch.

If he'd fallen asleep thinking about the times he'd made love with her when she'd been his girl instead of Joe's wife, no one knew it. And no one ever would.

During the past few years he hadn't allowed himself to think about those nights. He hadn't allowed himself to think about a lot of things. It was the only way he'd been able to face himself in the mirror every morning.

Suddenly bone-tired, Nick pointed the boy in the direction of the kitchen. "Help yourself to whatever you can scrounge," he said before he walked into the bathroom and closed the door.

Now what? Nick thought wearily as he turned on the tap and splashed cold water on his face with both hands. His cheeks stung, reminding him of the last time he'd seen Cory Kingston.

It had been a bleak day in February. The sky had been gray, the wind cold—a perfect day for a funeral.

Cory had been nine months pregnant and deathly pale. No one had been able to convince her to rest. Instead she had devoted herself to the mourners, trying to lessen the pain for Joe's friends and grieving colleagues.

Nick had been one of the pallbearers, along with four other fellow officers and twelve-year-old Joey, looking scared and uncomfortable in a new blue suit.

Joe's casket had just slid into the ground, leaving a hush over the hundreds of mourners, when he'd gone to her. With the swell of Joe's unborn child between them, he'd tried to express his grief.

Cold as a stranger, she'd looked at him with naked hatred shimmering like tears in her exotic cat's eyes. "I'll never forgive you, Nick," she'd said with a sob rending her voice. "As far as I'm concerned, you're as dead as my husband. Don't ever come around me or my children again, or I swear I'll use Joe's gun on you."

Her hand had caught him squarely on the jaw. The sound had carried over the hushed assemblage like the crack of a rifle, drawing the shocked attention of friends and strangers, people he respected, people who had once respected him.

He'd walked away then, the mark of her hand on his face like a brand. To this day he couldn't remember ever hurting as much as he'd hurt at that moment.

Nick closed his eyes on a spasm of pain. No one had swung on him since he'd learned how to defend himself at the age of twelve. No one but Cory had ever dared to risk his explosive temper. But he hadn't felt rage that raw winter morning. Only grief and remorse.

Newcomb's camera had captured his tears. But no one would ever see the raw agony he still carried in his gut.

Feeling old as death, Nick jerked aside the plastic curtain and turned on the shower full blast. Scalding water pounded into the tub, filling the small space with steam.

He stripped down quickly and stepped into the spray. The hot water was needle sharp against his sleep-starved muscles, but no matter how hot the water or how long he let it beat against him, he still felt dirty inside.

* * *

Cory dropped the receiver onto the hook and stared through the window at the towering eucalyptus in her backyard, her thoughts as bleak as the morning overcast.

Where is he? she thought with a fear approaching panic. Hours. He must have been gone for hours. He could be anywhere. Alone. Scared. Hurt. Maybe even dying.

She shivered, huddling deeper into her robe. It was nearly eight. Since Blount's departure, she'd made one phone call after another to Joey's friends, asking question after question. But no one had seen him. No one knew where he might have gone.

Dear God, don't let him be hurt, she prayed silently, covering her face with her hands. I promise I won't complain about those disgusting clothes he wears, or even about that awful earring, if you just bring him home.

"Momma, are you crying?"

Cory looked up to see Timmy standing next to the desk, a well-loved panda clutched tightly in the crook of his chubby arm. Blue-eyed and sturdy, he was more like the father he would never know than either Joey or Jennifer, her middle child.

Cory felt a rush of love. Born the night of Joe's funeral, Timmy was sweet-tempered and affectionate, her snugglebunny. He was the last gift Joe had given her—and the most precious.

"It's okay, sweetie," she said past the lump in her throat. "Sometimes Mommies cry, too."

Timmy padded across the rug and climbed into her lap. His silky hair stood up in tufts, and his cheeks were rosy. He smelled of soap and milk.

After she'd left a message with Theo's service, she'd called Mai Bui, her fellow teacher at the Sunshine School, to explain why she wouldn't be in until later, if at all. She'd kept Timmy home, as well, which was why he was still dressed in his Sesame Street pajamas and Big Bird slippers.

"Pandy needs a kiss, too," Timmy informed her solemnly, holding up the bedraggled bear.

It seemed like yesterday when Joey, too, had been small enough to cuddle in her lap. Now he was a head taller than her and considered his mother's hugs and kisses an embarrassment. Fighting a fresh rush of tears, Cory planted a kiss on the bear's threadbare head.

"Is it Sesame Street time?" the little boy asked after he'd settled Pandy comfortably in his lap.

"Not yet, darling." Cory glanced at her watch. "Momma will turn on the TV in a minute."

"'Kay," he said, snuggling against her breasts.

Cory hugged him tight, her heart thudding painfully. Most days she did just fine being mother and father to the kids. Sure, dealing with Joey's adolescent hormones had been a bit of a strain, especially when she'd found those awful pornographic magazines stuffed under his mattress.

And, yes, suffering through Timmy's endless bouts of colic during those first months alone had had her in tears most of the time. Because her children needed her, however, she'd found the strength to face each day. Little by little it had gotten easier.

Her school was the most successful in town, with a long waiting list. Joe's insurance had bought this house free and clear. The children were growing like weeds. She could even see herself marrying again—someday.

The bad times were behind her. Things were fine now. Or so she'd thought—until Blount had pounded on her door.

We'll get through this, she told herself, hugging Timmy closer. If she just stayed calm, everything would work out. Except that calm wasn't something she did well. That was Joe's department.

"My cute little volcano," he used to tease when her cheeks got pink and her eyes began to smolder. Only he wasn't here to tease her now. And he wasn't here to tell her what to do. No one was.

If anything ever happens to me, Nick will take care of you. He loves you almost as much as I do.

Love?

Cory felt her mouth pull into a cynical scowl against Timmy's silky hair. Joe had been such a good man, a decent man, almost as loyal to his partner as he'd been to her. So loyal that he'd had a blind spot when it had come to Nick. But then, so had she—once.

She'd been nineteen and still in college when they'd met. At twenty-two, a decorated Army veteran and already a cop, Nick had been bronzed by the sun, sinewy and strong, a lusty male animal in his prime. In his uniform, with his strong Italian features and strapping build, he had reminded her of a Roman legionnaire incarnate, a proud, honorable man willing to die for those who had neither his strength nor his courage. And when he'd smiled that sweet-sad, off-center smile, she'd wanted nothing more than to be his girl.

But ultimately, as the first blush of sexual passion had tempered into something deeper and richer, she had longed to see that same smile in miniature on the face of their child. A nester by nature, she had begun to spin a dream of marriage and a home of their own. And why not?

The handsome rookie cop was all that a woman could want, fun-loving, charming, and adorable. His kisses made her weak. His lovemaking was addictive, but gradually she'd come to realize that Nick Donatelli had a pathological fear of commitment.

He'd moved three times in the eleven months she'd known him because he hated coming home to the same place night after night. He changed cars for the same reason—boredom. He never wanted to do the same thing twice, never wanted to stay in one place, other than in bed with her, for more than a few hours at a stretch.

Why he was the way he was, she never knew. He had never talked much about his past. He'd grown up in L.A., flirted with juvenile delinquency before a kindly judge had set him straight, and had one brother, also on the force.

Bits and pieces of information here and there had given her a picture of an unhappy, unstable childhood turned into a battlefield by angry, vindictive parents who never should have had children.

Pathetically naive, Cory had been convinced that she could heal those wounds by giving him a warm, loving place to come home to every night.

To her shock, she'd discovered that Nick's dreams of the future were vastly different. He wanted the good times to go on and on—cookouts at the beach, beer and pizza parties on

Friday nights, skiing in the winter, scuba diving in the summer. Instead of saving for a house, he'd wanted a trip to Mazatlan for the sun and tequila. Instead of babies to love and cherish, he'd wanted endless weekends of sex and fun.

If he was hurting, he partied to forget. If he was happy, he partied harder. If she was unhappy, he tried to comfort her with his body instead of his understanding and his love.

Introspective and sensitive by nature, she'd needed him to share his feelings and thoughts and hopes, not just his laughter and teasing and passion. She had been so sure that he loved her enough to change.

Finally, worn out working two jobs and carrying a full course load, she'd proposed to him. She loved him, she'd told him, and although he hadn't come right out and said the words, she knew that he loved her. They would marry, pool their finances, get settled before starting a family.

No babies, Nick had declared emphatically. And no wedding. He wasn't the marrying kind. No one put chains on Nick Donatelli, not even her.

She'd been heartbroken. Joe had been there for her then. Homely and awkward and unsure of his own masculine appeal, he'd been the antithesis of his reckless partner, gentle where Nick had been rough-edged and hard, understanding where Nick had been impatient, stable where Nick had been mercurial. Most of all, he had been undemanding, offering friendship instead of seduction.

It had taken her a long time to heal, but Joe's devotion had helped her see that Nick was incapable of loving anyone, even if he had wanted to. In the end, she'd fallen in love with Joe, and never once in sixteen years had she regretted marrying him. During the last four years, however, there hadn't been a day when she hadn't regretted meeting Nick Donatelli.

Rousing herself, she lifted Timmy from her lap and rose. "Time for Sesame Street," she said brightly, settling him onto the floor in front of the TV.

"Can I have juice, like in school?" Timmy asked amiably after she'd turned on the set and adjusted the volume.

"In a minute, darling, okay? After Momma gets dressed."

"'Kay."

After that, she would take Timmy to school, then drive up and down every street in town until she found Joey. He had to be someplace close. He didn't have much money, and—

The back door slammed so hard it seemed to rattle the window panes in the den. "Mom? You here?" Joey's voice called from the kitchen.

Relief came in a rush, leaving her wanting to laugh and cry at the same time. "I'll be right there," she shouted hoarsely. "Don't you dare move."

Muttering a hasty prayer for calm, she hurried down the wide hall, her robe swirling around her bare legs.

Joey was standing by the kitchen table, his shoulders hunched into the worn denim jacket that seemed to have gotten too small overnight. There were circles under his eyes, and lines in his too-pale face. He tried to smile when he saw her, but he couldn't quite manage it.

"Are you all right?" she demanded in a rush. "You're not hurt?"

Joey shook his head, his guilty expression reminding her of the mischievous little scamp who'd been able to twist her around his chubby little finger with one crooked smile.

As soon as she realized he was safe, she felt a rush of anger. "Where have you *been* all night?" she demanded in a frazzled tone. "I must have called every kid in the eleventh grade, and no one had seen you since you left the movies last night."

Joey's gaze didn't quite meet hers. "Don't be upset, okay, Mom?"

Cory's breath escaped in a whoosh. "Are you kidding, Joseph? Of course I'm upset! What mother wouldn't be when she finds a policeman on her doorstep at the crack of dawn and her son nowhere in sight?"

At the mention of the law, Joey's face flushed. "Things just got too heavy all of a sudden," he muttered. "I needed to talk to someone who wouldn't yell at me."

Cory's chin came up, and her eyes narrowed ominously. "And who was that?"

Joey's gaze slid to the left. Hers followed, to widen in disbelief at the image of a man just closing the door behind him.

Shock took over. For an instant the distraught mother vanished. She was simply a woman made vulnerable by surprise. Her chest was so tight it hurt to breathe. Her heart seemed determined to escape her rib cage, so violently was it pounding.

"Nick," she whispered. He was wearing his usual working uniform, tight jeans with the cuffs fraying over worn-down boots, a faded blue sweatshirt with a torn neck, and an old leather bomber jacket that should have been thrown away years ago.

Everything about him suggested a man who lived on the edge—the tense, almost belligerent stance that hinted at tightly coiled energy barely restrained, the arrogant jut of his jaw, the chilling stillness in his midnight pupils.

"Hello, Cory." His voice seemed deeper, quieter, almost sad.

Hearing him, seeing him again after so long, hurt. But even though she felt as though she were strangling, she was determined to maintain control. "I told you never to come here," she said without even a pretense of civility.

"I remember," he said quietly, his mouth taking on a stiff slant that told her he remembered more than her words. "There didn't seem to be another way to get Joey home."

"Is that where Joey's been all night? At your place?"

"So he tells me."

"Don't you know?"

"I wasn't there."

Cory felt her face flame. Of course he wasn't. His apartment wasn't a home, merely a place to shower, change clothes, and grab a quick nap between parties.

"Why didn't you call?" She couldn't keep the bitterness out of her voice.

"I tried. Your line was busy."

Cory refused to acknowledge the shimmer of apology in his eyes. "Not all night."

"I pulled stakeout duty. Didn't get back until dawn."

I'll bet, she thought, eying the patch of adhesive on his forehead. More like a brawl in a bar.

"Thank you for bringing him home," she said with the same polite nod she reserved for door-to-door salesmen. "I'm sure you have things to do, so we won't keep you."

To her alarm, instead of turning to leave, Nick moved toward her, his stride controlled, like a man who had no need to broadcast his power. When he was close enough to touch her, he stopped.

Inexplicably, Cory felt a rush of panic. Only force of will kept her from taking a step backward, out of reach of those powerful arms.

"It's not that easy, Cory," he said in a deceptively gentle tone that sent shivers sliding down her spine. "I'm taking Joey in. He's under arrest."

Chapter 3

"Is this a joke?" Cory challenged, her voice sharp. "Because, if it is, it isn't funny."

Nick took a deep breath and forced himself to keep his gaze steady on hers. There was no warmth in her face, not even a hint of welcome. He was furious with himself for searching for it.

"You know me better than that, Cory. I never joke about my job."

"Yes, I know you all right. I wish I didn't."

Nick's jaw inched upward, only a fraction, but Cory recognized the sign. He always led with his jaw when he was angry.

"Careful, Cory," he warned. "Whether you know it or not, you need me."

"Oh, no, I don't, Nick. I would never let myself depend on a man like you."

He went absolutely still. "And what kind of man am I?" His voice was dangerously low.

"Irresponsible," she shot back. "You were hung over that morning, and Joe died because of it."

Nick felt her anger and made himself accept it. "I've never denied that."

But he had. Hadn't he? Of course he had. "Then why did the board exonerate you?"

"Ask them."

"I don't have to. I know why. You have a brother who's going to be chief someday."

The quicksilver flash in his eyes warned her that she'd gone too far. Joe had told her once that she never wanted to know the man Nick became when his temper was unleashed.

"I'll give you that one, because you're upset," he said. "Just don't push me. I'm not in the mood."

Cory refused to acknowledge the steely thread of warning in his deep voice. "Get out of my house," she ordered, pointing her small square chin toward the door.

"If I go, Joey goes with me."

"Just try and take him, Nick. I still have Joe's pistol, and I know how to use it."

"Mom!" Joey exclaimed, his features growing slack with shock.

With a rush of chagrin, Cory realized that she had forgotten her son was there. Turning to him, she said in a grim voice, "This is between me and Uncle Nick."

Joey's gaze swung from her to Nick. "Don't be mad, okay? She . . . says things she doesn't mean when she gets upset."

"Yeah, I know. I've gotten used to it." Amusement threaded Nick's voice, but his eyes didn't smile.

She refused to let herself feel remorse for her sharp words. Nick was the reason why Joe wasn't standing here now. Nick was the reason why her children had cried themselves to sleep for months after Joe died, the reason why Timmy was growing up without a father.

But she did feel a twinge of regret that Joey had glimpsed her anger. Later, when things calmed down, she would deal with that. Right now she had more immediate concerns.

She took a slow breath, reminding herself to stay calm no matter what happened. She could fall apart later. "Is Nick telling the truth, Joey? Are you under arrest?"

"Uh, yeah, I sorta gave myself up to him," Joey mumbled, his gaze fixed on the floor.

"Why?"

"'Cause he said Dad never ran away from anything and I shouldn't, either." Her son still refused to look at her.

"Is it true? Did you and your friends...beat up an old man last night? Is that why you ran away?"

As his head jerked up, the color left Joey's face, leaving it ashen. "No! I swear I didn't touch him!"

Cory drew a careful breath. She wanted to believe her son, but she had to be sure. "But you were there?" she asked, hoping against hope that Blount had been mistaken. When Joey nodded, her heart sank.

"It wasn't my fault, I swear, Mom. I thought we were going to the movies, just like I told you."

"Why did you run away, Joey? Why didn't you come to me and tell me what happened?"

"You would just have yelled, like always."

Cory started to deny his accusations, then remembered the heated discussions they'd had recently. About his grades. About his friends. Lately the house had begun to resemble an armed camp, with Joey on one side and the rest of the family on the other.

"You're right," she said with a sigh. "But it's not because I don't love you, Joey. You know that, don't you?"

"I guess," he mumbled, his gaze once again riveted on his sneakers.

Although she wasn't looking at Nick, she was acutely aware of his dark gaze fixed on her face. Inside, she felt a sudden tension forming, the same tension she always felt when Nick was near. Ignoring it, she plastered a reassuring smile on her face and said calmly, "Honey, your brother is in the den, watching TV. I need you to get him dressed, please, while I talk with Uncle Nick."

Instead of obeying as she expected, Joey directed a questioning look toward Nick. "Is it okay?"

"Go ahead," Nick said quietly, bringing a quick look of frustration to shimmer in Cory's eyes. "And then get yourself cleaned up. We'll leave in thirty minutes."

Joey looked resigned. "If you say so."

"I say so."

Joey headed for the hall, but a quiet command from Nick stopped him. "Be sure to wash that stuff out of your hair, and forget the earring."

Joey's expression turned mutinous. "Aw, Uncle Nick—"

"I mean it, Joe. And put on some halfway decent clothes. You look like sh—like a punk in that getup."

Joey's gaze jerked to his mother, red spreading over his face until even his ears were flushed. "I guess you're finally happy," he muttered.

Before she could answer, he spun away and loped out of the kitchen. Less than a second later, she heard Timmy's squeal of delight, followed by the thunder of footsteps on the stairs. Upstairs, a door slammed.

Cory rounded on Nick angrily, her eyes a vivid emerald with anger. "You hurt his feelings!"

"Better to hurt his feelings than have the booking officer peg him as a potential troublemaker."

Cory's pulse began slamming in her throat. "Booking officer?" she exclaimed in disbelief. "But . . . but the officer who came this morning said he was just wanted for questioning."

"When the detective handling the case found out Joey had skipped, he issued an arrest warrant."

"Arrest . . . *but he's not a criminal.* He shouldn't be treated like one, especially . . . especially not by his godfather."

"I didn't have a choice, Cory. I couldn't just forget I was a cop."

"Why not?"

"Would Joe have forgotten?" he shot back, his voice taking on an edge.

"He would have believed in his son."

Nick saw the obstinate tilt to her chin and knew she was beyond logic when it came to her child. But he made himself try. "Peer pressure is damned powerful, Cory, especially at Joey's age."

"Joe and I taught him to make his own choices."

Nick remembered making his own choices, too—the wrong ones. And he'd paid for the choices he'd made. Then, and now.

"He could have walked away," he said in a deliberately mild tone.

Cory had no answer for that. Still shaken by the emotions fighting inside her, she turned her back to him and moved to the counter. She needed time to think, to plan.

The coffee in the pot smelled burned, but it was still hot. Knowing that Nick was watching her, she took her time pouring herself a cup.

"Got any more of that?" he asked when she turned to face him, his gaze flickering to the mug she held against the knot of her sash.

"No," she said. Both could see that the pot was almost half full.

She's changed, he thought. Gotten stronger, more sure of herself. But her feelings for him seemed even more antagonistic than ever. The small hope he'd nurtured on the drive north withered and died.

"You're not going to make this easy, are you?" he asked, biting off his words the way he sometimes did when his emotions threatened to override his control.

"Look around, Nick. Survivor's benefits bought this house. It's a nice house, but I'd rather have my husband here. Maybe you've forgotten why he isn't, but I haven't."

He looked down at the floor, his jaw tight. "I haven't forgotten."

Cory warned herself not to trust the quiet note of humility in his voice. Nick Donatelli had never humbled himself before anyone. He never would.

Because the cup was in her hand, she made herself take a few sips of coffee. It was as bitter as her hatred. "I've left a message for my attorney. He and I will take Joey in as soon as he gets here."

Nick's head came up, and she saw that his face had been wiped clean of emotion. "I'm taking him in. I gave my word."

Cory knew that Nick always kept his word. In fact, in nearly every way but one, he was as solid and dependable as Joe had been. Unlike Joe, however, he was flawed. Because of that, she and her children were paying the price.

Damn him, she thought. And yet, he was right. She did need him. He knew about police procedures, booking officers, warrants. She didn't.

Careful to keep her robe from gaping open, she pulled out a chair and sat down. It was easier, somehow, having the expanse of the table between them.

"When you called about Joey, did Blount say... how is the man who was hurt?"

Nick hesitated, then pulled out the chair opposite hers and sat down. Over the years he and Cory had been together hundreds of times, but ever since their breakup, Joe and the kids had always been there, too—until that day eighteen months ago when he had been flat on his back in the hospital, hovering somewhere between pain-racked reality and wavering illusion. Cory had been with him then, or so he'd told himself over the years. But he'd never really been convinced.

This, however, was definitely real, the first time they had been face to face, alone. He wasn't sure why that made him tense as a school kid on his first date, but it did. Hating the feeling, he did his best to ignore it.

"You're not going to like it."

Cory's hand jerked, sloshing coffee over her wrist, but she scarcely felt the sting as she leaned forward to exclaim, "Oh no, he's not *dead*! Tell me he's not dead. Officer Blount said he was out of danger." Her words tumbled, one on top of the other, and her eyes went round with fear. "Oh, Nick—"

"He's fine." Nick blew out a stream of air. "I didn't mean to scare you."

"Well, you did," she returned, her voice trembling.

"Sorry."

Nick heard the sound of water running upstairs and glanced at his watch. Joey had fifteen minutes. Cory, too, and that lawyer of hers she was so anxious to have at her side.

"If... if he's not worse, what is it?"

"Way I hear it, the lawyers were lined up before the guy regained consciousness. Word is, he plans to sue."

"Sue?" Cory nearly choked on the word. "He can't do that!"

"Don't be naive, Cory. Everyone sues these days. The guy's lawyer is probably standing outside the county courthouse right now, with a brief in his greedy little hand."

"But . . . but who can he sue? Those boys are minors."

"The township, for one, and the parents of all the kids who are found guilty of assaulting him."

"I . . . you mean we could lose this house? And . . . and my school?"

"If what Joey claims is true, and he wasn't involved, the judge will probably find him not guilty. And then you won't have to worry about losing everything."

Losing everything.

If that would guarantee Joey's safety, if forfeiting all she'd worked for would mean keeping her son out of jail, she would give it all up gladly. But that wasn't what Nick was saying.

Feeling disoriented, she stared at the garish clown face grinning at her from the front of Timmy's cereal box. Mr. Smiley, Timmy called him. But to her, the face looked obscenely cheerful. She had a feeling she wasn't going to be laughing much in the next few weeks, not until this nightmare was behind them, and Joey was safe.

"I'd better get dressed," she said, her mouth firming into a determined line Nick had seen before. "Give me five minutes."

Before she could move, Nick's hand caught hers. "I'll give you anything you want," he said in a rough voice. "Just ask."

His words startled her into looking at him, really looking at him, for the first time. His features were familiar—the surprisingly sensuous mouth that didn't go with the strong bones and aggressive angles of his face, the eyes that changed with his mood, growing as black as obsidian when he was angry, burning with golden light when he was aroused. She knew that face. She should. It was the face of the man she hated.

And yet, it wasn't. This man looked tired, haggard, even, but she'd seen him tired before. Now the lines in his face and the silver in his hair hinted at a different kind of weariness, the kind that suffering imprinted on a person's soul.

Her gaze faltered and dropped. No, she thought, I won't feel anything for him. I've suffered, too. And my children. Because of him. All because of him.

"Cory? Look at me, please." His fingers moved on her wrist. "I'm trying to say I'm sorry."

The words came with hard edges, as though he'd had to force them out. But then, talking about his feelings was something Nick had always refused to do.

Something tore inside her, releasing a flood of emotions. Some of her anger gave way, leaving a raw wound. "Sorry doesn't help, Nick," she said, twisting out of his grasp and jumping to her feet. "Not this time."

Very slowly he withdrew his hands. "You used to be a compassionate woman, Cory."

Needing to deny the pain she heard in his voice, she said coldly, "I used to have a husband I loved dearly, too."

His face closed up until it was the same stony mask she'd seen at the funeral. "I'll wait in the 'Vette."

He stood and closed the distance to the door in three powerful strides. He jerked open the door, then turned to face her. "If Joey isn't outside in fifteen minutes, I'm coming after him." He slammed the door so hard one of the leaded glass panes cracked.

Nick was leaning against the car, and he had just glanced at his watch and seen that the time was up when Joey walked out the back door. The kid looked scrubbed and neat, as though he were on his way to church and dreading every minute of it.

Poor kid, Nick thought, watching him walk slowly across the grass, head down, shoulders slumped. Facing up to mistakes was a bitch. But, in a way, Joey was lucky. Cory would always forgive *him*, no matter what he did.

After taking a last puff of his cigar, Nick ground the butt under his heel and straightened his tired body, trying to ignore the twinges of pain that shot through him.

The cold pizza he'd washed down with a pot of coffee was now a lump in his belly, and his body craved sleep. But he had promised Joe, and God help him, this was one promise he would keep—even if Cory hated him for trying.

"Right on time," he said when the boy was within earshot.

"Mom wants me to ride with her," Joey said from the passenger side of the Corvette.

"You'll ride with me."

"She won't like it," the boy warned before opening the door and sliding in. After closing the door he slumped against the leather and crossed his arms in the classic picture of a sullen teenager. If Nick hadn't felt so rotten, he might have laughed, something he rarely did these days.

Less than a minute later the door of the house swung open again, and Cory came out with a chubby little boy, who was chattering a mile a minute. He was wearing a miniature backpack and had a bedraggled bear in a headlock.

Joe's son, he thought, born on the day of his father's funeral, a miniature version of Joe, right down to the cowlick on the back of his head. Joe had wanted another son. He had planned to name him Timmy.

Remembering, he pulled his emotions in tight before they could get a hold on him. But his chest felt heavy, making it difficult to breathe.

While Cory locked the door, the boy skipped toward the Corvette, his hair ruffling in the wind, his innocent blue eyes shining with excitement.

"Who are you?" he asked in a bright voice when he reached the spot where Nick stood motionless, towering over him.

"Name's Nick." Nick made himself smile.

The boy craned his neck, his small body arching backward at the same time. "Bet you don't know my name," he declared in a singsong, his freckled face alive with mischief.

"Bet I do." Nick hesitated, then went down on his haunches to bring them eye to eye. Closer now, he saw Cory in the shape of the boy's face and the set of the jaw. "You're Timothy Michael Kingston."

Timmy giggled. "Momma calls me that when she's mad."

Nick fingered the bear's foot where a rip had been neatly mended. "What does she call you when she's not?"

"Timmy!" the little boy shouted with a toothy grin.

From the corner of his eye Nick saw Cory approach, her high heels clicking on the sidewalk. She looked neat and elegant in black and white, her skirt long enough for modesty, short enough to show off her trim legs, her jacket tailored and fitted just enough to hint at the womanly shape it covered.

Classy, he thought, and just right for the occasion. No desk sergeant in his right mind would dare treat her like anything but the lady she was.

"Ready?" he asked.

Cory nodded. "My attorney returned my call. He's in San Francisco until this evening. He told me what to expect and how to handle anything that might come up."

A gust of wind swirled around them, ruffling Nick's hair and tugging at her chignon. Nick remembered when she'd worn it long and straight in a silky mane he'd warned her never to cut. The first time he'd seen her after they'd broken up, her hair had been shorter than his.

Timmy tugged on his arm. "Can me 'n' Pandy go for a ride in your car?"

Before Nick could answer, Cory answered for him. "Get in the van, sweetie. We're already very late."

The boy looked disappointed. "I wanna go with him," he said, his small chin jutting forward.

Stubborn little devil, Nick thought. Like his momma. Conscious that Cory was watching, he stood and looked at her over Timmy's head. "Another time, Tim," he promised Joe's son. "Right now you'd better do what your momma says."

Looking unhappy, the little boy wandered up the drive to the bright yellow minivan parked in front of the Corvette.

"He won't forget," Cory said disapprovingly. "About the ride."

In spite of the understated sophistication of her clothes, her body looked soft and vulnerable. Once he would have pulled her into his arms to comfort her. But no longer. One slap in the face was enough.

"Timmy looks like Joe," he said, shoving one hand in his pocket. "He would have been pleased."

"Yes, he . . . he was so sure it was a boy."

"Seems to me he wanted four more. A basketball team."

Cory felt the corners of her mouth curl. "I preferred a tennis team, mixed doubles."

Nick ran his hand over the back of his neck. "I remember."

"How . . . how did you know Timmy's full name?" she asked, keeping her gaze fixed on the street beyond the van.

"I kept track of you and the kids, just in case."

That brought her gaze to his face. "In case of what?"

"In case you needed help."

If anything ever happens to me, Nick will take care of you. He loves you almost as much as I do.

"Why?" she asked, her voice not quite steady.

"Because Joe was my friend. And because you're right. Sorry isn't enough." He turned and climbed into the Corvette.

As Cory walked toward the van, her throat was thick with the words that might have taken the pain from his eyes. But she hadn't been able to say them. Her own pain was too strong.

As Nick started the car, Joey acknowledged his presence with a nervous look. "You won't leave when we get there?" he asked, rushing his words. "No matter what Mom says? I mean, you promised you'd be with me."

"I won't leave." He backed into the street, then waited for Cory to do the same.

Driving up from the city, he'd been preparing himself to handle scorn from the lady, even words that would hurt. He hadn't been prepared for the near-violent impact that seeing her again had had on him.

She still had it, the subtle mix of cool class and sex appeal that messed with a man's mind until all he could think about was possessing her. Whenever he was near her, he found himself thinking of rare orchids and perfumed sheets—and a man's sweat drying on that small perfect body.

No matter how hard he'd tried, he'd never found another woman who could make him forget the touch of Cory's hand nestled in his. Or the music of her laughter in the darkness, chasing away the nightmares. Or the sweetness of her kiss after a brutal day. Bastard that he'd been, he'd driven her out of his life—and into the bed of his best friend.

God help fools and cowards, he thought. He was both.

Chapter 4

The interrogation room smelled of disinfectant and stale cigarette smoke. The table where Cory was sitting had long since lost most of its varnish.

The man in charge of the case, a slightly built, shrewd-faced Latino detective in his early thirties named Al Davila, sat across the table, his tie loosened and his shirtsleeves rolled up. Next to his elbow, a small tape machine whirred silently, recording every word that was said.

To her dismay, Nick was there, too, lounging at the end of the table, legs extended, arms crossed over his chest, saying little as he tilted his chair back. Even though she didn't want to be, she was intensely aware that he was there, watching, listening, thinking his own thoughts, thoughts no one would ever know unless he chose to reveal them.

She had a feeling Davila was as aware of him as she was. Several times she'd seen the detective's gaze sliding in Nick's direction before he'd caught himself. Intuition told her that Nick made the young detective nervous. She wasn't sure whether to be comforted by that fact—or frightened.

"Was your son upset after your husband's death, Mrs. Kingston?" Davila continued after consulting his notes.

"No more than you'd expect."

"I see." Davila was polite, even diffident, out of respect for her status as a policeman's widow. But it was becoming increasingly difficult for her to remain pleasant in return, when all she wanted to do was find her son and take him home—except she didn't know where he was.

Somewhere in the basement being fingerprinted and photographed, Nick had told her while they'd been waiting for Davila.

"You say Joseph was in therapy for a time, before you moved here?"

"Yes. We all were. The department provides it for all family members after a . . . death."

The detective made a great show of flipping through the papers in the folder in front of him before saying, "According to Joey's counselor at Chaparral High, he has a reputation as a troublemaker. In fact," he said slowly, drawing out his words for emphasis, "he was given detention twice last year for causing disruptions in class."

Cory fought down a sharp pang of fear. "I know all about those referrals, Detective Davila. You may not have noticed, but they came from the same teacher. He and Joey just had a personality conflict, that's all. As soon as Joey switched to another class, everything was fine."

More alert than he seemed, Nick heard the faint shimmer of anxiety in Cory's voice and clenched his jaw to keep from calling a halt to the questions, professional courtesy be damned. But the time wasn't right. Not yet.

While Davila was sizing up Cory, he was sizing up Davila. From the things Davila had said, Nick would have bet a year's salary that the guy was less than a year out of uniform. Looking to make points with the brass, too.

Green or not, though, the guy was good. Every skeptical glance, every slow lift of an eyebrow, was carefully calculated to frighten Cory into defending her son, and, in so doing, give away a lot of incriminating evidence Davila would hand over to the DA if this thing came to trial.

It was an effective technique, attack and retreat, bad cop one minute, good cop the next. He'd used it himself. Seeing it used on Cory, however, made him want to strangle the man with his bare hands.

Davila wrote something on the report form, then glanced up to say, "Actually, it was two teachers, Mrs. Kingston. He got another referral just two days ago. Perhaps you don't know about that?"

Looking into his eyes, she realized that Davila truly believed that Joey was guilty. The air in the room suddenly seemed too thin, the temperature too warm, making it difficult to breathe properly.

Hoping she wasn't being too obvious, she opened the top button of her blouse and pulled the collar away from her throat before saying with a disarming smile, "All teenagers have problems with authority at one time or another."

"Hmm, problems with authority," Davila repeated softly, his eyes never leaving her face. "Are you saying you had problems disciplining your son?" His voice was suddenly sharp and accusing, bringing a quick rush of blood to Cory's cheeks.

Something was dreadfully wrong here, she thought. This wasn't the way Theo had said things would be at all. "No more so than any other parent," she said stiffly. "Teenagers can be difficult."

"But not all teenagers assault old men!"

Nick's deep voice cut through her cry of protest. "Easy, detective," he said with a friendly grin. "Mrs. Kingston isn't a suspect."

Before she knew she was doing it, she sent Nick a look of gratitude, but his eyes were locked on Davila's face.

Davila's lips were stiff as they formed a smile. "No offense, Mrs. Kingston. I regret having to ask you these things, but I'm sure you understand that I'm just doing my job."

"It's nearly noon, detective," she said with as much courtesy as she could muster. "I'd like to take my son home now."

Davila leaned back in his chair. "The judge will hear a petition for bail tomorrow. Until then, I'm afraid your son will have to remain in custody."

Cory gasped. "*What?* You can't mean . . . jail?"

"Actually, he'll be in Juvenile Hall in Ventura."

Cory didn't realize she'd turned toward Nick, her expression beseeching, until she saw surprise glint in his dark eyes.

"What about the others, detective?" Nick asked in that same deceptively quiet tone, drawing Davila's attention away from her.

Davila hesitated, then said, "Released in their parents' custody."

"That's not fair, and you know it!" Cory cried, then realized she wasn't helping Joey by shouting at the man. Pausing, she made herself take a deep breath before she continued in a calmer tone. "He scarcely knows those... those other boys, and he certainly didn't know what they were planning. When he found out, it was too late, but he didn't *do* anything."

"Someone who's innocent doesn't usually run, Mrs. Kingston."

Nick didn't move. His expression didn't change, but Cory suddenly knew that he was dangerously angry.

"I told you, Davila. He came to me for help because he didn't want to upset his mother." Nick's tone was quiet. She couldn't remember the last time she'd heard Nick raise his voice. He didn't have to. People always paid attention to Nick.

"I'm not disputing your word, sergeant," the detective said smoothly, "merely pointing out that he's...inclined to leave town when things get hot. We can't take the chance he might run again."

Nick leaned back and eyed Davila thoughtfully, a faint smile playing over his mouth. Cory saw the tension in the corners and knew that he wasn't as relaxed as he seemed. "Mind if I look at your notes?"

Davila was caught off-guard, but recovered quickly. "They're confidential."

Nick saw Cory's eyes come to his again. He saw fear there, and a helplessness he'd never seen in her before. Something tore inside him. He couldn't walk away now. He wasn't certain he ever could have. Abruptly he let the chair drop onto four legs. It was time to let Davila know he'd just bought into Cory's trouble.

"Let's cut through the crap, detective. Who gave you Joey?"

That caught Davila by surprise. Frustration flashed in his eyes, followed by a grudging respect.

"Tobias Ramsay." Davila flicked a quick glance in Cory's direction. "He's prepared to swear that Joseph Kingston is the ringleader of this particular group of boys, and that this isn't the first time they've gone out to—" he consulted his notes "—'have a blast.'"

Cory felt the heat come into her face. "No, it's not true! I don't believe it."

Davila regarded her with a trace of pity. "No parent ever does, ma'am."

"I know my son, Detective Davila," she said with barely leashed fury. "He doesn't lie."

Davila glanced at his notes again. "Tobias Ramsay is the president of the sophomore class and an honor student. His record is spotless."

In contrast to Joey's, Cory finished silently.

Nick felt tension knot his spine. No wonder Davila looked smug. "That's damn thin, Davila, and you know it, one kid fingering another to save his skin. Any good attorney could break his story in five minutes."

Davila's expression acknowledged the truth of that statement. His half smile told Nick he'd been hiding an ace that he was about to play. "All of the boys involved are prepared to swear that trashing the school was Joey's idea."

Cory couldn't stand any more. Davila was wrong. Toby was wrong. She knew her son.

"I give you my word he won't run," she said, her voice breathy with urgency. "Just let him come home with me now, and I'll have him back here any time you say."

Davila closed the folder and placed both hands flat on the cover. "I'm sorry. It's out of my hands." The regret in his voice sounded genuine.

Without thinking, she turned toward Nick. "Can he do that?"

Nick heard her unspoken question. *Are you going to let him get away with this?* Frustration sliced his gut. For four years he'd prayed for a chance to redeem himself in her eyes.

Now, when he might just have a shot, there was precious little he could do.

"He can do that."

Nick saw Cory's mouth tremble, and her eyes mist. Thirty years on the streets had hardened him to just about everything imaginable—except Cory's tears.

With a silent, vicious curse, he grabbed his jacket and stood. At the sudden movement, the dull ache in his head exploded into sharp throbbing.

"Mrs. Kingston would like to see her son before she leaves," he told Davila, his glance brushing Cory's white face.

Davila picked up the folder and stood. "Sorry, sarge, he's already gone. No one but his attorney can see him until court tomorrow."

"No!" Cory cried, jumping up.

"That's bull, and you know it." This time Nick's voice was spiked with command. "You can arrange a visit, or I can. It would be better for you if you did."

Davila's face turned red. "Is that some kind of a threat?"

One side of Nick's mouth moved upward in a humorless smile. "No, a fact."

Davila tried to make himself taller, even though he topped Nick's six feet by several inches. "I checked you out, Donatelli, after you called," he said with a sneer. "I know all about you."

Nick moved toward him, his jacket hooked over one shoulder, his gaze locked onto Davila's. "Then you know I can be a good friend, or I can be a very bad enemy. Right now the choice is yours."

Davila took a step backward before he caught himself. "I don't need the kind of friend who freezes up on his partner."

Silence crashed around them. Cory waited for Nick to explode. Instead, he simply smiled. "Very original, Davila," he said in a voice as smooth and hard as sword steel. "Only I've heard that before, and from people I respect a hell of a lot more than I respect you."

Davila said something crude before stalking toward the door and jerking it open. A second later he was gone.

Trembling inside, Cory pushed back her chair and stood. "He shouldn't have said that."

Nick pulled on his jacket. "I've learned to live with it," he said before walking past her to the door.

"Where are you going?" she cried out.

"To see Joey."

Cory blinked, her hands crushing her purse against her belly. "But you heard Davila. They won't let us see him."

"Wanna bet?"

As grins go, it was pure dynamite, catching Cory off-guard and sending something swift and hot shooting through her. Suddenly she saw again the fun-loving rookie who had charmed her into his bed on the second date. Until she looked into his eyes. Shadowed and weary, they looked like the eyes of a very old man.

An hour later, when they arrived at Juvenile Hall, the visit had been arranged. Since the rules allowed only one visitor at a time, Nick was waiting for Cory in the small reception area.

Just once he would like to walk into a government office and find a decent chair, he thought sourly, trying without much success to find a comfortable position. This one was too hard and too narrow in the back to accommodate his shoulders.

Lord, he was tired. Deep down tired, the kind that never went away, no matter how many hours he piled up in the sack. No more than twenty minutes, the duty officer had warned Cory. Time was almost up. And then what? Then he went back to Santa Monica and got on with his life, that was what.

Biting off a curse, Nick surged to his feet and walked to the window, too restless to sit still any longer. Outside, the overcast had thickened and the wind had picked up. Bits and pieces of dead leaves and discarded paper swirled over the parking lot, collecting in the gutters, where the first rain would turn them into a sodden, ugly mess.

Maybe that was why he hated fall. Rain in the city brought out the worst in everyone, himself included. He hated being confined indoors, hated the claustrophobic feeling the overcast gave him.

He hated winter worse. All those damned holidays. Halloween, Thanksgiving, Christmas. Happy times. Family times. Times he used to spend with Joe and his family.

Nowadays, he spent holidays someplace else. Mexico, Hawaii, any place where it was hot enough to burn his skin and dull his mind. No matter where he went, however, it was never hot enough to steam the loneliness out of him.

Maybe this year he would try Australia, he decided, staring at the Corvette he should have sold years ago. The oversize engine got lousy mileage and cost him a fortune in tune-ups. Only a fool would keep a damn car because a woman with smokey green eyes had liked the way he looked behind the wheel.

Nick braced one hand against the window frame and dropped his head. Since Cory had chosen Joe, he'd made himself think of her as Joe's wife. It had kept her off-limits. Safe.

Thou shalt not covet thy neighbor's wife.

What about your best friend's widow? Shouldn't that be a sin, too?

"Nick?"

Turning, Nick saw her standing in the doorway. She looked steady enough. But her lips were white, and her breathing was much too rapid. She was terrified, but not for herself. For Joey.

Once upon a time, before he'd blown it, she had whispered to him in the dark about the child she wanted to give him someday. He hadn't had the guts to accept the precious gift she'd been offering, and she'd left him.

He'd never doubted that he'd been right. He wasn't cut out to be a father. At the moment, he wasn't even all that crazy about being a godfather.

"How's he doing?" he asked.

"Scared." Looking at him was a mistake. His eyes imprisoned hers, drawing her toward him. He didn't move, but she had a sensation of power under great restraint.

The room was too warm, and he'd removed his jacket, revealing his gun and his badge, worn, as always, on his belt.

"My partner, the cowboy," Joe used to say. "Nick scares the bad guys into surrendering. I just bore 'em to death."

But Joe hadn't been boring to her. He'd been solid and dependable, her rock. He had made her feel safe. With Nick she'd never been safe. Not emotionally, anyway.

There was something wild about him, something that couldn't be tamed, something that made her catch her breath every time she saw it in him. She saw it now.

"He's tough, Cory. He'll be okay."

"Okay? How can he be okay in a place like this?" Tears filmed her eyes, and she searched in her purse for a tissue. "The only time he's been away from home was to sleep over with friends."

Her mouth wobbled, drawing his gaze. He knew that mouth in all her moods. Laughing, teasing, pensive, naughty, angry. But no matter how angry she'd been at him, her mouth had always softened under his. It wasn't a mouth a man forgot easily. God knows, he'd tried. He shifted, trying to ease the tension in his back.

"Juvenile Hall isn't all that bad. He can do one night without raising a sweat."

"How many nights did you spend there?"

"Three hundred and sixty-four," he said without having to think about it. Each one had been served in sullen resentment, winning him more than his share of grief from the guards and staff. Even then, he'd never been one to make things easy on himself.

"Was it awful?" She didn't want to ask, and yet she had to know.

"Naw, a piece of cake."

Cory saw his quick smile come and go. It was meant to reassure, nothing more, and yet she felt its impact. She always had, even when she'd been deeply, totally in love with her husband.

Leave now, she thought. He's poison, remember? Irresponsible, shallow, selfish—all the things you hate. You can't afford to care about him anymore.

"I didn't expect you to wait," she said stiffly, wadding the tissue in her fingers.

Worried about the pinched expression around her eyes, Nick told himself that she shouldn't be alone and ignored the lack of warmth in her tone. "I thought you might need a friend to buy you a good stiff drink."

"Thanks, but I have twenty-five little ones waiting for me when I get to school. I need a clear head."

"How about lunch, then?"

"I couldn't manage a thing."

"Sure? I'll buy. Anything but pizza."

Cory shook her head. He was acting as though the four years of silence had never happened. But it had. Still, he'd been there when she needed him, and she owed him a thank you, at least.

"I'm grateful for all you've done," she said, close to tears again. "I know it wasn't easy for you." She turned away, her heels tapping hollowly on the linoleum as she headed for the door.

Nick followed her outside. "I'll walk you to your van," he told her as he fell in step.

They walked in silence until they reached the van with the bright logo of the Sunshine School painted on the side. Nick waited while she unlocked the door, then opened it for her.

As she turned to say goodbye, the wind whipped a pale strand of hair against her cheek, and she tried to push it back, drawing his gaze. Immediately his hand came up to smooth the soft wisps. Surprised by his touch, she flinched.

"Damn it, Cory," he said with what sounded like pain lashing his voice. "I'm not going to hurt you."

"You already have." His mouth was close to hers. Too close. It had been twenty years since he'd been this close to her.

"Don't you think I know that? If I could change that, I would. But I can't. All I can do is try to make it up to you in any way you'll let me."

Because he was so close, he saw the vulnerable softness in the corners of her mouth. Before he could stop himself, he brushed that faint tremble with his thumbs.

Cory felt the shiver start in some deep, hidden part of her. By the time it reached her skin, she had managed a measure of control.

"Nothing will change the way I feel about you, Nick," she said in a strangled voice. "No matter what you do."

Nick felt his head begin to pound again. "Maybe not, but I'm not leaving until this thing with Joey is settled. Whether you like it or not, I'm trying to save the kid's butt."

"Like you saved Joe's?" Cory regretted the words as soon as she said them, but it was too late.

Not even a muscle moved in his face, but his eyes were alive with some savage emotion. "What do you want from me, Cory?" he demanded in a low, seething voice. "Do you want me to eat my gun because I let Joe down? Would that make you happy?"

Something tore inside her, releasing a flood of emotions. Unable to escape, she turned her head away, her skin becoming clammy. The few sips of coffee she'd downed were threatening to come right back up again. "That's a terrible thing to say," she whispered.

"But true. Isn't it?"

She looked up to see Nick watching her steadily, a look of tension around his eyes and an unfamiliar vulnerability around his mouth.

Cory felt a tug of pity for this man she had hated for so long. "I don't wish you were dead, Nick. I just want you out of my life."

Very slowly, like a man in great pain, he stepped back, his shoulders rigid, his expression unreadable. "Joey wants me in court tomorrow. Like it or not, I intend to be there."

He turned and walked away from her.

Chapter 5

Nick had been twelve and already in trouble at school when he'd followed his older brother, Tony, into Handleman's Gym. The walls were nicotine yellow, and the linoleum was worn through in spots. The air smelled of wet towels and sweat. He'd fallen in love with the place on the spot.

But kids weren't allowed in the place, orders of Old Pops Handleman, a burned-out ex-pug from Brooklyn, who eked out a living teaching the fundamentals of boxing to anyone with a pair of gloves and a few bucks for lessons. Pops had thrown Nick out bodily every day for two weeks before he'd finally given in and offered him a job washing towels and cleaning up.

Pops became a surrogate father to the two Donatelli boys, who would rather spend their time on the streets than go home to a house filled with vicious bickering and angry outbursts that invariably spilled over onto them.

Full grown by the time he'd been sixteen, Tony had been Golden Gloves champion, and the prize money had enabled him to go to college.

By the age of fourteen Nick had been as big as his brother and even stronger, but he'd lacked the rigid discipline Tony had imposed on himself.

While he'd been serving his sentence in reform school, he'd used boxing to keep himself sane. In those black days his temper had made him his own worst enemy, making him forget the finesse Pops had tried to pound into him. When that happened, he'd relied on guts and his ability to withstand punishment long enough to find a way to win.

Tony had used boxing as a means to an end. Nick had used it to vent the rage that living with parents constantly at war had instilled in him.

Army discipline had taught him how to put that seething anger to good use. Working as a cop did the same thing. But sometimes, especially when he was tired or fighting too many battles at one time, it came close to taking over. When that happened, he hauled his gloves out of the trunk and headed for Handleman's.

Pops was in his usual spot by the ring, an unlit cigar butt clamped in one corner of his scowl. His face was bony, his skin cratered and mapped with lines, but his shrewd blue eyes could still cut into a man's soul.

"Hey, Nicky, long time no see," he called when Nick walked out of the shadows into the bright lights over the ring, his gloves slung over one shoulder.

"How's it goin', Pops?"

The old man shifted his cigar to the other corner of his mouth. "Can't complain," he grated in a voice made hoarse by sixty years of cheap cigars. "Working with this here kid Williams reminds me of you when you was trying to put them big fists of yours through everything that moved."

Pops squinted upward toward the ring, where two well-developed black men in their early twenties were sparring. Nick knew the one with a long scar on his shoulder, a former gang member who went by the name of Billy T.

He and Nick had met on the street eight years ago, when Nick had slammed him up against the nearest wall to keep him from going after the rival gang member who had just shot his sister by mistake.

Nick had arrested him, then gone to visit him while he'd been serving time. A few weeks after he'd been paroled, Nick had taken him to Handleman's one Tuesday night to the boxing clinic his brother Tony ran for former offenders. So far Billy T. hadn't given him a reason to regret it.

"Billy T. looks good," Nick said, wincing at a particularly vicious left hook.

Pops grunted. "Tony's been teachin' him some moves. Thinks he might be ready for the Olympic tryouts by spring."

"Tony ought to know." Nick's eyes shifted to the referee. When they'd been kids, he and Tony had looked enough alike to be mistaken for twins, even though Tony was six years older. Now Tony had iron-gray hair and a look of bleak anger about him that aged him beyond his forty-seven years.

"Hey, ref, how about going a few rounds—if you're not too tired?" Nick yelled over the slap of leather on flesh.

Captain Anthony Donatelli, the head of an elite task force taking on gang warfare in the city, gave his brother a quick grin that didn't quite reach his gold-brown eyes. "You're on, *fratello*. Better say your prayers."

Nick laughed because he knew Tony expected it. "Not on your best day."

Tony pushed his powerful body between the two fighters and forced them apart. "That's all for tonight, guys. Good job, both of you."

Instant allies now, the exhausted boxers began to protest, their glistening bodies dripping sweat onto the canvas.

"C'mon, Tony. I got 'im on the ropes."

"No way, man. I woulda won a decision easy!"

Tony caught each man around the neck with his big hands. "Stick around and watch me teach my cocky little brother a lesson or two."

He crossed to the far corner and wiped his face with a towel before slipping through the ropes to climb down from the ring. "I'll get my gloves," he called over his shoulder. One of the boxers followed him toward the locker room.

The other came toward Nick, a grin pushing at the helmet hiding half his face. "Hey, sarge, you see me whip that wimp?" he exclaimed as he jumped to the floor.

Nick pretended indecision. "I don't know about that, Billy T. I saw your eyes spin when he connected with that last right cross."

Billy T. ducked his head. "Never could fool you, could I, man?"

"I didn't know you tried."

The young boxer turned serious. "No way, man. I owe you."

Clearly uncomfortable with any kind of sentiment, Pops punched Billy T. on the shoulder with a gnarled fist. "Get showered, then come see me. You fight like that with a pro, your butt would be on the canvas right now."

"Yes, sir." Billy T. waved a glove at Nick and loped off.

When he was gone, Pops turned his rheumy gaze on Nick again. "You don't look like you're in shape to spar with my grandmother, let alone take on your brother's left jab. You got troubles again, Nicky?"

"I'm handling it."

Nick saw genuine worry in the old man's watery eyes and drew a hard breath. He hadn't allowed himself to care for too many people in his life, but he cared for Pops.

"You and that damn-fool brother of yours." Pops clucked his tongue in disapproval. "Stubborn bastards, both of you. Can't admit you're hurtin', even when it's as obvious as blood on your gloves."

Nick raised on eyebrow. "I agree. Tony really is a stubborn bastard."

Pops mouthed his cigar butt, his seamed face settling into another pattern of wrinkles. "Have it your way. You know where to find me, if'n you want to talk." With another look that was half-affection and half-disgust, Pops shambled off.

Turning away, Nick found his brother standing by the corner of the ring, watching him with that penetrating way he had come to expect. In the month since Nick had seen him last, Tony had lost some weight, giving his six-foot frame a mean, dangerous look.

People in the know swore he would be chief someday. Nick thought Tony would make a good one. As for himself, he knew he would never go higher than sergeant, no matter how many cases he closed or how many bullets he took. A dead partner under controversial circumstances was too heavy a chain to break.

"Rough day?" Tony asked, his gaze flickering to the bandage on Nick's forehead.

"Something like that, yeah."

"I heard about Morena. Word is you're going to get another commendation."

"No doubt the brass is choking."

Tony sighed. "You're your own worst enemy, *fratello*. You think everyone holds Joe's death against you, but they don't. The Board met, considered the circumstances and cleared you. Let it go, Nicky."

Nick hesitated, then asked in a cold tone, "You didn't have anything to do with the Board's decision, did you, Tony?"

Tony's eyes narrowed. "You know me better than that."

"Just checking." Nick hung his gloves over one of the ropes and shrugged out of his jacket.

"How's Stacy?" he asked before pulling his shirt over his head.

Tony dropped his gloves to the canvas and began to strip, his jaw hard. "She's seeing a lawyer."

"Divorce?"

"Yeah, so she told me when I finally managed to get her to say anything to me at all." Tony's voice was harsh, his expression controlled. "One mistake, Nick, one stupid roll in the hay with a woman I barely knew, and fifteen years of marriage get shot to hell."

Nick plucked his gloves from the rope and ran his palm over the smooth leather. "I've got a flash for you, Tony," he said, his voice razored with cynicism. "Once you hurt a woman, really hurt her, it'll be a cold day in hell before she ever forgives you." He pushed one fist into a glove and jerked the laces tight.

Tony's head came up so fast his hair flashed silver in the light. His gaze whipped toward his brother. "You saw Cory?"

Nick tried to swallow the bitter taste in his mouth. "I saw her."

"And?"

"And nothing's changed." He slammed his fist into the other glove and pulled the laces tight with his teeth.

Without seeming to, Tony studied his brother's face. What he saw made him hurt inside. Nick would never find peace until he could learn to forgive himself for what he'd done. That didn't seem likely. Ever since he'd been a kid with dirty knees and a stubborn streak, Nick had shown tolerance and compassion to everyone but himself.

"How come you saw her?" Tony draped his shirt over the bottom rope and reached for his gloves.

Nick separated the ropes and climbed into the ring. For the first time since he could remember, he didn't feel at home there. "Joey's in trouble with the law in Ojai. He thought I'd fix it for him."

"Did you?"

"You know better than that!" Nick said with a disgusted look. "I called Ojai PD and took him back. They had a warrant for assault, malicious mischief, flight to avoid arrest."

"Sounds serious."

"Serious enough. Ojai is keeping him overnight. A bail hearing is set for nine tomorrow morning."

Tony whistled softly. "How old is the kid now? Fourteen, fifteen?"

"Sixteen."

"That's heavy."

"Yeah."

Tony untangled the strings on his gloves. "You should have married her when you had the chance."

"Oh yeah? So we could live happily ever after like Mom and the old man?"

"Not everyone screws up, Nick."

"He did. You did. Half the guys I know are divorced, some more than once. I don't need that kind of pain."

Tony knew better than to argue with his brother when his eyes turned the color of slate. He'd seen that same look when his father had used a belt on Nick one too many times. Guido Donatelli had ended up in the hospital, and Nick had left home for good, at age seventeen.

Tony had a feeling that was the reason Nick had sworn never to get married. He and the old man were too much alike, too volatile, too stubborn, too independent to accept the limitations imposed by a wife and children. Guido had made four people miserable. Nick kept his misery to himself.

"I'll get us someone to help with the gloves," Tony said, glancing around the cavernous gym. It was late. The place was nearly empty, except for a burly Latino shadowboxing in front of the mirror next to the dressing room and a young black man who had just emerged from the back room, a stack of white towels in his arms.

"Hey, Jimbo," Tony called when he spied Pops' latest favorite. "Come lace us up, okay?"

"Sure thing, Tony. Just let me get rid of these towels, okay?"

Tony nodded, then climbed into the ring. Nick was spread-eagled against the ropes, his corded arms spread wide. The right side of his chest was slashed by a long scar where the surgeons had removed the bullet that had collapsed his lung. The scar had faded during the last eighteen months, but not the memory of Nick's suffering still deeply embedded in Tony's mind.

It had been touch and go, especially when Nick had gone into cardiac arrest during the operation. He'd been out of his head with fever for three days, and Tony had heard enough of his delirious rambling to know what Nick had gone through after Joe's death. He also had a pretty good idea of Nick's feelings for his partner's widow, perhaps more than Nick himself had.

"So, are you going to the hearing tomorrow?"

Nick stared at the smoke-stained ceiling. "Cory never wants to see me again."

"So?"

Nick pushed away from the ropes. "So I'm going to give her exactly what she wants."

The sound of running footsteps cut through the silence, and both men stiffened. "You guys look serious," Jimbo said as he entered the ring. "Is this some kind of grudge match?"

Tony laughed. "Naw. Nick and I just need to dull a few sharp edges," he said, extending his arms toward the young man.

"I get your drift," Jimbo said, bending to tie the laces. When he finished, he tied Nick's. "You guys need a ref?"

Nick shrugged. "Okay with me."

While Nick watched Jimbo, Tony watched him. The knot in his gut told him that his little brother was close to losing it, the way he had after Joe's funeral. He'd gone on a five-day drunk that would have killed an ordinary man. As it was, Nick had been sick for a week.

Tony wanted to help, but he knew Nick wouldn't let him. "Ten rounds?" he asked Nick when Jimbo finished.

Nick slammed his fists together. "Fifteen. And don't hold back."

Cory led the way to the front door. It was nearly eleven. She and Theo Kennedy had been talking since he'd arrived at a little past eight, mostly about Joey, and the threat of a lawsuit.

"Thanks for the friendly shoulder, Theo," she said with one hand on the doorknob, the other pressed to her stomach, which hadn't stopped churning since morning. "I know all my questions must have sounded pretty neurotic, especially since a cop's wife is supposed to know all about the law."

Tennis trim and boyishly handsome at fifty, Theo had a look of down-home honesty about him and a way with words that had mesmerized his share of juries during his twenty-five years as a criminal attorney.

He set his briefcase on the floor and rested both hands on her shoulders. His hands were warm and strong, but his touch signaled no more than warm affection between good friends. At least, that was what she told herself.

"First of all, get rid of that idea right now. Lawyers don't even know all there is to know about the law." He smiled, coaxing a small smile from her in return. "As for sounding neurotic, you sounded exactly like a mother whose son is spending the night locked up in a strange place. I only wish I could have been there to convince Al Davila to release him into your custody."

"I know you would have tried."

Theo withdrew his hands and picked up his briefcase. "I'll see you outside the courtroom at eight-thirty, okay?"

Cory glanced up the darkened staircase, where only two of her children were sleeping in their own beds. Where was Joey sleeping? she wondered with a quick flash of pain. In some dingy bed in a crowded dormitory? With a bunch of half-crazed drug users and gang members as roommates?

"He'll be home tomorrow, right?" She had lost track of the times she'd asked that same question.

"There are no guarantees in the law, Cory," Theo said in that meticulous way she had come to expect. "But, as I've explained, the odds are definitely in our favor. Juvenile judges almost always release first offenders into parental custody."

Cory tried, but she couldn't detect even a small crack in his confident expression, and some of the butterflies in her stomach quieted.

"Thanks again for coming, Theo," she said as she opened the door. "I really appreciate it."

The grandfather clock in the corner began to bong the hour, and the deep-throated sound seemed to reverberate through her like a series of blows.

"Try to get some sleep," Theo said when the clock was finished.

"I think that's going to be impossible," she said with the briefest of sad smiles. "Every minute until the hearing tomorrow is going to seem like an hour."

He shifted his briefcase from one hand to the other and leaned down to kiss her cheek. She caught a whiff of expensive aftershave, the kind that suggested vacations on the

Riviera and three-hundred-dollar champagne. "Trust me, Cory. I'll make sure your boy comes home."

Cory nodded, her eyes filling with tears. "I know you will, Theo. Thank you."

When he disappeared into the darkness beyond the light, she closed the door and leaned against it, suddenly too spent to move. Eyes closed, she tried to summon the energy to lock up the house and go to bed.

After Nick had left her, she'd gone through her day like an automaton, keeping her fear at bay by devoting herself to the children at school. After that, she'd forced herself to put on a calm facade for Jen and Timmy.

After the fifth call from well-meaning friends—some whose sharp tones made her wonder just what they'd heard—she had let the machine take her calls.

To occupy her mind, she'd fixed an elaborate Mexican meal, then hadn't been able to eat a bite. Listening to Timmy's prayers, hearing him ask God to take care of his big brother, had torn her apart, but she had managed to escape to her room before the tears had come.

"Mom, can I go with you to court tomorrow?"

Cory opened her eyes to see her daughter standing on the bottom step, huddling into her candy-striped pajamas, her feet bare. At thirteen, Jennifer was painfully shy with everyone but family. Tall for her age and plump, she wore thick glasses and had made straight A's since the second grade. She had inherited Cory's fair skin and green eyes, but Jen's hair was mousy brown and coarse instead of silky blond.

Cory told herself that her daughter would be pretty someday—when she'd shed the thirty extra pounds she'd put on after her father's death.

"You know you can't miss school," Cory told her with a tired smile.

"Joey is."

Cory smiled. "Jen," she said in her best warning tone.

Jennifer grinned and held up both hands. "Okay, okay. Only kidding."

"Give me a break, will you? I'm too tired to deal with teenage humor." Cory pushed herself away from the door and walked toward the stairs.

"You should be asleep," she chided as she brushed the girl's wispy hair away from her face.

Jennifer regarded her with eyes that looked huge behind the round lenses of her glasses before sinking down to sit on the stairs. "Are you going to marry Mr. Kennedy?"

Taken aback, Cory sat down beside her daughter and put her arm around the girl's shoulder. She had never seen her daughter look more lost or more in need of reassurance and love. "Why in the world would you ask that, sweetie?"

"I saw him kissing you." Jen began pleating the striped cotton over one knee.

"Mr. Kennedy's just a friend, Jen, and that was just a friendly kiss."

Jen sliced her mother a sideways glance. "You never let any man but Daddy kiss you before, not even Uncle Nick, and he was a friend."

Careful, Cory, she told herself with an inner sigh. "That . . . was different. Daddy was alive then."

Jennifer's face twisted. "Why doesn't Uncle Nick come around anymore? Doesn't he like us?"

She'd always known that Jennifer idolized Nick. When she'd asked about his abrupt absence from her life, Cory had given her every answer but the real one. When she'd been nine, she'd been too young to understand. Cory still wasn't sure she was old enough.

"Jen, look at me, please." Cory touched her shoulder.

Slowly, the girl turned her face toward her mother.

"Are you really sure you want to know the truth?" Cory asked in a quiet tone. "It might hurt."

Jen nodded, but her expression was uncertain. Cory took one of Jen's hands and folded it into hers. "Remember how Daddy used to talk about cops and their partners? That they never let each other down, no matter what?"

Jen nodded again. "He told us the story about the *Three Musketeers* and said he and Uncle Nick were the two musketeers, only they had guns instead of swords."

Cory felt a pang of deep sadness, but she made herself smile. "That's exactly right." Her smile faded, and her throat tightened, making her words sound hollow.

"Well, when Daddy and Uncle Nick went into that liquor store that morning, Uncle Nick wasn't feeling well and... and he made a mistake."

Jennifer's pale brows pushed together in a frown above the frames of her glasses. "What kind of a mistake?"

Cory took a shaky breath. "Because the...the robber was so young, Uncle Nick didn't draw his gun right away. And so...and so Daddy got shot." Tears clogged her throat, and it hurt to breathe.

Jen blinked at her, bewilderment shadowing her face. "But you always say that it's no sin to make a mistake, as long as you're sorry and you learn from it."

Cory nodded slowly, stalling for time. Now what? she thought. It wouldn't do any good to tell Jen her adored uncle partied too much and so he'd had a wicked hangover that fatal morning. It wouldn't serve any purpose to tell Jen that he just might be an alcoholic by now, the way he'd been going.

"Jen, it's late, and I'm so tired I can't keep my eyes open any longer. Let's go to bed, okay?"

Jennifer didn't budge. "Mom, do you think Uncle Nick is sorry?"

Cory stared at her, the silence in the old house closing in around them. The clock ticked steadily. Outside, the wind blew a branch against the shingles. Familiar sounds. Lonely sounds.

What do you want me to do, eat my gun?

Cory's fingers dug into the nap of the carpet. "Yes," she said in a nearly inaudible tone. "I think he is."

"Well," Jen said on a quick indrawn breath, "you always said that God forgives us when we're sorry for what we do. How come you can't forgive Uncle Nick?"

Cory drew a shaky breath. And another. "I wish I could forgive him, Jen, for your sake. But I... just can't. Daddy's gone because of him."

Jennifer lowered her gaze to their entwined hands. "I guess I should hate him, too," she said very quietly. "If you do, I mean."

"Oh, baby, I don't want you to hate anyone," Cory whispered. "Please don't think that I do." She pulled Jennifer into her arms and closed her eyes on a wave of anguish. What was she doing to her child? What had she already done?

Cory smoothed the girl's hair, trying to swallow the tears that filled her throat. God, she didn't want her little girl to be hurt.

If she could, she would wipe away all the memories her children had of the man who had been their honorary uncle. If she could, she would wipe away her own memories of the lusty young man she'd loved. But life wasn't like that. All she could do was try to protect her children against more hurt.

"I miss him," Jen mumbled against Cory's breast.

So do I, Cory thought, and then was aghast. Worry was making her lose perspective. A good night's sleep would put things right again.

"Go to bed, sweetie," she said, her tone putting an end to the discussion. "I need to check the phone machine, and then I'll be up." She gave her daughter a quick hug and got to her feet. Behind her, Jennifer scrambled to her feet and ran up the stairs.

Cory walked slowly down the hall to the den and crossed to the desk. The red light was blinking on the machine, and she punched the play button.

"Cory, this is Nick." His voice came out of the machine hard and fast, without a hint of the humility she'd sensed in him earlier. "About tomorrow. You win. You want me out of your life, I'm out of your life. Tell Joey to remember the things his dad taught him and he can't go wrong." He hung up without saying goodbye.

As the machine recycled itself, Cory sank down on the chair and stared at the blinking light.

If God can forgive him, why can't you?

With a soft moan, she buried her face in her hands.

* * *

The moon was a cold disk of silver slicing through the cloud bank. The fathomless Pacific stretched like an inky void toward the horizon, where it seemed to bleed into the blacker sky.

The tide was coming in, bringing waves tipped with phosphorous to crash into the breakwater like frenzied soldiers beating themselves against an impenetrable fortress before sliding inexorably into the depths again.

On the deserted beach Nick ran through the seething foam, his bare feet leaving angry gouges in the wet sand. A vicious onshore wind tore the breath from his lungs and spattered his face with icy drops of brine.

At the edge of the breakwater he stopped, too exhausted to take another step. Bracing one hand on a jagged piece of granite, he bent double and tried to drag more air into his burning lungs. His belly ached, and his head was buzzing from the combined effects of sleep deprivation and pain from the bullet crease.

After he'd left the gym, he'd gone home exhausted enough to sleep for a couple of restless hours before the familiar nightmare jerked him awake. Impenetrable and black, the walls of his bedroom had closed in on him until he felt as though he were choking, and he'd gone to the only place in the city where he could find enough air.

Spitting a curse into the wind, he sank down onto the boulder and stared into the seething eddies below the breakwater. Posttrauma syndrome, the department shrink had called it, then told him that the flashbacks and insomnia would eventually go away. Nick knew better. His conscience was punishing him for being alive.

Somewhere behind him, a siren began to wail. Some poor cop hurrying to a call, he thought. God only knew what he'd find when he got to his destination. A drug buy gone bloody, maybe, or a liquored-up husband taking out his pain on his wife. Or some strung out thirteen-year-old trying to boost the price of a fix.

He ran his hands down his face, feeling the whiskers scrape his palms. Was it Fate that had put them close to that liquor store that morning? Or plain bad luck?

He could still see Joe's reproachful look when he'd dragged himself into work that morning. "Hey, Nicky, you look like hell warmed over," he'd chided. "Maybe you'd better cut out those late nights for a while."

"Are you crazy, man?" he'd answered with a grin that had turned into a wince. "I've got this flight attendant who's crazy for my body."

Joe had shaken his head at that. "You're going to kill yourself before you're fifty, partner. Now me, I plan to die in bed at the ripe old age of a hundred, with Cory beside me and a satisfied smile on my face."

Nick had laughed, even as he privately envied his partner's happiness. Two hours later Cory had been a widow—because Nick Donatelli had been too hung over to do his job.

On another muttered curse he pushed himself to his feet and began to retrace his steps. As he passed a fire ring, he smelled the embers that were all that remained of a beach party. Kids, he thought. College students, surfers, locals—the usual beach mix.

He'd been in that mix once, and so had Cory. He'd been one of the locals; she'd been a sophomore at UCLA. They'd collided, literally, at a pickup volleyball game.

Nick's steps slowed, then swerved toward the net hanging bedraggled and forlorn between two steel posts anchored in buckets of cement. It had been here that he'd first seen her.

He'd been half-drunk and randy as hell. She'd been caught up in the boisterous play, fighting for the ball, yelling encouragement to her teammates, shouting good-natured insults to his, holding her own against the larger players. Watching her lush, suntanned body in a bikini had driven him crazy most of the afternoon.

After the game, he'd done his best to charm her out of those two scraps of material. To his shock, she'd been immune to the line a lifetime on the beach had honed to perfection, giving him the brush-off politely but firmly.

He'd gone home that night so horny he'd resorted to measures he'd rarely used since puberty. Forget her, he'd told himself. There were plenty of women who would be happy to share his bed.

His resolve had lasted until the next Saturday. He'd just come off duty, and his head had still been filled with the agonized screams of a six-year-old accident victim who had died in his arms by the side of the Hollywood Freeway while the fire department struggled to free her legs from the mangled wreckage of her father's car.

The hot stench of blood was still in his nostrils when he'd gone to the beach to try to decide if he had the stomach to remain a cop.

He'd kept to himself that day, methodically working his way through one beer after another. At sunset, he'd found Cory sitting next to him. If she had said one word, he would have gotten up and walked away.

She'd said nothing, but eyes as green and deep as the sea had told him that she understood. A loner by nature even then, he'd tried to drive her away by making a crude pass.

"If you want me to get upset and leave, I will," she'd said. "But you look like you could use a friend."

He wanted her body, he'd told himself, not her sympathy. Yet, without knowing why, he'd begun to talk about that little girl. When he'd finished, she'd taken his hand in hers and told him she was proud of him for caring.

Before he'd figured out that he wanted her for more than sex, she'd slipped past that legendary guard of his to touch the part of him no one else even knew was there.

As soon as he'd realized how vulnerable he was to her soft smiles and understanding words, he'd closed up tight, shutting her out. That had been the beginning of the end for them. That and his fierce need for freedom.

The great Nick Donatelli was still free, he thought grimly. And so was Cory, for all the good it did him. In his mind, she was still Joe's wife. In hers, he was the man who had killed her husband.

Nick's palm smashed into the steel upright, toppling it to the sand. It didn't help.

Chapter 6

Juvenile Court was located on the third floor of Ventura County Courthouse. As Cory walked through the front doors, her watch said eight-thirty, exactly the time she was to meet Theo.

Riding up in the elevator, she straightened the collar of her blue silk dress and ran her tongue over her dry lips. She had been up since five, too nervous to stare at the ceiling for one more second.

While the children had been around, she had managed a semblance of calm, even a smile or two for Timmy as she'd helped him dress and a comforting word for Jen before the worried girl had left to catch the bus. But as soon as she'd dropped Tim at the Sunshine School, her facade of composure had crumbled. Twice she'd had to pull over to the curb in order to calm herself.

Chin up, Corinne, she told herself as the elevator doors slid open. You're all Joey has.

Upstairs, the corridor was strangely hushed, magnifying the click of her heels on the terrazzo floor. Theo, garbed in pin-striped navy, was seated on a bench at the far end, not too far from the double doors leading into the courtroom.

A group of men in similar dark suits, along with a marshal in khaki, stood together near a marble statue of Blind Justice tucked into a niche in the wall. As soon as she recognized Davila as one of the men, her heart began racing, and her eyebrows pulled into a frown.

"Good morning," he said as she passed.

"Good morning," she replied with as much aplomb as she could summon. Walking toward Theo, she could feel the detective's eyes boring into her back. He didn't seem unfriendly, exactly, more like coolly professional.

As soon as she was within speaking distance, Theo closed the briefcase on the bench next to him and got to his feet. As he indicated that she should sit, she saw that he wasn't smiling.

"We've got trouble," he said in a confidential tone as soon as he settled next to her.

"What? Tell me," she pleaded with a quick look toward the men talking among themselves.

"Judge Bieberman had to go out of town on a family emergency. Judge Macias is taking her place on the bench this morning."

Cory saw the glum look in Theo's eyes and knew there was more to it than the simple substitution of one judge for another. "You don't like this Judge Macias?"

"It's not a matter of that." He took a deep breath. "I might as well give it to you straight. Macias has a reputation as a hard-nose, especially when someone has been hurt."

"What does that mean?"

"I'm not sure. Let's wait and see."

"I feel as though that's all I've been doing for two days—waiting. I—" She stopped abruptly, her attention riveted on the man who had just stepped out of the elevator. Even before she saw his face, she felt a sensation like a shiver pass down her spine.

No one but Nick walked into a strange place as though he had a divine right to be there. No one but Nick had the ability to charge the air in a place just by entering.

Her heartbeat moved into a faster rhythm, and her hands felt numb. "He said he wasn't coming."

"Who?"

"Nick Donatelli. Remember I told you about him, Joey's godfather?"

"The man who arrested him?"

"Yes. He said he wasn't coming."

Theo's gaze followed hers. "Impressive man," he said, giving her an odd look. "Looks tough."

"Yes."

He was wearing a blue blazer that must have been altered to accommodate his big shoulders and narrow waist, along with tailored gray slacks that only partially camouflaged the muscle in his long legs. His white shirt was starched and crisp, his silk tie conservative. His loafers gleamed.

Automatically checking out his surroundings and the people around him, Nick saw the surprise in Cory's eyes, along with something he couldn't identify. Nothing good, he told himself before focusing his attention on the group of men with Davila. Before he did anything else, he might as well get the formalities over with.

Davila noticed him first. He said something short and succinct, and all conversation stopped.

"Morning, gentlemen," Nick said when he joined the now silent group.

Unable to hear the words, Cory saw the wariness in their faces and the stiffness in their stances, like large powerful animals sensing an even more powerful intruder in their territory.

Catching her eyes on him, Nick gave her a brief impersonal nod before returning his attention to the group.

"You here officially?" Davila asked with an unfriendly smile.

"Let's say I'm an interested party," Nick said as he pulled his ID wallet from his back pocket and showed it to the marshal.

"Are you armed, sergeant?" the marshal asked after a thorough inspection of Nick's credentials.

"I'm carrying a regulation .38." He opened his jacket to show his pistol. "Any problem?"

"No, sir, but you'd better wear your ID in court."

Nick nodded and returned his badge to his pocket before clipping his ID card to his lapel. "Thanks for the help yesterday," he said to Davila. "I owe you one. Feel free to call in the marker any time."

Before Davila could get his tight jaw unhinged enough to reply, Nick nodded again and walked toward the bench where Cory was sitting.

Theo stood and extended his hand. After a split-second's hesitation, Nick took it in his. Theo's hand was slender and well kept. Nick's was knotted with muscle, and one of his knuckles was misshapen and bruised. Nothing had changed, Cory thought. Nick attracted violence the way other men attracted good luck.

"Sergeant Donatelli, I'm Theodore Kennedy, Joey's attorney."

"Mr. Kennedy."

"Good morning," Cory said when Nick's gaze lowered to her face.

"You look tired," he said by way of greeting. Unlike yesterday, the unruly curl in his glossy hair had been partially tamed, and the bandage was gone from his forehead. Cory had been around cops long enough to recognize a bullet crease when she saw one, and her empty stomach twisted.

"Why didn't you tell me you'd been shot?" The tension in her voice made her words into an accusation.

"Because I haven't been. He missed." Shifting his weight onto one cocked hip, he shoved one hand in his pocket, revealing a flat torso under the starched white cotton. He looked leaner than she remembered and even more powerful.

Uncomfortable staring at his belly, she got to her feet and slung her purse over her shoulder. "I got your message on my machine."

"I thought you would." His eyes were steady on hers, showing nothing but the shadowed sadness she remembered. She felt her throat go dry, and she swallowed, but the pinched feeling remained.

"You changed your mind."

"Evidently."

Cory waited, but he didn't explain. Nick never explained.

"Joey will be pleased."

Her voice was calm, but she was nervous. Nick saw it in the sudden press of her fingers against her purse and the flutter of her long eyelashes when she looked up at him.

"Actually, I stopped by Juvenile Hall this morning to see him before I came here," he told her.

Without thinking, Cory reached out to clutch his arm. "Oh, Nick, is he all right? I tried to call last night, but they wouldn't put me through."

Nick wondered if she knew how tightly she was holding on to him, and then realized she had acted on impulse, not by deliberate choice. He could have been anyone who had talked to her son.

"He was pretty shaken, but he's handling it."

"I wish I were. I'm so nervous my knees are knocking like castanets."

"Don't try to hide it. You want the judge on your side." Nick caught a whiff of roses, and the familiar scent rippled through his senses like a swift jolt of desire. It hurt to remember. That kind of pain was useless; it made a man face regrets that were better left buried.

Cory felt his muscles contract under her fingers and realized how intimately they were connected. "Sorry, I didn't mean to . . . to, uh . . ." She pulled her hand away and curled her fingers into a fist against her belt.

"I know," he said with the first sign of a smile she'd seen. When she didn't answer with one of her own, his stiffened and died.

Theo, who had been watching the two of them with speculative eyes, interrupted to say in a low voice, "Cory, if you want to see Joey before court convenes, we'd better get inside. They'll be bringing him in any minute now."

"Oh, God, yes!" she exclaimed, glancing around eagerly for a glimpse of her son. "Let's get inside."

Theo hefted his briefcase and turned to offer his arm, but Cory was already walking toward the doors, Nick beside her, one square hand hovering over her back.

Possessive bastard, Theo thought, and wondered if the cop from L.A. was as coldly dangerous as he looked. Even as his mind formed the question he knew the answer. He'd seen men like Donatelli before—on death row.

The marshal opened the door and nodded to Cory, a faintly apologetic smile on his face. "Sorry about this, Mrs. Kingston."

"I appreciate that, Fred," Cory answered with an attempt at her usual warmth. Fred Baxter and his wife were two of the Sunshine School's biggest boosters.

"I want to thank you for what you've done for Fred, Jr. He comes home every day all excited about the things you're teaching him, 'specially his drawing."

Cory managed a smile. "He's very talented."

The marshal beamed, softening his bull-like jaw. "The wife says he takes after me. I do some painting in my spare time, you know."

"Really? Maybe you could come in some day and give the children a lesson."

"Sure I could, Mrs. Kingston. You name the day."

"I will, as soon as...as...you know." Cory felt her smile slip.

"Sure, sure, I understand," Baxter said hastily, looking uncomfortable.

Nick saw the panic flare in her eyes. "Excuse us, marshal," Nick said with a nod to the other man. "Mrs. Kingston wants to see her son."

"Sure thing, sarge." He turned to Cory, saying in a confidential tone, "I'm pullin' for you and your boy."

"I appreciate that, Fred," she said, managing a small smile. "Thank you."

As she moved forward, she felt the firm pressure of Nick's hand through the silk of her dress. Surprise sifted through her anxiety, but she managed to keep from showing it.

The courtroom was small, with a wide center aisle bisecting six rows of uncomfortable-looking benches. Ahead was a small railing setting off an area containing the judge's bench and the witness stand, as well as two long tables, one on each side of the aisle, and a small table shared by the bailiff and the court reporter, who were already seated. The empty jury box was off to one side. According to Theo, it would remain empty, since juvenile cases were decided by the judge only.

Nerves leaping, Cory glanced around the room, looking for Joey's familiar blond head. She didn't know whether to be worried or relieved that he hadn't yet arrived.

Not many people had. Most of the benches were empty. She recognized a reporter from the *Ojai Gazette* who had done a story on the gala opening of her school. Susan...Susan Something-or-Other. They exchanged nods, and Cory thought she saw a look of sympathy on the young woman's face.

As they approached the front, a short balding man with a scholarly stoop and thick wire-rimmed glasses left his seat at one of the tables and came up to Theo.

"Morning, counselor," he said with a nod for Cory and a longer than necessary look at Nick.

"Mr. Prosecutor," Theo said with a friendly smile. "Albert Slovik. Cory Kingston, Sergeant Donatelli, LAPD."

Cory answered the man's nod with one of her own. Nick and the man exchanged a perfunctory handshake. "I heard LAPD had an interest in this case," Slovik said. "I'm flattered."

"Strictly unofficial," Nick said in a neutral tone.

"But not casual."

Nick saw the sharp curiosity in the man's myopic eyes and knew exactly what Davila had told the county prosecutor about one Nick Donatelli.

"Doesn't seem like it, does it?"

Cory felt her muscles knot with tension. She felt naked, vulnerable, in this place, as though everything she'd ever taught her son, everything she'd done while raising him, was also on trial.

"How come you're handling a petty case like this one yourself?" Theo asked Slovik after they'd exchanged the usual banter between lawyers.

"Assault with intent isn't petty, Theo my man. The county commissioners have tagged this high priority all the way."

"Oh yeah? I didn't know you took orders from politicians."

Slovik's friendly grin grew strained. "I don't. But the people have a right to be protected from street gangs and violence." With a curt nod, he turned and returned to his place.

"I hope you've got muscle, counselor," Nick said as they made their way to the front row. "This smells like trouble."

Theo nodded. "You notice he didn't mention a deal?"

"I noticed."

Cory stared from one to the other. "A deal? What are you talking about? Joey is innocent."

"Standard procedure," Theo tossed off. "Don't worry about it."

Cory shifted her gaze to Nick's impassive face. "Nick?"

"It's the system, Cory."

Nick tried to ignore the tug in his gut as she looked up at him, her eyes shimmering with concern the way they had been that long ago day on the beach. Then she'd been worried about him instead of her son, trying to ease the agony that only she'd had the insight—or was it caring?—to sense in him.

That had been the real problem between them. She'd sensed too much in him, too much he'd fought to keep protected and safe. And yet, when she'd left his life, she'd opened a hole he'd never been able to fill.

"I'll see if I can find Joey," he said when he couldn't stand the worry in her eyes an instant longer.

"Thanks," she said in a shaky whisper.

He looked as though he were going to say something, but whatever it was stayed locked inside where no one had ever been allowed to go.

Theo led her to the middle of the front bench on the left and sat down with her, his briefcase safe at his feet. Nick spoke a few words to the bailiff, who motioned him to the door by the jury box. A few rangy strides and he had disappeared behind the oak panel.

Cory ran her hand over the rail in front of her. It was hard and unyielding, like the contempt she'd felt for the man who was doing everything he could to help her—in spite of the angry words she'd thrown at him.

"He took your husband's death hard, didn't he?"

For an instant Cory had forgotten that Theo was there. "Why do you say that?" she asked, turning to regard him quizzically.

"He carries his pain in his eyes. I'm surprised you didn't notice."

But she had, and she had hurt when she'd seen it. "Nick and Joe were very close."

"Partners usually are."

"Yes. I hear Nick's gone through three since…Joe died." She hadn't asked, but friends in L.A. had told her about Nick's troubles.

Theo nodded, but privately he doubted that friendship was the entire reason Donatelli had bought into this. The man had the look of someone who had more than a casual interest in his partner's widow.

Fortunately, he thought, Cory didn't seem to return that interest. As soon as this problem with her son was taken care of, he would make sure she never did.

"I'd better take my seat." He put extra warmth in his lawyer-to-client smile. "Judge Macias is very punctual."

Cory nodded and let him press her hand. "Good luck," she managed.

"Don't worry. Joey will be home by noon."

Seconds later, just as Theo was arranging his papers in front of him, Nick and Joey came into the courtroom through a door to the left of the jury box. Dressed in stained blue coveralls, the boy was accompanied by a deputy sheriff, who had one hand on his shoulder, the other on his gun.

As soon as Joey saw his mother, he started to veer in her direction, but the marshal pulled him up short, earning a swift look of anger from the boy's green eyes.

At a quiet word from Nick, the marshal glanced at Cory, then shrugged and removed his beefy hand from Joey's shoulder.

"Joey," Cory called in a choked voice as she got to her feet and leaned over the rail. "Oh, baby, I'm so glad to see you."

"Hi, Mom," he said with a shaky smile.

With the thick wooden railing between them, it was difficult to hug him, but she managed. From the corner of her eye she saw Davila and the other men with him slip into the opposite bench.

"How are you doing, sweetie?" she asked when they drew apart. He smelled as though he needed a bath, and his face was paper white.

"Get me out of here, Mom." His voice cracked, bringing a flood of red to his pinched features. His eyes were bloodshot, and Cory tried not to think about the night he must have spent.

"We will, sweetie. I promise." Cory clutched his hand tightly, afraid to let go. It helped to touch him, to feel the warmth of his skin. His fingers were trembling almost as much as hers. Before Joey could say anything further, the burly marshal stepped forward.

"Excuse me, ma'am," he said to Cory before urging Joey to his seat next to Theo. "Court's about to convene."

Cory sank back into her seat, then glanced up to see Nick standing at the end of the bench, waiting. "Sorry," she muttered, sliding sideways with a rustle of silk.

"No problem." He sat next to her, careful to keep a good foot of bench between them. Even so, she caught a whiff of soap and sandalwood, two scents that always reminded her of Nick.

"This is old stuff to you, I guess," she said, slanting him a look that held the memory of the words they'd flung at each other at their last meeting.

"If you mean being in court, yes. If you mean being worried as hell, no."

Cory saw the hard truth in his eyes and drew a long slow breath. "Theo said everything would be all right."

"He's your attorney. You should listen to him."

The band of tension running along his shoulders tightened. He hated to sit and wait, hated to feel powerless the way he was beginning to feel around this woman. The hell of it was, she wasn't the one taking the power. He was giving it to her, because he cared too damn much, and that made him furious with himself.

"Nick, do you think Theo is wrong?"

"What I think isn't important," he hedged. "It's what Theo can make the judge think that counts."

Feeling rebuffed and knowing she deserved it, Cory sat stiffly, her gaze fixed on the bench where the judge would be sitting in just a few short minutes, listening to a man she didn't know say terrible things about her son.

On the stroke of nine the bailiff straightened to attention and glanced at the clock above the rear doors. At the same instant the rear door opened again and the judge entered.

"All rise," the bailiff droned. "The Juvenile Court of Ventura County is now in session, the honorable Homer Macias presiding."

The low buzz of conversation ceased, and the feet of the half-dozen spectators made scuffling noises on the wooden floor as everyone obeyed.

The judge took his place and nodded his thanks to the bailiff, who barked, "Be seated."

The judge's gaze swept the courtroom, stopping for what seemed like an extra beat on her face before moving on. How many mothers had he seen sitting where she was? she wondered with a small tremor of anxiety. And how many of those mothers had left brokenhearted and in tears?

"Mean-looking bastard, isn't he?" Nick whispered close to her ear.

Cory's throat was so tight she could only nod. Macias was a few years shy of sixty, with a stocky body and a stern face. As he read aloud the charges against Joey, she looked for compassion in those chiseled features and found none.

The proceedings went very much as Theo had predicted. Slovik spoke first, presenting the evidence that Davila had compiled.

"As Your Honor can plainly see," the prosecutor concluded in ringing tones that made Cory cringe inside, "Joseph Kingston, young as he is, has shown himself to be a danger to the community. Moreover, by leaving the city in such a precipitous manner, he has demonstrated that he's a flight risk. Therefore, the county respectfully requests that he be held in custody until the trial."

Theo was on his feet immediately. "I object, Your Honor. My client has never before been in trouble. His mother is a respected teacher and businesswoman with deep ties to the community, and his late father was a policeman who died in the line of duty."

As Cory sat rigid on the edge of her seat, he went on to list additional reasons, precedents from similar cases, why Joey should be released. "And as for his being a flight risk, I submit that he went to Los Angeles to seek advice from his godfather who, if Your Honor will notice, is also the arresting officer. I submit further that Joseph would not have gone anywhere near an officer of the law if he had intended to flee."

The judge's expression turned thoughtful as he peered at Joey over his steel-rimmed glasses. "You have a point, Mr. Kennedy. However, the court is still not convinced that your client won't run away again."

Theo glanced behind him, his expression mirroring indecision. His eyes met Nick's, and his face cleared. "I realize this is an informal hearing, Your Honor, but if I may, I'd like to put the arresting officer on the stand."

The judge hesitated, his gaze going from Theo to the prosecutor, who frowned. "I object, Your Honor," Slovik said, getting to his feet. "Mr. Kennedy can present his witnesses at the trial."

As soon as Cory saw the judge's eyebrows rise, she knew Slovik had made a mistake. "Proceed, Mr. Kennedy," Macias said with a nod.

Sitting so close, Cory saw a muscle tighten in Nick's jaw and sensed that he wasn't happy to be called to the stand. Puzzled, she gave him a questioning look, which he answered with a swift frown.

As he walked to the stand and took the oath, Cory felt the atmosphere in the courtroom change. It was as though everyone was holding their breath—including her.

"State your full name and title for the record, please," the judge instructed.

"Dominic Franco Donatelli, Sergeant, LAPD."

"I'm sure you know that this is an informal hearing," the judge said in a stern tone. "Please keep your remarks brief."

"Yes, sir."

Nick felt his heart thud against his ribs. He couldn't begin to remember the number of times he'd been on the witness stand, but this was the first time Cory had been sitting a few feet away, looking at him with anxious eyes that cut into his soul.

"Sergeant, when did you learn of Joey's, er, problem?" Theo asked in a confident tone.

"Around seven a.m. yesterday morning at my apartment in Santa Monica. I came off a stakeout to find him waiting for me."

"He told you about the incident at the school?"

"Yes, he did. He asked for my help."

"What kind of help?"

Nick chose his words carefully. "Mostly I think he wanted me with him when he explained to his mother what kind of a mess he'd gotten himself into. He was worried about her."

Theo glanced toward Cory and smiled, drawing everyone's attention to her small erect figure and pale anxious face. Nick's opinion of the lawyer rose a few notches.

"What did you do then?"

"I called Ojai PD and found out that a warrant had been issued, so I told the watch commander that I would be bringing him in."

"Which you did."

"Yes, a few hours later."

"So you're saying that Joseph willingly surrendered to you as an officer of the law? So that you would be the one to go with him to the local authorities?"

"Yes, that's right," he said, hoping Kennedy had the good sense not to push too hard for the complete truth. Joey *had* surrendered to him—*after* he'd told the kid he didn't have a choice. If he was asked, that was exactly what he would have to say.

"Thank you, sergeant, you may step down."

Slovik surged to his feet again. "Your Honor!"

The judge gave Theo a reproving look. "This may be an informal proceeding, Mr. Kennedy, but Mr. Slovik is entitled to cross-examine your witness."

"Yes, Your Honor," Theo said before sitting down.

Slovik moved toward Nick with the glint of battle in his eyes. "When Joseph Kingston came to your apartment, was he armed?"

Cory gasped, drawing a quick glance from Nick before he answered. "No."

"Did he resist arrest?" Slovik persisted, and this time his gaze lingered pointedly on the scrape above Nick's eyebrow.

"No, he surrendered voluntarily."

"Did he surrender before or after you called here to ask about the incident at the high school?"

Smart question, Nick thought with a rising feeling of dread. "After."

"Counselor has suggested that Joseph came to you with the express intention of asking you to accompany him to the Ojai police. I ask you now, did your godson specifically ask you to go to the police with him?"

"He asked me to contact the Ojai authorities, yes."

At the subtle change of wording, Slovik's expression sharpened. "Did he ask you to accompany him to the police so that he could give himself up?"

Nick saw Cory's eyes shift to his, and he knew what she wanted him to say. What she *expected* him to say.

Trust me, he wanted to beg. I won't let you down this time. But even if he could make himself say the words, he knew he couldn't keep that kind of promise. He would die for her or her children. But he wouldn't lie for anyone, not even her.

Nick took a deep breath and met the man's gaze squarely. "No, he didn't."

A light glinted behind Slovik's thick lenses. "Did he tell you why he came to see you?"

"Yes."

"Tell the court, please."

"He asked me to fix things with Ojai PD."

Respect glinted in Slovik's small eyes for an instant before he turned away. "Thank you for your honesty. That's all."

Nick left the stand and walked toward Cory, feeling her scorn with each step. As he sat down, he made himself meet her eyes.

"How could you?" she whispered, her mouth pale.

"I had no choice."

"You bastard."

The judge's gavel came down on the block, startling her into silence. "Bail is denied. Trial is set for December second. The defendant will be confined in Juvenile Hall until that time."

"No!" Cory cried, jumping to her feet. "December is two months away."

"I'm sorry, Mrs. Kingston," the judge said in a surprisingly kind tone. "I would be remiss if I ignored the evidence."

"But he's not a criminal, Your Honor. I swear he isn't!"

She started to move toward the aisle, but Nick's big body blocked her way. "Get out of my way," she snapped. "I want to see my son."

"Don't, Cory," Theo said in alarm. By this time nearly everyone in the courtroom but the judge and Joey was on their feet.

"Your Honor," Nick called over the buzz of comment. "May I offer a suggestion?"

Macias's eyebrows raised. "It is a bit irregular, but since this is an informal hearing, go ahead."

"Release the defendant to my supervision until the trial. I'll be responsible for him."

The judge looked surprised, but not displeased. "I admit your suggestion has merit, Sergeant. Unfortunately, however, I can't allow the boy to leave the county."

Nick heard Cory's strangled moan and knew he would hate himself forever if he failed her now. "Then I'll move here."

Chapter 7

The judge tentatively agreed to Nick's suggestion, providing his credentials checked out. Before he had called a temporary recess, he'd instructed his clerk to get the name and phone number of Nick's immediate superior. At the moment, Macias was in his chambers conferring with Theo and Slovik, deciding Joey's fate.

Cory and Nick were waiting in a small anteroom off the judge's chambers. Joey was downstairs somewhere with the marshal. Cory could still see him looking back at her as he was led away, his eyes as wide and frightened as a lost little boy's.

Every instinct she possessed urged her to run from floor to floor, from room to room, until she found her child. But even if she found him, she couldn't sit in a cell with him, and she couldn't protect him from the men who held him. It was tearing her apart.

"What's taking so long?" she muttered, her impatience showing in the quick little glances she sent around the room.

"It's only been twenty minutes," Nick told her, angling his thick wrist so that he could see his watch. "Give 'em time to make the calls."

Calls? The judge had only asked for one number, Lieutenant Bill Frazier's. She knew him, of course. In fact, he had been standing very close to her when she'd said those things to Nick at Joe's funeral. Now she wondered if Bill would describe that scene to the judge. And if he did? Then what?

"Theo promised that Joey would be home for lunch," she said with a look at her own watch.

"He should have known better."

Cory glared at him before returning her attention to the blank wall in front of her. She wanted to be angry with Nick. She *needed* to be angry with him. Otherwise, there were too many other things she might feel about him, none of them wise, or particularly safe.

Nick shrugged out of his jacket and tossed it onto one of the benches. With one hand he loosened the perfect knot of his tie and wrenched the starched collar away from his throat. It helped some, but not enough. Cooped up with Cory in a space hardly big enough for one was making him as tense as a cornered animal.

From the corner of her eye Cory watched him unlink his cuffs and roll them halfway to his elbows. "You don't have to baby-sit me, Nick. Go outside for some air if you need it."

"The air's fine." He walked to the window and looked out, one hand braced against the wall. The other hand rubbed the back of his neck as though the muscles had seized up on him.

"You were right the first time, Nick," she said in a tension-strained voice. "You should have stayed away."

"You never give up, do you, Cory? No matter what I do, it's wrong."

Cory was too anxious to think about her words before she spoke them. "If it hadn't been for your testimony, the judge would have granted bail, and Joey would be home by now instead of God only knows where."

"No way. Macias was set against the kid from the moment he walked in."

Cory shook her head. "You're wrong," she insisted. "I saw his face when he looked at me. He seems like a very nice man, once you get beyond that stern look."

"You think everyone is nice."

"Most people are."

"In your world, maybe. Not in mine." One side of his mouth lifted in a sardonic smile that chilled her worse than the most dangerous frown.

Before she caught herself, she slid her legs backward and tucked her hands more firmly around her purse. Terrific, Cory, she thought. Five minutes alone with the man and you're in the fetal position.

"I hate waiting," she muttered to the opposite wall. Much as she hated to admit it, she was glad she wasn't alone. She would talk with the devil himself to ease the agony of waiting.

"Me, I'm used to it," he said with a shrug that settled his shoulders into a deceptively casual angle. Nick never really relaxed.

"Joe said you used to tell him dirty jokes."

"Naw, he told them to me. Claimed he got 'em from you."

Her head jerked around so fast she felt a twinge in her neck. "He did not," she protested with an indignant flash in her eyes.

"No?"

"No! I hate dirty jokes."

Nick's eyes crinkled into shallow laugh lines. "Besides, you always laugh before you get to the punch line."

Cory looked away, but not before he'd seen a faint softening in her mouth. It wasn't quite a smile, but he felt a quick shift in the air.

Strung tight and close to his limit, he turned back to the window. A mother was pushing her little boy in one of the swings in the park across from the city hall. Her long honey-colored hair blew in the breeze, reminding him of Cory when she'd been a young mother. She'd had a glow about her then, making her so beautiful it had taken all his control to be happy for his partner.

Now, at thirty-nine, she possessed a different kind of beauty. It was softer, gentler, as though it came from within, and carrying three children had rounded her figure in a way that made him wonder how she would feel in his arms.

"Nick?"

He heard the ragged edge to her voice and wondered what she would say if she knew that he'd never stopped wanting to make love to her. He turned away from the window to confront her.

Sunlight angled through the window, highlighting the gold in her hair and touching her cheeks with color. He felt a stir inside, an emotion that, unlike most of his feelings, he had no trouble labeling. Hunger, the raw, clawing kind Cory always managed to arouse in him.

He cleared the sudden tightness from his throat. "It'll work out, Cory. I know patience is hard for you, but try, okay?"

"What if the judge doesn't like what Bill Frazier has to say about you? What if he decides you're not a good role model?"

"Then we're all in for a rotten eight weeks."

Cory had no answer for that. Silence dripped between them like a Chinese water torture. She stared at the wall again, aware of Nick's brooding eyes on her.

When Joe had been alive, he'd been a natural buffer between them. Now that he was gone, she felt strangely exposed around Nick. Without Joe's presence, Nick suddenly seemed more like the man who had been her first love.

Then, as now, he'd possessed an earthy virility that reminded her of wild moonlit nights roaring along back roads in his Corvette, the wind blowing in her hair and his arm heavy on her shoulder.

Down the hall a door slammed. Nerves already raw, Cory jumped as adrenaline spurted into her bloodstream. "What are they doing in there?" Leaning forward slightly, she strained to hear the sound of voices beyond the door but heard only her own breathing.

"Arguing, most likely. That's what lawyers do best."

She looked up to find Nick watching her. "I keep thinking that this has to be my fault," she said in a shredded voice. "So much happened to the kids all at once. Joe's death. Selling the house and relocating up here. Making the kids change schools, find new friends. I wanted us to have a new start. Now I'm wondering if I wasn't really trying to run away."

"From what?"

Her shrug was self-conscious. "Pain, grief, I don't know," she murmured. "Too many ghosts, maybe. I thought we could leave them behind."

"Nice idea, if you can manage it." The cynical twist to his mouth told her he'd tried.

"I thought so then." She thought about Jen's weight problem and Joey's troubles. She thought about her almost obsessive cheerfulness whenever loneliness got her down. "Now I'm not so sure."

Nick saw the faint trembling of her mouth and knew she wasn't nearly as composed as she wanted him to believe. "Don't be so hard on yourself. You did your best. Maybe it was a mistake, maybe it wasn't. Doesn't matter much either way, because you can't change it." He knew better than most how much it hurt to want desperately to correct a mistake and know that you never could.

"No, I can't change it. I . . ." Suddenly it all seemed to come at her at once. The memory-jarring appearance of a man in uniform on her doorstep, Joey's disappearance, his arrest, Nick's sudden reappearance in her life. Perhaps that was the worst of the uncertainties tormenting her, reopening old wounds and forcing her to face things better left forgotten.

His face blurred, and she made herself look away. Hands twisted together in her lap, she sat rigid as marble, trying to force back the tears. But the dampness spread from her eyes to her cheeks.

"I . . . he seemed happy here, honestly he did. He had new friends, a girl . . . and now this." She began to shake. "I'm so afraid for him."

She buried her face in her hands, sobs shaking her shoulders beneath the silk. Nick took it as long as he could, his hands knotted at his sides. He looked at the floor, at the wall, at the forlorn curve of her neck beneath the sleek coil of her hair.

Cursing Joey, himself, the judge, he crossed the room in two strides and pulled her to her feet. Before she had time to do more than direct a watery gasp of surprise his way, he wrapped her in his arms.

Cory stiffened and tried to pull away. "I'm all right," she protested, but her mouth trembled as she spoke the words.

"No, you're not." The rough edge of understanding in his voice undid her.

"No, I'm not," she whispered, overtaken by a sob. "Darn, I hate to . . . cry," she muttered through a hiccup.

"You always did." Fierce, stubborn Cory, he thought. She hated weakness of any kind, especially in herself.

"Did I?" Another half-stifled cry.

He'd forgotten how delicate her body felt next to his. Not that she was skinny. Far from it. The soft breasts pressed against his chest were nicely full, and her hips had a decidedly feminine curve to them. Because he wanted to trace those curves with his hands, he kept them pressed firmly against her back.

"Cory, stop talking and cry before you explode." His voice was edged with the kind of tension frustration puts in a man when his body wants what his mind says he can't have.

His arms tightened, and she felt the steel beneath the starched shirt. It had been so long since she'd felt protected, so long since she'd felt safe, really deep down safe. At the moment it didn't seem to matter that the strong, sheltering arms were Nick's.

Cory let herself relax into those arms and stopped fighting the tears. They stung her tired eyes and flowed onto his shirt, soaking the expensive material, but Nick didn't seem to mind. Instead, he stood perfectly still, his big hands pressed against the small of her back. It was only seconds, but it seemed like hours, before she managed to swallow the last of the sobs.

"Better?" Nick murmured against her hair. She nodded against his chest, and her forehead brushed his chin. Her hair was soft and clinging. He remembered the way it had felt fanned over his chest after they'd made love.

Hunger clawed deeper, reminding him that he'd never had any control over his physical desires when he was around Cory. He edged backward, breaking the contact of their thighs. It helped, but not enough.

"Joey's a good kid, Cory. He knows what's right and what isn't. He just got a little off track, picked the wrong friends, didn't come home when he should have."

Cory raised her gaze to his face, her shimmering eyes searching his. "Like you did once?" she asked, her voice barely above a whisper.

"My reasons were different, but yes, like me." Framing her face with his hands, he wiped away the tears with his thumbs, but the violet smudges of fatigue remained, tearing at him.

Cory would go through hell and back for her child and never stop to think about herself. Once she'd felt the same way about him. A man only got lucky like that once in his life. God didn't give second chances.

Seeing the shadows shift in his eyes, Cory wanted to weep. Nick had suffered, too—because of Joe, because of countless other tragedies he hadn't been able to prevent. But he was still a compassionate man under the hard-forged exterior, and he was trying to make up for his mistake by helping Joey. And her.

"I was wrong," she said in a low, soft tone. "You were right to come. Joey... Joey needs you."

Before he could stop her, she pulled out of his arms and turned away. Nick breathed in against the need to pull her back against him and wondered why she always managed to catch him off guard.

"What about you? Don't you need an old friend to lean on right now?"

"No," she said, "Yes. Oh, Nick, I—"

Whatever she'd intended to say was lost when the door suddenly opened and Theo appeared. He was smiling. "The judge would like to see you both."

Cory felt adrenaline rush through her. The inner shaking that had gone away in Nick's arms began again. "Does that mean . . . is he going to let Joey come home?"

"Yes, under one condition." His smile faded as his gaze went from Cory's face to Nick's.

"What's that?" Nick asked, his eyes narrowing in anticipation.

"Yes, tell us," Cory urged, her words tumbling over Nick's.

Theo cleared his throat. This time his gaze fastened on Cory's face as he said without inflection, "Joey has to live with Nick."

"No!" Cory cried.

Theo looked uncomfortable. "He won't budge, Cory. He wants Joey supervised in the evening hours."

"But . . . but he belongs at home."

Both men looked at her. No, she thought. I can't. I won't. But she had no choice. Joey's safety meant more to her than anything else in the world, including her own peace of mind.

"Then Nick will just have to move in with us."

Cory unfolded a clean sheet and spread it over the mattress of the bed that would be Nick's for eight weeks while Joey moved into the spare bunk in Timmy's room.

Joey grabbed the other end of the sheet and haphazardly tucked in the end. "Why can't Uncle Nick sleep on the couch like always?"

Because he sleeps half-nude. "Because it's better this way."

"Timmy snores," Joey groused. Since they'd arrived home shortly after two, Joey had done little else but complain. What scant patience Cory had managed to salvage after three hours of bureaucratic red tape at the courthouse was long gone.

"You'll get used to it." Cory tucked a pillow under her chin and pulled on a case. It smelled of fabric softener. Nick's sheets had always carried the clean scent of his skin.

With a silent curse she threw the pillow against the headboard and picked up its companion and a fresh case. She hadn't thought of those long-ago nights in a very long time.

"Why can't Uncle Nick sleep with Timmy?" her son persisted.

"Enough, Joseph," she grated in her sternest tone. "If it wasn't for Uncle Nick, you would be spending the next eight weeks in juvenile detention. So I think a little consideration and gratitude might be in order, don't you?"

"I guess."

Cory threw the pillow onto the bed and took a deep breath.

"Finish moving your clothes and then vacuum the closet for me."

"Aw, Mom..."

Cory rested both hands on his shoulders. "Joey, don't push it, okay? You've caused enough turmoil around here."

Joey's gaze slid away from hers, and color flooded his cheeks. "Okay," he mumbled in the direction of her left ear.

Cory pulled his head down and kissed his forehead. "I love you, Joey, but I'm not going to pretend I'm not upset, because I am."

Joey edged away from her, his expression a mix of defiance and guilt. "You're not gonna ground me, are you, Mom?"

"What do you think?"

"I think it would be a big mistake."

Cory blinked at him, her brow wrinkling into a frown. "I can't wait to hear your reason for that statement," she said with a weary edge of humor in her voice.

Joey's expression turned earnest. "See, if you ground me, everyone will think I'm guilty, and I'm not. You believe that, don't you, Mom?"

"Of course I do! That goes without saying. But you also made some bad mistakes. If I don't punish you, you'll think I approve of what you did, and I don't. Not any of it."

Joey winced but held his ground. "Don't you think spending a night in that stinking jail is punishment enough?"

"Do you?"

"God, yes!" he exclaimed with a shudder. "That place was the rankest, a real pit. Half the guys in my dormitory were stoned. The other half spent the night telling me what they were going to do to me when the guard wasn't looking."

Cory gasped, and his face turned bright red. "Ask Uncle Nick what it's like if you don't believe me," he added in a thin voice.

Cory watched his nervous hands pick up a cassette tape and turn it over and over. His brush with the law had changed him. His face had lost the last signs of boyish innocence, and his eyes seemed different, somehow. She had a feeling it would change him even more before the nightmare was finally over.

"I believe you," she said with an inner shiver. "That's one of the reasons I wanted you home."

The strained lines in his face eased into a tentative, lopsided smile. "So you won't ground me?"

Cory hesitated. Was Joey right? Had he been punished enough? Yes, she thought. He had.

"If you promise you'll be on your best behavior," she said with a stern look.

"I promise!" Breaking into a grin, he gave her a clumsy hug that nearly bent her double, then loped toward the door. "I'm going over to Skip's."

"Joey—"

"Don't worry. It's just to get my homework assignments, that's all. I'll be back for dinner."

He was gone before Cory realized he hadn't moved his clothes or vacuumed the closet as she'd asked him to do.

"Damn," she muttered, smoothing the pillow Nick would use tonight. She needed a nap.

Cory was putting the last of the dinner dishes in the dishwasher when she heard the Corvette pulling into the driveway, followed seconds later by the muffled thud of the sports car's heavy door slamming.

It wouldn't be long before her neighbors began to wonder about the lethal black car and the equally lethal man driving it. She would have to explain before the rumors started. Most of the time she loved small town life. This wasn't one of those times.

Cory had expected Nick to walk right in, the way he'd done in the past, so she'd made certain the door was unlocked and the porch light switched on. He knocked instead.

"Hi," he said with a grin when she opened the door. "Is this the Hotel Kingston?" Cory recognized his attempt to lessen the tension and was grateful. Trying to pretend everything was normal was the only way they would get through the next two months.

"Do you have a reservation?" she asked, trying to ignore the nervous flutters in her stomach.

One eyebrow lifted. "So they tell me."

He stood in the circle of light, his black hair tossed every which way. He had changed into jeans and a red *V*-necked sweater worn without a shirt. The tie he'd worn earlier was slung around his neck, as though he'd grabbed it as an afterthought. A garment bag was slung over one shoulder, a duffel over the other. He carried a suitcase in one hand. In the other, he carried his bulletproof vest.

"You don't have to knock," she said, stepping back to let him enter. He brought the scent of autumn leaves and wood smoke into the kitchen with him.

"The last time I was here, you threatened to shoot me, remember?" Nick's grin came and went, the lopsided, boyish one that few people saw and always remembered when they did.

"Don't worry. You're safe until December second."

"That's something, anyway." He looked pale and tired.

She closed the door and managed a deep breath. "Was the traffic bad?"

"Yeah, a bitch."

And he would be fighting it both ways for two months. Gratitude tugged at her, making her feel stiff and uncomfortable.

"I'm sorry," she said. "About the inconvenience."

"No problem." Nick shrugged and gave the kitchen a quick once-over. If asked, Cory thought, he would be able to give an accurate accounting of the layout, furnishings, and accessories, including the nearly full pot of coffee warming on the burner. Along with the superior eyesight that had won him every sharpshooting medal offered by the department, Nick had a photographic memory, something Cory had always envied.

"Where's Joey?" he asked, training those enigmatic dark eyes on her face again.

"In the den, studying."

"Hey, I'm impressed!"

"Don't hold your breath," she said with a laugh that sounded almost natural. The flutters in her stomach had settled into a slow rolling that was almost as unnerving.

"*Uncle Nick!*" Jennifer came barreling into the room and launched herself at him. Nick dropped his suitcase and the garment bag fell to the floor as he managed to grab her with one arm.

"Whoa, you've grown up, squirt," he said when he settled her on her feet again.

Jenny giggled at his pet name for her. "I'm taller than Mom now."

"I can see that." She was also far heavier than he remembered. Too heavy for her small bones and delicate features. Poor kid, he thought. Some people ate to ease their pain. Others, like him, tried the bottle. He doubted that Jenny's solution had worked any better than his had.

Jenny clung to his arm, her face pink with excitement and her eyes shining behind the thick glasses. "Mom says you're going to stay with us until Joey's trial."

Nick felt a lump come to this throat. "Think you can put up with me that long?" From the corner of his eyes he saw Cory turn away.

"Sure." Jenny angled a quick look at her mother. "Longer's all right with me. I missed you."

"I missed you, too, squirt." He slid his free arm around her waist and hugged her. She grinned, her eyes shining up at him. As always, when he saw Cory's daughter, he felt something soften inside him. On those rare occasions when he'd allowed himself to think about fathering a child, he'd always pictured a little girl with freckles. And Cory's eyes.

"Maybe we can play Monopoly later?" Jen said in a hopeful tone.

"Sure, if it's okay with your mom."

"Mom never wants to play anymore. She says she's no good at it, but that's because you always made her laugh so hard she forgot to charge you rent when you landed on her stuff."

Nick glanced over Jen's head toward Cory's set face. "Seems to me I still owe you twenty-seven thousand, give or take a few thou."

"That was a long time ago," she said, feeling her mouth begin to soften into a smile to match his.

For four solid years she'd tried to forget the way his laughter used to fill her house, the way his grin had flashed while he was regaling her and Joe with a detailed description of his latest conquest.

For four solid years she'd tried to forget the man who had been closer than a brother to her husband, the man she had once thought she loved. She had almost succeeded. Almost.

When she saw that brooding, almost wistful look in his eyes, it was too easy to remember why she had wanted to love him. Remember why you stopped, she told herself with a mental shake. That hasn't changed.

Her gaze swung to Jenny and became stern. "Honey, Uncle Nick will be here a long time. Give him a chance to settle in before you pounce."

"Sorry," Jenny said with an abashed look.

"It won't take me long," he told her with a wink. "I'll just throw my stuff in a corner someplace, and I'm home."

Jenny giggled. "Don't let Mom catch you doing that. She's got this thing about keeping things neat."

"Yeah, I remember."

"I'll show you to your room," Cory said, turning away from those shadowed brown eyes.

Nick slung the garment bag over his shoulder and reached for his suitcase. At the open door to the den, Cory stopped and looked in. Joey was stretched out on the couch, his attention riveted on a scantily clad blonde gyrating across the

TV screen. No sound came from the set, but Joey was mouthing the lyrics just the same.

"Studying, huh?" Nick said with just the slightest hint of humor creeping into his low voice.

Cory found herself smiling. "It's a new experience for him. He doesn't have all the bugs worked out."

Nick laughed, taking years off his face. She had forgotten how very masculine and full of fun his laugh was. Feeling her own laugh bubble in her throat, she turned her attention to her son.

"Joseph!" Her voice was sharper than she intended and nearly tumbled her son from the sagging couch.

"Just taking a break," he said as he bounded forward to snap off the set. "Hi, Uncle Nick. Looks like you got enough stuff for a couple months."

"Feels like it, too," Nick said before directing a dubious look at the couch Joey had just vacated. "I see you still have old-faithful."

"I keep intending to replace it, but somehow, I just never get around to it."

"Just my luck."

Cory met his amused glance, and something that felt like sadness twisted inside her. In her mind, she realized suddenly, Nick and that old couch had become inseparable. The realization that that might be the reason why she hadn't been able to part with the ratty old thing shook her more than she wanted to admit.

"Don't worry, you won't suffer," she said, not quite able to resist a smile. "Joey is giving you his room. This time you'll be sleeping upstairs."

Nick looked up from his half-empty suitcase to see Joey walk through the bedroom door and head for the closet.

"Just came to get my jacket," Joey said when he saw Nick's eyebrows rise. "Mom forgot to move it to Timmy's room."

"Going someplace?" Nick asked with a quick look at his watch. It was nearly nine.

"Me and the guys are going to shoot a couple games of pool down at the rec center." Joey shrugged into an expensive-looking jacket, then opened his desk drawer and pulled out some folded bills.

Nick took his spare pistol from the suitcase and slipped it under the pillow before turning to confront the boy. "Sorry. You're staying in tonight."

"Mom says it's okay." He shoved the money into his jacket pocket and edged toward the door.

"I say it's not."

Joey's grin faltered at the corners. "Hey, man, you sound serious."

"I am."

"Did I do somethin' wrong?"

Nick dropped an arm on the boy's shoulders and felt him stiffen. "You're grounded, Joe. Until December second. I want you home right after school, and you're not to leave the house without my permission."

Belligerence flashed in the boy's eyes. "No way, man! You got no right to give me orders."

"Joey!" Cory's shocked protest cut through her son's. Both men turned. Nick saw her first. She was wearing the same robe she'd worn earlier and fuzzy slippers that showed off pink toes. Her face was scrubbed clean, and her hair was a shiny tumble of curls against her shoulders.

"Did you say he could go out tonight?"

"Yes, I did. Is there a problem?"

Nick took his time answering, hoping that he didn't sound as irritable as he felt. "You heard the judge the same as I did, Cory. If Joey so much as jaywalks and gets caught, he's in for more trouble than you want to know about. Neither of us wants that."

"He's just going down to the rec center for an hour. What's the harm in that?"

"No harm. He's not going."

"He's my son, Nick. You don't have the right to tell him what to do."

Nick felt his head begin to throb. He was so tired his vision was fuzzy, and the burritos he'd wolfed down while he'd been throwing his things into a suitcase hadn't done much to take the edge off his hunger.

"The paper I signed in court today said I do. If you object, fine. I'll take him back to Juvenile Hall tonight. Your choice."

Cory took one look at the rigid line of Nick's jaw and gritted her teeth against an impulse to order him out of her house again. You're doing this for Joey, she reminded herself with grim resolve.

Cory slowly turned toward her son. "Uncle Nick is right," she said in a stiff tone. "We have to do what he says."

"Aw, Mom."

"No arguing, Joey. Take off your jacket and go watch TV until bedtime."

Joey shot Nick a look that dripped with resentment before he marched out. "Shut the door, please," Cory called after him and he did as he was told.

As soon as she heard Joey's footsteps on the stairs, she turned to Nick and said in what she considered a reasonable tone, considering how angry she was, "We have to come to some agreement here. My kids are upset enough as it is. We need to keep things calm."

"I'm calm," he said, crossing his arms over the width of his chest. "You're the one with fire in her eyes." His grin slashed white. "I have a feeling this is going to be an interesting eight weeks."

"More like impossible," she muttered. She glanced impatiently around the room, then did a double take as she saw the buxom raven-haired centerfold tacked to the back wall of the closet. The languidly posed model had breasts the size of balloons, and a see-through Valentine strategically placed. Miss February, no doubt. "Is that yours?" she demanded with a fierce frown.

"Nope. You know I've always been partial to blondes." He lifted a strand of her hair and let it sift through his fingers. An absorbed expression came over his face as he fingered the silky thickness as though nothing were more important than its texture. Cory tried to brush away his hand and found her fingers caught by his.

"I guess you want me to take it down, huh?" he asked, holding her hand against his shoulder.

"Of course—" she began, but the sensuous gleam in his eyes hit her like a blow. Nick hadn't looked at her like that in twenty years. Not once, in all the times they'd seen each other. It threw her off balance. "I . . . do what you want," she managed to finish. "This is your room while you're here."

Nick saw the faint tint of pink creep into her cheeks and wondered if she was as aware of the sudden sexual tension crackling between them as he was.

"If I keep it clean, do I get a reward?" he asked, thinking about the time she'd called him a sloppy pig and made him clean his place while she sipped Coke and issued orders. When he was done, she'd slowly stripped off his dusty, sweaty clothes and made love to him so thoroughly he'd been weak from it.

Cory saw the glitter in his eyes and knew they were both remembering that same rainy Sunday in his apartment. "Don't, Nick," she said in a low tone, pulling her hand free. "That was a long time ago."

"Remember, Cory? Remember how I used to go crazy when you touched me?"

Had his mouth always turned soft when he said her name? "No, I don't remember." Her voice was strained, bringing a quick slanted smile to the mouth that was so close to hers.

"*I* remember. I've always remembered."

Cory stared at him, the low intimate tone of his voice thrumming in her in time with the racing beat of her heart. "Stop it, Nick," she whispered, and her breath warmed his face. "I'm not interested in picking up where we left off."

"Is that what you think I want?" His voice was low, intense.

"Isn't it?"

He bit back an oath, even as he made himself smile. His pride was all he had left, all that kept him from using his gun on himself.

"I'm going out for a while. Lock the door. I'll take Joey's key." Before he could change his mind, he turned and walked away from her.

Chapter 8

Nick stared at the streetlight beyond the skeletal tree branches outside the open window. The breeze was cool, but his skin burned, and sweat beaded his forehead.

Dumb move, ace, he told himself, thumping his pillow into shape. Eight weeks in the woman's house smelling her perfume, watching her move, hearing the husky lilt in her voice, was going to be the worst kind of torture.

He mouthed a curse into the darkness, stretching out his legs until the muscles threatened to cramp. Even his blood felt hot and heavy as it pushed through his veins. With an impatient sigh, he dragged his wrist over his eyes and tried to sink into the too-soft mattress.

God, he'd been a fool at twenty-two. A damned idiot to turn away from the only real love he'd ever known. And Cory *had* loved him, he realized now, when it was too late.

She would never have given herself to a man she didn't love. All that sweetness, all that hidden fire—it had been his first. He had been the first man to watch her eyes glitter like sun-warmed gems under his caresses, the first man to hear the wild, sweet moans she made in her throat when his hands found secret places never explored before, the first man to feel his body slide into hers.

She'd been so sleek and moist, so ready for him. When she'd climaxed that first time, the tiny convulsions that pulsed against him had driven him into a frenzy that had exploded in a savage, almost unbearable pleasure.

Sex had never been as good for him since. He knew now that it never would be. With other women, he'd made love for the physical release. With Cory, he'd crossed some kind of line inside himself, some kind of private barrier that made him want to give more than a rational man should give any woman.

It wasn't love he'd felt for her. As a child, he'd learned that love wasn't an emotion that was safe to feel, and he'd never changed his mind. But with Cory, sex was more than simple physical release. Raw need came closest to describing it, a primitive, gut-deep ache of one man for one woman that had never gone away.

Being with her had settled him in some quiet way deep inside himself, and yet, at the same time, she had made him feel more alive, more like a man, than the roughest language or the grittiest work could do. With her at his side, he would be willing to face down the insults and snide remarks of the whole damn department, from the chief on down. With her at his side, her forgiveness tucked someplace next to his heart, he just might learn to forgive himself.

"Damn, I need air," he muttered, throwing off the sheet and climbing out of bed in one violent motion. He jerked on his jeans, then looked around for his shirt. Unable to find it in the dark, he shrugged and headed downstairs half-dressed. No one was awake to care what the hell he had on, anyway.

The red numbers on the clock said twenty to four, and Cory's bedroom was pitch black. Disoriented, she held her breath, trying to figure out what had jerked her awake.

The old house creaked and sighed around her, comforting sounds, sounds that wouldn't have signaled alarm.

Straining to hear, she sat up and clutched the blanket close to her throat.

Lightning zigzagged into the window, startling her half-closed eyes into a wide-awake stare. Thunder rolled over-head, soothing and alarming her at the same time. A storm was coming, and the child's desk she'd been refinishing for Tim was outside on the patio with only a latticework over-hang to protect it.

"Rats," she muttered as she stretched across the bed to turn on the bedside lamp. "Now the darn varnish will never dry."

Yawning, eyes slitted against the glare, she stumbled out of bed and fumbled into her robe. Lightning flashed again, and the first drops hit the window.

Directing a few choice words toward the wisecracking TV weatherman who'd predicted clear skies for the next three days, she opened her door and hurried across the dimly lit landing, noticing as she did that Nick's door was ajar.

He was home. She'd heard him come in around mid-night. How long she'd lain awake after that, fighting the past, fighting herself, fighting him, she didn't know. Too long, anyway.

Hand skimming the bannister, she fled down the steps, her bare feet making little sound. At the bottom of the stairs she started to flip the light switch, then froze at the sight of light spilling from the half-open door to the den.

Joey, she thought with an exasperated shake of her head. That kid was going to fry his brain, watching those darn videos hour after hour like some kind of zombie.

But it was Nick she found stretched out on the sofa, clad only in jeans, a book steepled on his bare chest as though he'd fallen asleep while reading.

His face, framed by one thick forearm thrown over his head, was turned toward her. His cheeks looked gaunt in the shadowed light, and fatigue was etched in deep lines along his mouth. His hair curled over his forehead, the way it of-ten did when he'd toweled it dry and neglected to brush through the rebellious thickness.

As though his dreams troubled him, he groaned and muttered something indistinguishable, his voice hoarse.

Surprise filtered through her uneasiness. During the nights they'd spent together, Nick had always slept like a rock, scarcely moving, his breathing even and controlled.

Even though the room was cool, his broad chest glistened with a fine film of sweat, and the triangle of black hair darkening his chest was curled into damp ringlets. One side of his rib cage was bisected by a long pink scar that looked tender against the olive tinge of his skin.

Cory drew a long breath and tried not to think about the pain he must have suffered from the slug he'd taken. She'd seen the headlines when he'd been shot. For the third time in as many years, the article had claimed. The other wounds had been superficial, but a bullet in the lung was life-threatening.

The paper had given the name of the hospital where they'd taken him. Without really knowing why, she'd found herself standing outside the cubicle in intensive care, watching while the hospital priest administered the last rites over Nick's still as death body. Sick inside, Cory had said her own prayers for him, but she hadn't let herself think about how she would feel if he died.

He groaned again, then drew up one long muscular leg, stretching the soft, faded denim over the heavy bulge of his sex. Even as she jerked her gaze upward again, she realized that he was partially aroused.

A disturbing excitement shivered through her, bringing a scowl to her face. Feeling like an intruder in her own house, Cory started to tiptoe backward, then realized the window over the desk was open. The wind whipped at the curtains, and several papers had blown to the floor. Better shut the darn thing before the rain soaked everything, she thought with a quick look at the sleeping man.

Before she'd taken more a few steps forward, Nick's eyes snapped open and he sat up, sending the book crashing to the floor.

"Nick? It's me, Cory," she called out, accustomed to defusing a cop's initial instinct to expect danger.

Nick fought through the fog of exhaustion, his body awake before his mind. Senses alert, he was ready to fight—until he saw that it was Cory who had awakened him.

"What's wrong?" he demanded, his thick black lashes sweeping up and down as he struggled to focus.

"I didn't mean to wake you," she said, watching the threat of violence clear from his eyes. "I need to close the window before it starts to rain any harder."

As though to prove her words, lightning flashed against the dark pane, followed almost instantly by thunder. Turning her back to him, she hastened to the window and slid it closed. When she turned around again, Nick still looked slightly disoriented.

She told herself that the sudden shivering of her skin had nothing to do with the way Nick's gaze had ever-so-briefly flowed down her body like an intimate brush of his hand.

"What time is it?" he asked with a yawn.

"Almost four."

Nick remembered hearing the clock strike two while he'd been reading. He must have fallen asleep shortly after that. Two hours, he thought. Better than last night.

He rubbed the back of his neck, far too aware of the flush of sleep on her cheeks. Her skin would still be warm from the blankets, while his was cold where the wind had blown over him. He was always cold these days when he slept. *If* he slept, that is.

Cory saw what looked like a wince pass over his face and wondered if his forehead was as sore as it looked. "Can I get you some aspirin? I have extra strength."

"No need, thanks." His head hurt like hell, but sympathy was the last thing he was trying to win from her.

"I . . . there are blankets in the hall closet. It feels like it's freezing in here."

"I'm fine." Nick felt the heavy warmth in his groin and tried not to think about the especially vivid dream of Cory that had put it there. Trying to ignore the womanly curves under the pink robe, he reached down and picked up the book.

He looked up to find Cory watching him, a look of drowsy confusion in her eyes. She was never one to wake easily, he remembered, images of her sleepy good-morning kiss prodding him. Few men could resist eyes like that. The lucky ones didn't have to try.

"What are you reading?" she asked when their eyes met.

"*A Tale of Two Cities*," he said with a slight shrug. "I flunked a test on it in tenth grade. Maybe this time I'll understand what it's about."

She inhaled a shallow breath. Nick was looking down at the book in his hands, so why did she feel as though his eyes were still resting on the curve of her breasts?

"Well, I guess I'd better, uh, you know, get back to bed," she said, edging backward. Just then rain began pelting the panes, loud as buckshot.

Cory jumped, and her head turned in the general direction of the patio. "Oh, good heavens, I forgot," she muttered, flying across the room and out the door toward the kitchen.

"Now what?" Nick muttered as he whirled around to follow her.

Cory had the heavy back door unlocked and had just pulled it open when Nick clamped a hand around her arm. In her dash to the kitchen, the sash of her robe had loosened, and the front fell open, revealing a long stretch of silky skin below the hem of her skimpy cotton gown. Before she could cinch the robe closed again, something flashed in his eyes, reminding her of moonlit nights and a hard masculine body pressing hers into the sand.

"What the hell are you doing?" he asked in a graveled voice.

"Bringing in Timmy's desk before it gets ruined."

Nick kept his gaze on her face, but his mind was still filled with the sight of her creamy thighs. "Where is it?"

"On the patio, but—"

"Stay here," he muttered shoving open the screen door and slipping into the night. Raindrops slanted through the slats of the overhang, gleaming silver in the porch light. The wind blew drops through the screen, dampening her face. The air smelled like wet leaves and rain.

Less than a second later, he reappeared, carrying the desk with one hand, the miniature chair with the other. As soon as she saw him approaching, Cory pushed open the screen door and stood with her back to it, holding it wide.

Nick moved by her, flattening himself awkwardly to avoid brushing against her. "Where do you want it?" he asked. His face and chest were slick with rain, and his hair had been plastered to his head by the force of the deluge.

"Uh, by the pantry, please."

Cory watched the muscles ripple across his back as he leaned forward to set the desk down. It had been a long time since she'd been in the same room with a half-naked man.

Not any man, a little voice prodded. The first man to see you naked. The first man to become a part of you. The first man you loved.

While her body had become more rounded by childbearing, his had gotten more muscular, his proud shoulders and corrugated torso seemingly sculpted from granite, and his skin burned bronze by the sun.

Much too aware of the changes, even more aware of her body's involuntary response to them, she busied herself closing the door and locking it again.

"The finish is tacky. You'll either have my fingerprints enshrined forever, or you're going to have to redo it."

"I'll redo it," she said, and her voice came out oddly sultry before she quickly cleared her throat. "Inside, this time."

"Good idea." He wiped the moisture from one arm and then the other before running his palms over his hips like a gunfighter pulling his guns.

She pressed her own hands together. "Uh, it's late. I'll say good-night."

"Wait," he said in a quiet voice. "There's something I have to say."

"What?"

How long would it be before he could look into those smoky green eyes and not remember what it had felt like to make love to her? Nick wondered.

"I know this isn't going to be easy for either of us, but I think it would help if we both try to give each other some room. Okay?"

Cory didn't pretend to misunderstand. "I agree. I know family life is...confining, so please don't think you have to fit your schedule into mine…ours. I…we're flexible around here.''

But not flexible enough to offer a former lover the comfort of her bed, Nick added silently, absentmindedly rubbing his belly, where an emptiness that had nothing to do with hunger had settled.

"I shouldn't have brought up the past," he told her, his voice deep with regret. "I was out of line."

He had expected to see anger in her eyes, perhaps even hatred, but not vulnerability. That, and a touch of some other emotion he couldn't quite identify.

"Yes, you were. What we had was over a long time ago."

"Right," he said with the faintest of smiles. "You married the other guy."

"Only after you told me you weren't the marrying kind." Her words came out a half-beat too quickly, but perhaps Nick would put that down to anger.

"Looks like I was right."

This time Cory was the one to smile. "I married Joe because I fell in love with him, Nick. Not because you didn't want me."

He continued to rub his belly as though it hurt. "I wanted you. It was the gold ring and kids I didn't want."

"And I did."

"And you did."

Feeling sad for all that he'd missed, Cory reached out to straighten a cinnamon-colored mum in the arrangement on the table. "I have no regrets, Nick. I wouldn't trade the life I had with Joe for anything."

Nick dropped his gaze. "I know that, Cory. I've always known."

Was that sadness she heard in his voice? she wondered. Had he been harboring second thoughts all these years? If he had, she couldn't let that matter. She and Nick would never have made it as husband and wife.

Cory wiped a smudge from the table and felt her fingers begin to shake. "I know I seem ungrateful for your help. I don't want to be. I just can't seem to help it."

Nick took a deep breath. "Can we settle this, Cory? Really settle it?"

Touched by the raw sound of his voice, she felt an almost unbearable need to cry. "I want to, Nick, but every time I look at you, I remember the reason why you're here and Joe isn't."

He moved toward her slowly, his eyes fixed on her as though he were afraid she would bolt. When he was close enough to touch her, he stopped.

"You were there, in the hospital, when I was in intensive care," he said quietly, surprising her.

"No," she said with a quick shake of her head. "Why would I be there?"

"I saw you. You were crying."

"Don't Nick." Her lips trembled over the words, giving them a breathless quality that struck a golden spark in the brooding darkness of his gaze.

"Don't what?"

"Don't make me say things that will hurt you."

"If hurting me gets you closer to forgiving me, I can take it."

Just as he'd taken her bitter words at the funeral, she thought. He hadn't even tried to duck when her hand had lashed out at his face. Because he believed he deserved the pain, he had let her humiliate him in front of his peers. And he was still carrying the burden of that day on those wide shoulders that never completely relaxed.

"I wish I'd never met you," she said, turning away from those dark, mesmerizing eyes.

"But you did."

A sound whispered into the silence, and then his hands came down on her shoulders. She stiffened, and his fingers tightened, letting her know that it would be useless to struggle.

"Cory, look at me."

His palms exerted pressure, forcing her to turn. His big chest was very close, so close she could feel the heat of his skin. The thick thatch of hair trapped the light and absorbed it, just as it had absorbed her fevered cries when they'd made love.

He waited until her gaze slowly lifted to his, and then he smiled. But Cory saw the tension riding along his jaw and felt it in the hands still resting on her shoulders.

In the hall the clock began to count the hour, four mellow bongs. Outside the rain pounded the parched earth, and the wind whipped the silvery eucalyptus leaves into a frenzy.

When the resonant echo of the last bong faded, Nick began to speak in a voice that was flat, empty of emotion. "When you came to the hospital, I was dying. I knew it, and I didn't care. It was easier that way. No more...regrets. And then I saw you standing over me."

Cory bit her lip, remembering how pale he'd been that day. And how his eyes had seemed to search hers when he'd opened them for just a minute. He'd said her name, or tried to. But when she'd answered, he'd been unconscious again.

"I knew you hated me, and yet you were crying because I was dying. It nearly tore me apart."

His hand slid across her shoulder to her neck, his fingers resting on the pulse beating there. "You were so beautiful, Cory, like a dream. I was afraid to say anything, afraid you would fade away."

Her pulse leaped against his fingers, and his voice turned raw. "There I was, with tubes everywhere and hurting like a son of a gun, and all I could think about was making love to you."

Shaken, Cory took a slow, deep breath. It didn't help. She felt disoriented, strange. After years of hating this man, she found she didn't feel quite so certain that he deserved her hatred.

"No," she whispered. Or maybe she only thought she did.

His other hand came up to cup her shoulder. Cory felt the pressure of his palm through two layers of clothing and tried not to think about how warm his skin would be against hers.

"I decided then and there that I was going to live. And that I would find a way to win your respect again."

"Oh, Nick, I wish..." She broke off, her lower lip clamped between her teeth.

"I understand. I wish it hadn't happened, too, more than you can imagine'. But it did. All I can do is ask you to forgive me."

Nick looked into the eyes that had haunted him, half-afraid of what he would see. Only he knew how much he was shaking inside. "Please, Cory. Let the past go."

It was the rough masculine plea that held her. Nick was not a man to ask for anything. But he was asking her. To her shock, she wanted to give him what he asked.

"I'm trying, Nick. I don't want to hate you anymore. I just don't know what I *do* feel."

The shadow of memory had turned her eyes dark and turbulent. "Remember the good things we had," he said in a rough whisper. "The days we spent together. And the nights."

Cory watched his eyes begin to smolder, and she knew he intended to kiss her. Her pulse leaped, and her throat was suddenly tight.

"It's late," she whispered.

"Is it?"

"Yes. We both have to work tomorrow."

"Not me. I'm on recuperative leave for a week." His voice had rough edges that shivered her skin.

She swallowed hard and took a step backward. But he moved with her until she was pressed up against the counter.

"Smile for me, Cory. The way you used to when you were waiting for me to come off watch." His throat hurt with the effort he was expending to be gentle. "I waited all day for that smile. Just thinking about it got me through more than one godawful day."

His thumb brushed her lower lip, and her mouth began to tremble. His fingers feathered along her jaw, sending warm sensations rocketing through her.

She dropped her gaze to the thick mat of curly hair spread across his chest. That was a mistake, she realized, even as her fingers curled into her palms at the memory of stroking that soft pelt with sensitive fingertips.

Nick saw her gaze dart to his chest and then away and wondered if she were remembering the way he had coaxed her out of her virginal fear of touching him the way he'd always longed to be touched.

At the thought of those small, gentle hands stroking him, his body began to quicken. Blood surged to his groin, and he felt a rush of heat.

Shifting his position didn't help. Neither did telling himself to think about something else. He needed to feel Cory against him. He needed to be inside her. But it was too soon. Way too soon. He had to wait until he'd won her back. If he ever succeeded in winning her back at all.

Gritting his teeth, he cupped her chin in one palm and tilted her face up to his. Her long lashes fluttered, then rose, tawny spikes against her lightly tanned skin.

His eyes turned dark and stormy, and his thick black lashes lowered until all she could see was sizzling need. Her heartbeat rivaled the thunder overhead.

His big, scarred hands framed her face, holding her, caressing her. Muscles rippled in his chest as he shifted to bring them closer. How strong he was, she thought, and yet how gentle. The paradox had always fascinated her. Now it sent shivers cascading like warm rain down her spine.

"Don't turn away," he whispered as his head descended toward hers. "I couldn't stand it if…God, Cory, I've missed you. So much."

His mouth brushed hers, once, twice, again, sending sweet memories rippling through her. Strong fingers threaded into her hair, arching her neck backward. His mouth opened, and his tongue slowly slid along the curve of her lower lip. Heat began burning under her skin, arousing a feverish need to feel that hard mouth against hers.

Nick heard the faint moan she made, and the rigid restraint he'd imposed on himself shuddered into a violent need to taste, to feel, to possess.

His mouth grew hungry; his hands roamed over her shoulders, her back, the feminine curve of her waist. It had been so long since he'd had a woman, so long since he'd wanted one. Tension prowled his lower body, tearing at his control.

"*Cara mia*," he whispered in a voice as rough as a groan. His mouth took hers again, and this time his tongue was hot and insistent as it gently pried her lips apart.

Cory willingly, eagerly, opened her mouth to his, wanting more. His mouth was warm and seeking, his tongue teasing hers and drawing a sound more like a plea than a moan from her throat.

Her arms circled his neck, and she arched against him. Her breasts felt hot and swollen, and the nipples throbbed to feel his tongue swirling over them.

When he had tasted his fill, he began trailing kisses along the sensitive line from her ear to her shoulder. Her fingers dug into his shoulders, sending a shockwave through him like a shudder.

"Yes, *carisima*, yes," he whispered into the hollow of her throat. "I need to feel you. I need..."

Straining to withstand the desperate need to plunge into her now, without gentleness, without her permission, he slid his hands to her buttocks and began rocking her against him, trying to ease the heavy, punishing ache tormenting him.

Cory felt the thrust of his hard flesh pressing against her, and a heady feeling of excitement began swirling inside her. Nothing mattered but the pleasure building in her.

She was hot where she had been cold for so long; she was alive and wanting, needing. She rubbed her breasts against him, and his arms turned to steel, forcing her closer.

Yes, she echoed silently, giving him her mouth again. Oh, yes. She felt his kiss in every part of her body, intoxicating her like the fieriest wine. Desire thrummed through her veins, making her strain to get closer to the long, lean body braced against hers.

Close to his limit, he buried his face in her hair and breathed in the exotic scent of her. It had been so long since he'd held her like this, her thighs soft against his, her arms clinging and yet bold, her breasts warm and enticing.

His body swelled, stretching the skin to the point of pain. He needed to be inside her, to ease the constant tension that never left him in her sweet, warm moistness.

Caught in his arms, Cory felt a shudder pass through him. With a hoarse groan he drew back, easing his grip on her at the same time.

His face was flushed and his brows drawn in a taut line over his half-closed eyes. He was breathing hard, and his expression was tortured.

"I want you," he whispered in a hoarse, almost strangled tone. "Now. Here, in your bed, anywhere. Everywhere. Whatever you want."

His hands kneaded her shoulders, his fingers biting deep, reminding her of the line he walked between violence and gentleness.

She drew in a steamy, ragged breath and tried to clear her head. Between her thighs a warm dampness began to spread, urging her to take what he was offering.

Her lashes felt heavy as she slowly lifted them for a better look at his eyes. She saw hunger, black and fathomless and seductive, so different from the pure, gentle light of love she'd seen in Joe's clear blue eyes.

She blinked, drawing a smoldering look from those brooding, dangerous eyes. He dipped his head so that he could nuzzle her neck.

"Come to me, *bellisima*. Be mine tonight. Only mine."

His? The way she had once been Joe's?

The thought hit her like a sudden plunge into icy water. Her hands shook as she took his face and pushed it away from hers. "No, it's wrong," she whispered through lips that still throbbed.

Confusion filled his eyes until they were shot with silver. "Wrong? How can it be wrong?" he asked in a thick, barely controlled voice. "I can feel how much you want me."

Cory fought to bring order to her tumbling, erratic thoughts. Want him? Oh, yes, she wanted him. It was all she could do to keep from begging him to take her right here on her own kitchen table. It had always been that way with them.

His big, powerful body had given her the greatest of pleasure. But he had also given her the deepest pain, the soul-scarring kind that never completely went away. Remember the pain, she thought as she groped for reason in the seductive haze of desire.

"Please, Nick. I didn't start this." The heat of passion was leeching from her body, leaving her shivering inside.

"You didn't stop me, either." He wanted her so much he was shuddering with it.

"I tried."

"How? By winding your arms around my neck and trying to climb inside me?"

Heat bloomed in her face, and her gaze faltered. Guilt made her reckless. "I . . . I was missing Joe. You were here. I just needed to feel a man's arms around me. Any man's."

Nick stared, his jaw getting tighter and tighter. His hands lifted from her shoulders and moved slowly, carefully, to his sides, where they curled into large, tight fists.

"You want me staked out and bleeding, don't you?" he asked in the coldest voice she'd ever heard. "Well, you got your wish. Are you happy?"

A wave of shame rose from someplace inside to clog her throat. She took a step away from him, somehow resisting the urge to huddle into her robe for warmth. "No," she whispered with difficulty. "I haven't been happy for a long time."

Cory saw what looked like raw pain flash in his eyes for an instant before the shutters slammed down. "Go to bed, Cory."

She stood rooted to the floor, her conscience warring with a desperate need to protect herself from the same unbearable pain that had nearly destroyed her once before.

"Nick, I—"

Fury bunched his jaw before he controlled it. "I get the message, Cory. Now you get mine. If you're not out of here in five seconds, you won't leave."

He turned his back to her and leaned over the sink. A vicious twist of his strong wrist sent cold water pouring from the faucet even as he stuck his head under the rushing water. It cascaded over his cheeks and stung his eyes.

The muscles of his shoulders and back bunched as he fought the need clawing at him. He closed his eyes, waiting for the cold water to cool his burning skin. His fists clenched, straining the tendons in his wrists and forearms until they felt ready to pop. Finally, feeling he had a semblance of control, he turned slowly, his eyes narrowed in warning.

The kitchen was empty. Cory was gone.

Chapter 9

Cory wiped the last of the cereal from Timmy's face and kissed his forehead. "Play with your trucks and don't get dirty. Momma has to clean up, and then it's time to go to school."

It was an effort to get out the words. Her head felt as though it were filled with cotton, and her eyes stung from lack of sleep.

It had been getting light outside when she'd finally dropped off. Consequently she'd slept through her alarm, and the older children had made a mess of the kitchen by the time she'd thrown on some clothes and managed to make herself presentable.

"Can we go in the black car?" Timmy asked as he climbed down from his chair.

Head buzzing with tiredness, Cory tried for a bright smile. "Not today, sweetie, but soon, okay?"

"Okay." Balancing precariously on tiptoes, he pulled open the pantry door. Inside was a wicker basket filled with toys.

"Timmy don't—" the sound of metal trucks crashing to the floor interrupted her "—upset that basket," she finished with a sigh.

Thank God it's Friday, she thought as she finished wiping the table. Her hand was reaching for the carton of milk when she saw the unused place setting on the table. Breakfast had been its usual boisterous affair, but Nick had slept through it. At least, she assumed he was still asleep, since his door had been pulled nearly closed when she'd gotten up.

"Mom, where's my math book?" Jenny called as she rushed into the kitchen, her arms full of books and the flute she played in the high school band.

"I don't know, sweetie. Where did you leave it?"

Her daughter stopped long enough to give her a long-suffering look. "If I knew that, I wouldn't be looking for it, would I?"

"No, I guess not." Cory glanced toward the clock. She had to leave in five minutes. Otherwise she would be late for her own school.

"What's wrong?" Jen asked with a curious look. "You sound funny."

Cory managed a cheery smile. "I'm fine, just tired." Her gaze went to the clock again. "Uh, have you heard Uncle Nick up and about yet this morning?"

Jenny's curious look sharpened. "He left before I got up. Didn't you hear the Corvette?"

"No, no, I didn't."

Left? she thought in sudden alarm. But he'd said he was on recuperative leave for a week. Surely he hadn't walked out on them. Or had he?

Cory rubbed her throbbing temple and tried not to think about the look in his eyes when he'd turned away from her last night. She'd hurt him. Badly.

Alone in her bed she'd tried to tell herself that he deserved to be hurt. In the cold light of day, she knew that he didn't. Not after the things he'd done to try to make amends.

Guilt sifted through her, sharp and accusing. Apologize, a small voice ordered. Do as he asked and settle this, so the two of you can find a way to live together for eight weeks.

A horn sounded outside, rousing her. "There's the bus, Jen. Better run."

"My book!" Jennifer glanced around frantically, then shrugged. "Oh, well, it's only math," she muttered as she headed for the door.

"Have a good day," Cory said in a distracted tone.

"You too. And, Mom, can we have something special for dinner tonight?"

Dinner? At the moment that was the last thing on her mind. "Uh, okay. Any requests?"

Jenny opened the door and waved toward the yellow bus idling at the curb. "Yeah, spaghetti and meatballs. It's Uncle Nick's favorite!"

The driver tooted again. Jenny flashed her mother a pleading smile. "Please?"

Cory felt something tear inside her. "Okay, okay," she managed in a halfway normal tone. "Now, get going before Mr. Williams drives off without you."

"Thanks, Mom. Isn't it great to have Uncle Nick around again?"

She was gone before Cory had to answer.

The desk sergeant, a Sylvester Stallone look-alike named DiCiccio, held his hand over the mouthpiece of the phone pressed to his ear and gave Nick a startled look. "Hey, *paisan,* I thought the doc sent you home."

"He did. Now I'm back," Nick said without stopping.

It was nearly an hour before shift change, and half of the six desks crowded into the detectives' squad room were empty. Just as Nick expected, however, Bill Frazier was already in his cubbyhole office, his big feet propped on his desk, a jelly doughnut in one hand, a report in the other.

"Got a minute, Lieutenant?" Nick asked from the open doorway.

Frazier glanced up, his eyebrows shooting above the rims of his reading glasses. "What the hell are you doing here, Donatelli?" he exclaimed in a voice that was bull-frog deep.

"Reporting for work."

"No way! Dr. Wiseman gave you a week off, and department policy says you have to take it."

"Screw policy. I feel fine."

Frazier pulled his feet from the desk and sat up, his chair creaking beneath the two hundred pounds tightly packed into a body that was only slightly taller than average.

"You look like hell," the lieutenant drawled, "and you know it."

Nick shot a glance over his shoulder at the three men watching his every move. Just once he would like to blend into the damned woodwork, he thought as he moved into the office and closed the door behind him.

"I need to work, Bill."

Frazier's gray eyes regarded him thoughtfully. "This have anything to do with the call I got from a Ventura County judge by the name of Macias?"

"It might."

"What happened?"

Nick told him about moving in with Cory and her children until Joey's trial.

Frazier whistled through his teeth. "You've got more guts than I do, I'll give you that. If I'd been the one she'd slapped in front of God and most of the LAPD, I'd never want to see Cory Kingston again." His voice carried a rough edge that Nick identified as pity. His jaw tightened, even as he made himself stand and take it.

"What about it, Bill? Can you put me back on the board?"

Frazier's mouth flattened into disapproval. "Nick, I wasn't kidding when I said you looked like hell. Are you sure you can handle a regular duty schedule?"

"I can handle it."

Frazier sighed. "Okay, you got it. But if you need time off, take it."

Nick felt some of the tension raking his spine ease. "Thanks, Bill. I appreciate it." He opened the door and started to leave, but Frazier stopped him.

"How is she? Cory, I mean."

The sound of her name twisted Nick's gut. A few hours ago he'd been holding her in his arms, with only a couple of layers of cloth separating them. Now he realized that nothing could breech the distance he'd put between them.

"She's fine. Doing great." He cleared his throat. "She's got herself this preschool up there, one of the best in the state, I hear."

"Joe always said she was good with kids." Frazier's gaze slid away from Nick toward the row of school pictures lined up on his desk. He had five kids, by three different wives. "They were lucky, those two. They made it work."

Nick felt a thickness in his throat. "Yeah, they were lucky."

Frazier leaned back and propped his feet up again. "You're smart not to get married, Nick," he said in a voice edged with bitterness. "Saved yourself a lot of grief and alimony payments."

Yeah, I'm damn smart, Nick said to himself as he walked out of the office and headed for his desk. So smart he'd let himself hope for a damned miracle. Some guys never learned. Looked like he was one of them.

His desk was in the corner, under a large blowup of Jack Webb's scowling face. One side was piled high with manila folders; the other was relatively neat. A stack of pink messages had been stuck in one corner of the blotter. The desk butted up against his was clean. He was between partners again.

Nick felt the eyes of the others in the room bore into his back as he opened the bottom drawer and pulled out his coffee mug. Cracked and coffee-stained, it was oversize and still carried the yellow smiling face that had been the rage twenty years ago when Cory had given it to him for his birthday.

He ran his finger over the slashing black grin, his own mouth hard. Pain hammered his temple like a sledge, and his eyes stung from lack of sleep. For two cents he would call Macias and tell the judge he'd changed his mind. Why should he put himself through hell for a kid who thought he was crooked enough to put in the fix and a woman who could tear him apart with just a few quiet words?

With a silent curse, he opened his hand and let the mug fall into the wastebasket by the desk. Five minutes later he fished it out. The handle had broken, but he used it anyway.

"Momma, I'm hungry."

Cory turned away from the stove and gave her younger son a coaxing smile. "I know, sweetie. We're all hungry." Her voice was edged with annoyance she was too tired to hide.

"Can't we eat now?"

"Not yet, Tim. Have another cracker, okay? And leave the napkin rings alone."

Jennifer had insisted on a tablecloth and candles to go with the mums, and Cory hadn't had the heart to refuse her, even though she herself felt anything but festive.

"Maybe Uncle Nick isn't coming home for dinner," Joey muttered before sneaking another olive from the tray of antipasto already on the table.

Jenny looked up from the basket she was busily filling with the toy trucks scattered over the kitchen floor. "That's a stupid thing to say, Joey," she said in a disgusted tone. "Why shouldn't he come home? He lives here now."

Joey gave his sister a superior grin. "Don't be such an airhead, Jen. It's Friday night. He's probably got a hot date."

The spoon Cory was holding clattered into the pot, splashing scarlet tomato sauce onto her wrist. "*Joseph Kingston!* You know I hate talk like that."

"Sorry," her son mumbled. "I forgot."

"Don't forget again," she ordered, holding her stinging wrist under a stream of cold water.

Behind her back, Jenny gave her brother a triumphant look and stuck out her tongue. Joey's face turned red, and his eyes narrowed. "Mom, it's almost seven," he grumbled, still directing a menacing look at his sister. "I'm starved."

"Me too, Momma," Timmy chimed in with a hopeful look.

"We can't start without Uncle Nick," Jennifer protested, jumping up with a small red dump truck still clutched in her hand. "This whole dinner is for him, to celebrate us all being together again."

Not all of us, Cory thought, then let her shoulders slump. The thought of crawling between cool sheets and pulling the blanket over her head was nearly irresistible.

"Mom, Joey's making faces at me again."

"I am not! You need your glasses changed is all."

Cory spun around to give both older children warning glares. "Enough, you two," she ordered sharply. "Sit down. We'll eat."

"Mom!" Jennifer wailed. "We have to wait."

Timmy climbed into his tall youth chair and reached for his milk. "Let's eat," he said with an impatient look toward his mother and the pot on the stove.

Just then they heard the rumble of the Corvette's engine as Nick swung into the driveway. "He's here," Jenny shouted, her eyes lighting up. "I'll get the matches."

She ran to a chest under the window and began searching through the top drawer.

Cory busied herself with the pasta, thankful that the steam hid the sudden flush she'd felt bloom on her cheeks. Behind her she heard the lock click and the door open.

Even though her back was to him, she knew the moment Nick walked in. The atmosphere in the kitchen changed until it seemed suddenly charged with new energy. A man's restless, potent energy.

"Hi, Uncle Nick," Jenny called. "Dinner's ready. Mom made your favorite, spaghetti and meatballs. I hope you're hungry."

"Hey, you know I would kill for some of your mom's special sauce," he said with a quick glance in Cory's direction. "Smells great, Cory."

"Thank you." Her back was straight, too straight. She didn't turn.

Nick took in the flickering candles and the hovering children. Was this what it was like to be the daddy? To see smiles flash just for you? Something inside him tore.

The smiles, the warmth, the pretty table—all those right-fully belonged to Joe, not him. Cory couldn't have made that any plainer. And she'd been right. He was a selfish bastard, trying to use another man's wife and another man's family to ease his own pain.

"Sorry I'm late," he said as he shrugged out of his jacket and looked around for a place to put it. "I tried to call, but the line was busy."

"Joey was talking to Melissa," Jenny said in a singsong voice. "He's always talking to her."

"Shut up, Jen. I've had it with you."

"Stop it, both of you," Cory said, her tone edging toward a blowup.

Nick smiled his apology. "Next time, just go ahead, okay? I'm used to potluck."

"We didn't mind waiting, honest," Jennifer said as she took the worn leather jacket from his hands and carried it to the pantry, where she carefully hung it next to Cory's bright red sweater.

"Did we, Mom?" she asked with an impatient look in her mother's direction.

"No."

Nick took a deep breath and walked over to the sink to wash his hands. Cory's face was pink from the steam pouring up from the draining pasta, and her hair had curled into enticing little tendrils against her neck, making her look as young and innocent as her daughter.

As he leaned over the sink, he caught a whiff of her perfume mingling with the Italian spices. Hunger spiked in him, but it wasn't for the meal.

"Can I help?" he asked as he dried his hands.

Cory's glance rested briefly on his face before shifting to the food in front of her. "Everything's ready, thanks."

She knew she sounded wooden, but she was fighting a sudden need to cry. It was too familiar, having Nick in the kitchen, offering to help, complimenting her on her cooking. Joe should be here, too. Ragging Nick about this or that, giving her an absentminded hug now and then. But Joe wasn't here. And the casual friendship between Nick and her was gone.

"Jen, get the bread, okay?" she said, her voice hollow.

"Sure." Jenny opened the oven and took out a foil-wrapped loaf, which she carefully unwrapped before carrying it to the table. "The candles were my idea," she said with a shy look at Nick.

"Very classy. Like you," he said, giving Jenny a hug that she returned with a grin before straightening the already perfectly aligned mat at Nick's place.

"It's just like old times, right?"

Nick glanced at Cory's stiff back. "Almost," he said, his voice roughened by the regret he couldn't quite hide. He would rather face a drug-crazed killer than the sadness in her eyes.

Joey avoided his eye as he pulled out a chair and sat down. Timmy watched him with a look of childish fascination on his round little face. "Hi," he said with a bright smile. "I know you. You're my new Uncle Nick."

Nick swallowed hard. "And you're Timothy Michael Kingston."

Timmy giggled. "No, I'm *Timmy!*"

Her chest suddenly tight, Cory dumped the spaghetti into a large bowl and carried it to the table. "There's no Chianti," she said, feeling a flutter of nerves. "If you want some, you'll have to run down to the liquor store on the corner."

Nick glanced at the four glasses of milk already poured. "Milk is fine," he said, hoping he wouldn't gag getting it down.

That startled her into looking at him directly. "You hate milk."

"Yeah, but I'm already in the doghouse for being late, so I'll drink whatever you want to give me."

Aware that all three of her children were watching, Cory said with a calm she didn't feel, "You're not in the doghouse."

"Aren't I? Somehow I thought I was."

He watched the corners of her pale mouth curl into a frown and remembered the taste of those soft lips. He hadn't done a thing worth a damn all day. Every time he tried to concentrate on work, thoughts of Cory intruded. In his mind he kept feeling her body stretched warm and yielding against his. He knew enough about sex to know when a woman was faking arousal. She hadn't been.

He'd felt the tremors shake her when his tongue had found hers. He'd heard the catch in her throat when he'd rubbed against her, his body as hard as it had ever been.

Hell, no, she hadn't been faking, he thought with grim acceptance. Why should she? In her mind, it had been Joe holding her, Joe kissing her, Joe's body hard and aching for hers.

He turned away and pulled out her chair. Ignoring the polite gesture, Cory wiped the sweat from her face with her apron and tried not to think about the next hour, the next day, the next two months, with this man. Her hand shook as she picked up the bowl of sauce and meatballs.

"Everyone sit down please," she said, veering wide of the place where he stood. Nick took a step sideways, intercepting her.

The flush on her cheeks had deepened, and her eyes held a brittle look Nick couldn't read. Tension skated across his broad shoulders. The unknown was always dangerous, especially to a man who counted the people he allowed himself to trust on one hand.

"Sit down, Cory," he said. "You look like you're ready to drop." He reached for the bowl, and their hands brushed. Nick saw the slight betraying flicker of Cory's eyelids at his touch before she jerked her hand away from his.

Before he could catch it, the heavy dish crashed to the floor. Cory gasped and stepped back, but it was too late. Her sneakers were covered with red. So were Nick's boots and most of his shins.

"Uh, oh," Timmy shouted, clapping his hands.

"Oh, Mom!" Jenny wailed before her hand went to her mouth.

"Told you we shouldn't have waited," Joey grumbled with a quick upward glance of disgust.

Cory heard all those things, but her attention was riveted on Nick. He was staring at the floor, his face slowly draining of color, his eyes glazed. His throat worked, but no sound came out.

"Nick? What's wrong? Are you burned? Talk to me."

His eyebrows slid together, and his face tightened until his teeth were bared in a grimace of what appeared to be anguish. "Blood," he whispered, his voice torn by pain. "Mother of God, why can't I forget the blood?"

Cory's hand flew to her mouth. "Oh, no, Nick. It's not blood. Listen to me, it's spaghetti sauce, that's all."

Slowly his head came up, and his torment-darkened eyes found her face. But she knew he wasn't really seeing her. "I tried, but I couldn't stop it. I . . . it was so quick. I . . ." His voice choked into silence and a shudder ripped his rigid body.

Cory began shaking, but she tried to remain calm as she glanced past his rigid shoulder to the children sitting frozen and wide-eyed at the pathetically bright table. Jenny's napkin was twisted between her tight fists, and she was biting her lip to keep from crying.

"Jen, you and Joey take Timmy into the other room. Now," she commanded in a hushed tone.

Timmy started to protest, but Jenny scooped him from his high chair and ran with him from the room. Joey nearly knocked over his chair in his haste to follow.

"Nick, listen to me," she said when they were gone. "It's all right." She was crying openly. For him, for her, for all of them.

If Nick noticed, he gave no sign. Agony twisted his mouth and contorted his face. He started to turn away, but Cory walked into his arms, blocking his way.

"Hold me, Nick," she said in a quavering voice. "Please."

His arms came around her, crushing her against him. He buried his face in the curve of her neck, his pain a living thing. He began to shake with hard, vicious tremors that were only partially absorbed by her smaller body.

The moment Nick felt her touch him the flashback itself ended, but the memories remained hauntingly vivid. This time, unlike the others, he couldn't push them back.

Tears stung his eyes. His throat ached with the need to release the sobs trapped there.

"I'm sorry," he said, pulling away. "You'll never know how sorry." He disentangled her arms and turned away, ashamed that he'd broken in front of the one person whose opinion he valued above all others.

"Nick, wait!" Cory called. "Don't go."

"I just need some air," he said from the door. "Don't worry. I won't let you down again. I'll be back."

Cory heard the harsh tremor of self-loathing stain his deep voice and bit off a sob. "Please, Nick. You shouldn't drive."

"Funny," he said with a ghost of a smile. "You've said that to me before."

Cory drew in a shaky breath. "I'll go with you, then. We'll...we'll talk. There are some things I need to say, things I should have said a long time ago."

He dropped his gaze, then looked up, his face taking on weary lines again. "If you came with me, we wouldn't talk, Cory. And I have enough sins on my soul as it is."

He walked out into the night. He no longer went to Mass. Why should he? No amount of penance, no earthy absolution, could save him. He was already in hell.

Chapter 10

Half-Vietnamese, half-American, Mai Bui was only two years out of USC and the best preschool teacher Cory had ever met. She'd hired the younger woman without experience and never been sorry.

"So, how's Joey?" Mai asked as she wiped down the last of the pint-sized tables and tossed the rag into the bucket of disinfectant.

Cory glanced up from the fat pumpkin she was cutting out of orange construction paper and shrugged. "Okay. He's still grounded."

"Must be rough, with the Homecoming game coming up and all the Halloween parties."

"We've had our moments," Cory admitted, starting on another pumpkin. Halloween was only five days away. She and Mai were planning a party for the children on Friday and had stayed after the end of the afternoon session to decorate. Zipped into a new red parka, Timmy was playing in the sandbox outside.

"How's it going with your houseguest?"

Cory stabbed the paper with the point of the scissors and began on the pumpkin's mouth. "Fine, just fine."

"Hmm. Is that why you've been as grumpy as Wanda Witch these days?"

"I'm not," Cory protested. She caught Mai's appraising look and frowned. "Am I?"

"To be blunt, yes. In all the time I've known you, I've never seen you so uptight." Looking suddenly ill at ease, Mai picked at a thread on her long cotton skirt. "I'm sure you know it's all over town, about the man who's been living with you for the past three weeks."

"Terrific," Cory muttered with a deep sigh.

"My husband's friend, Pete—you know, the one who owns the bar on Signal—said your, uh, houseguest came in alone one night and ordered a triple whiskey, which he stared into for a couple of hours before he pushed it away and left."

"He didn't drink it?"

"No, Pete did. Said the guy left him a big tip, too."

Cory closed her eyes on a wince. No doubt that had been the night Nick had suffered the flashback. Since then he'd been quiet and introspective, two things that were completely out of character for him.

"Take this as fair warning, Mai. As soon as Joey is acquitted, I'm going to stay in bed for a week," she muttered as she threw down the scissors and rubbed her aching neck.

Mai's eyebrows wiggled. "Alone?"

Cory gave her a warning look. "Yes, alone."

Even if she had wanted to change her mind, it was obvious that Nick had lost interest. He was polite, she was polite, but the tension between them grew with every night they spent under the same roof.

Not that he was a difficult guest. He wasn't. He made his own bed, washed his own clothes, and tried to stay out of her way. When she was downstairs, he was upstairs, or outside shooting baskets with Joey. When she walked into a room, he made an excuse and left. At night, he prowled the house at all hours, sometimes reading in the den, sometimes sitting in the dark in the living room.

After a few restless forays of her own, during which she'd run into him in various stages of undress, Cory had learned to stay curled into her blankets at night, no matter how claustrophobic she felt.

"Are you inviting him to the party?" Mai asked as she positioned the ladder under the light fixture and began attaching orange and black crepe paper to the ceiling with thumbtacks.

Cory jumped up to help. "No, why should I?"

"Well, for one thing, he is acting in loco parentis for Timmy, and all the other fathers are invited."

"He's working."

"Uh-huh."

Cory handed Mai another roll of crepe paper, and their eyes met. The speculation Cory saw in the other woman's expression made her scowl. "He'd hate it, all the noise and confusion and sticky little fingers."

"I see. That's why he took Timmy to Fiesta Days, because he hates kids."

"He was bored and wanted to get out of the house. Nick can't stand to stay in one place for very long."

"He could have gone alone," Mai said in a bland voice.

Or he could have asked her to go along. But he hadn't. Cory gave the orange strip a savage twist. "Oh, for heaven's sake, Mai. If you want him here so badly, you invite him."

Mai pushed the last tack in place and climbed down. "See what I mean?" she said with a grin. "You're acting just like I did when I was falling in love with Tran and didn't know it."

Cory felt her face freeze. "I'm not in love with Nick," she said in a stiff tone.

"Unless my inscrutable Oriental intuition has suddenly short-circuited, you were once."

"Well, I'm not now."

Cory walked to the window, her footsteps echoing in the empty space. Outside, Timmy saw her and waved. Heart swelling at the sight of his guileless grin, she waved back.

It had only taken Tim a few days to accept Nick as a father figure. Cory had watched helplessly as the little boy followed Nick from room to room, chattering endlessly.

She'd expected Nick to avoid him. Instead, he treated Tim with a gruff affection that nearly broke her heart.

Cory stared at the black crepe paper in her hand. Seeing Nick's grief displayed so starkly had forced her to examine her own feelings honestly.

She missed Joe, but she no longer grieved for his loss with the force of the newly bereft. What had happened was tragic and she wished with all her heart that it hadn't. But Joe wouldn't have wanted her to spend the rest of her life longing for the past.

If anything happens to me, Nick will take care of you. He loves you almost as much as I do.

No, Joe darling, she thought. He doesn't. He never did.

"No, Momma. A *big* smile."

Tongue clamped between her teeth, Cory erased the grin she'd sketched on the fat pumpkin with crayon and tried for an even grander one. "Better?" she asked, giving Timmy a fond glance.

"Yep," he said, bobbing his head up and down.

It was the night before Halloween, and the two of them were alone in the kitchen. Neither of the other children had any interest in creating the family jack-o'-lantern.

"Now you do the eyes," she said, handing him the crayon.

"'Kay," he agreed, screwing up his little face into a fierce expression of concentration. His stubby fingers gripped the crayon so tightly they were white.

"How's that, Momma?" he asked when he was finished.

Cory pursed her lips and pretended to ponder. "Terrific, sweetie. Now I'll cut around the lines for you, and then—"

"No, no, that's Uncle Nick's job," Timmy protested. "He said that's the part he wants to do."

Cory cast a quick look in the direction of the den, where Nick and Joey were watching a Thursday night football game.

"He's busy, sweetie. Why don't you and I do it?"

"I promised, Momma," Timmy said with a reproving look before he slid from his chair.

"Uncle Nick, Uncle Nick," he called as he ran pell-mell down the hall, his sneakers squeaking on the bare wood. "C'mon. We saved the lines for you, like you said."

Cory stood and folded up the newspaper piled with the seeds she'd scooped from the pumpkin's innards. She was turning away from the trash basket under the sink when Nick came into the kitchen. Timmy was riding on his shoulders, his small hands clutched in Nick's thick hair.

Surprise flickered in his eyes when he caught sight of her standing stiff and uneasy by the sink. She could count on one hand the number of times they'd been together outside of meals.

Seeing him now, she noticed that his jeans rode lower on his hips than she remembered, and his waist seemed leaner beneath the red flannel shirt. His tan had faded in the weeks during which he'd been away from the beach, and the scar over his eyebrow was less livid.

He swung Timmy to the ground and ran a hand through his disheveled hair. Looking as pleased as a little Buddha, Timmy leaned against Nick's long leg and popped his thumb into his mouth.

"Tim saved the lines for me," Nick said, his gaze lingering on her flushed face for a beat too long before shifting to the pumpkin on the table.

"I understand that's the favorite part you've been looking forward to," she said in a dry voice that brought his gaze jerking back to her face.

"Let's say I'm better with a knife than a crayon." His voice was equally dry, and Cory couldn't help smiling. He looked ill at ease but determined.

Cory wanted to tell him how much she appreciated the time he spent with the children, but the strained distance he'd put between them kept the words locked inside.

Forcing a smile for Timmy's sake, she edged toward the door. Just being close to him made her feel strangely vulnerable, and she didn't like the feeling. She wasn't supposed to be vulnerable to a man she didn't love.

"Well, I'll leave you two alone," she said as she reached the entrance to the hall.

Nick's face registered alarm. "Oh, no, you don't! This is virgin territory for me. I need help." He pulled out a chair and cocked one black eyebrow in her direction. "You wouldn't want me to make a mistake and massacre the kid's Halloween pumpkin, would you, Mom?"

Some of the old teasing warmth had crept into his voice, making her realize how much she'd missed it. She knew it was for Timmy's sake, but she couldn't help responding.

"Heaven forbid," she managed to joke around the lump in her throat. He waited until she slipped past him into a chair before settling into the one next to hers and pulling Timmy onto his lap.

He picked up the knife, then drew an exaggerated breath. "Wish me luck," he said, his grin flashing.

"Good luck," she murmured, remembering the insistent pressure of that hard mouth on hers. As kisses went, Nick's were as potent as fire—and just as dangerous. All her life people had said that Cory Kingston was not a person to court danger, so why did she yearn to be wrapped in those strong arms one more time?

Sexual frustration, she decided, dismissing the idea firmly as she listened to the conversation Nick was carrying on with her son. Perfectly natural in a woman who had been celibate for four years.

"That bad, huh?" Cory heard the rumble of Nick's deep voice and jerked her head toward the sound. He was watching her with the guarded look she had come to expect from him.

"I'm sorry. Did you say something?"

"Tim and I want your opinion of good old jack, here," he repeated. "Don't we, Tim?"

Timmy beamed, bouncing up and down on Nick's lap. Cory dropped her gaze to the pumpkin. The face was lopsided, and the toothy grin was definitely ragged.

"Isn't it the bestest you've ever seen?" Timmy exclaimed with a grin nearly as broad as the pumpkin's.

"Absolutely," she said in a bright voice. "I love it."

"I wanna show it to Jen, okay, Momma?"

"Sure, she's in her room. Go tell her to come down."

Timmy's brows drew together. "No, no, I wanna take it to her."

Cory's attention was fixed on her son, but she was very aware that Nick's attention was fixed on her. "Honey, it's too heavy. You might drop it."

"No, I won't," Timmy said, sticking out his chin. "I'm strong. Uncle Nick says so." He twisted around to give Nick a dimpled grin. "Tell her, Uncle Nick."

Nick's gaze met hers over Timmy's flaxen curls. "He's right, Mom. Feel those muscles." His big hand wrapped Timmy's biceps and gently squeezed.

Seeing Timmy's expectant look, her hand hovered over Nick's. Slowly he drew his away, and she put her fingers where his hand been. Timmy flexed his arm, and she felt the small muscle bunch beneath his shirt.

"Uncle Nick is right," she said with an emphatic nod of her head. "You *are* strong."

"See, I told you," he said as he slid from Nick's lap and reached for the pumpkin. Even though he rose on his tiptoes, his arms were too short to manage.

"Here, tiger, let me try," Nick said as he lifted the pumpkin and put it in Timmy's arms. Holding her breath, Cory noticed the way Nick's hands stayed around the jack-o'-lantern until he was certain the proud little boy could manage.

"I'll be back, and then we'll have milk and cookies," Timmy said as he walked out of the room, leaning backward to balance the load in front.

Cory and Nick were suddenly alone. He shifted in his chair, his shoulders rising and falling as though to ease a sudden stiffness. One arm rested on the table, his fist loosely bunched against the paper holding the chunks his knife had sliced from the pumpkin face.

"He's all excited about this party you're having tomorrow at school."

Cory smiled. "We had one last year, too, but he doesn't remember it."

"Am I really invited?"

Cory's smile wavered. "I . . . sure, if you want to come."

"What about you, Cory? Do you want me to come?"

His fingers began playing with the wicked-looking butcher knife, drawing her gaze. He was using his left hand, the one with the scar where he'd had a tattoo of a gory dagger removed because she'd shuddered every time she'd seen it.

He'd done a lot of things for her then. Bought the car she adored, even though it cost more than a rookie cop could really afford. Given up scarce football tickets he'd moved heaven and earth to get in order to accompany her to the ballet because she adored dancing and hated football.

"It would mean a lot to Timmy if you could come," she said with quiet sincerity. "He's crazy about his Uncle Nick."

The smile that briefly curved his hard mouth didn't make a ripple in the dark stillness in his eyes. "I'm crazy about him, too," he said, his voice edged with rough affection. "Jenny, too. It takes a little more work with Joey."

She was discovering how affectionate Nick could be—with others. Jen asked his advice on everything from clothes to rock stars. Even Joey, after an initial period of sullen silence, had begun to seem more like his old self when Nick was around. To her surprise, her son hadn't worn the earring she abhorred since Nick had ordered him to remove it.

In every way but one, they were becoming a family, her children and Nick. Only she was left out of the warm circle forming around him.

"Sometimes I think teenagers should be frozen at thirteen and not thawed out again until their twenty-first birthday," she said. "I'm sure I wasn't as difficult as my two are."

"I was. I gave my mother fits. She got so she stopped talking to me at all."

His fingers slid down the steel blade to the handle and began rubbing the smooth wood. His head rose slowly until he was impaling her with brooding dark eyes that seemed so deep and so still.

"How do *you* feel about me, Cory? Do you still hate me?"

"No," she admitted softly, lifting her gaze to his again. "Not anymore."

"But you still blame me for Joe's death." It was a statement, not a question.

Cory stood and walked to the sink, looking out into the night. "After Joe died, I think I needed to blame someone in order to diffuse the pain I was feeling. Now...I don't want to blame anyone. It hurts too many people, people I care about."

Nick pushed back his chair and went to her. "If I could make it be me in that box in Forest Lawn instead of Joe, I would. I need you to believe that."

Cory turned to look at him. The remorse she saw in his eyes made her draw a shaky breath. "I believe you," she said in a low voice.

"Can you forgive me, Cory?"

Cory looked at the rigid line of his strong shoulders and wanted to cry. Her grief had been blunted by time. Nick's had only grown more intolerable, driving him relentlessly day after day, night after restless night. No wonder he always looked so lonely, even when he was surrounded by her children.

"I think we both need to forget the past," she said in a voice that she couldn't keep steady.

"And forgive?" His voice was urgent, his gaze intense.

Cory took a deep breath. "Yes, and forgive," she whispered.

A spasm of some emotion twisted his features. "Twenty years ago you were my best friend, Cory. I miss that."

"I do, too," she admitted. "You were different then. More...more human."

Nick's gaze fell, and a muscle twitched along his jaw. "I'm human, Cory. I make mistakes. Bad ones, sometimes. But I never make the same mistake twice." His voice was rough with emotion, his eyes very dark.

He leaned closer, and his fingers framed her face, tilting her head until her mouth was perfectly aligned with his. His head lowered, and he pressed his mouth to hers in a gentle kiss.

He drew back, his dark gaze sweeping over her. A tender smile played over his mouth. "Cory," he said, his deep voice wrapping her name in warmth before his mouth touched hers again. And then he was raining soft kisses on her face, her neck, the tender place behind her ear.

His hand found the pins in her hair, removing them one by one until her hair fell to her shoulders. His fingers combed through the heavy tumble, separating the glossy strands.

Nick felt the softening of her body, heard the change in her breathing. Hunger ripped through him raw and potent.

Since he'd been sixteen, he'd never had to postpone satisfying his needs, never had to deny himself physical release. He wanted, he took—always making sure his lover of the moment got what she wanted, too. Patience came hard for him, self-denial even harder, but, if he had to, he could wait for Cory. But not too long.

"Be my friend again, Cory," he whispered, his voice hoarse.

"I'd like that," she murmured, touching the corner of his mouth with her fingertip. Nick closed his eyes for a long moment, savoring the feel of her hand against his face with an intensity that was close to pain.

Her hands went around his waist, and she hugged him, resting her cheek against his heart. It was beating fast and hard, but his hands were gentle as they stroked her hair.

They stood silently, wrapped in each other's arms, until they heard a thump overhead, followed by Timmy's urgent wail.

Cory lifted her head and looked into Nick's face. A drowsy smile of contentment had replaced the worn look of tension around his mouth, and the harsh lines around his eyes had eased. He looked at peace for the first time since Joe's funeral.

Warmth flooded her. Was that what she had given him with just a hug and a few words? Was that what he needed from her?

"I think Timmy just dropped the pumpkin," she said, her voice unnaturally husky.

His lashes slowly parted. "Sounds like," he agreed, his voice a contented rumble.

Timmy's footsteps sounded on the stairs, accompanied by a wail of indignation.

"Do you suppose the convenience store on the corner still has pumpkins for sale?" she asked with a deep sigh.

"Something tells me I'll soon find out," he said, chuckling. She laughed softly, hugging him for a moment before stepping away.

"That's what friends are for," she said, swallowing hard.

Or fathers, he thought, kissing her one last time. That realization both tempted and terrified him.

Cory darted another look at her watch. Quarter to two. At three, the party was over.

Her gaze went past the laughing, teasing children to the little boy hovering by the window, his blue eyes fixed on the parking lot beyond. Timmy was dressed as a clown, but the cheery smile she'd painted on his face with lipstick couldn't hide the forlorn droop of his mouth.

"He'll get over it," Mai said in a low tone when she caught Cory's eye. "Kids are tough."

Cory watched Fred Baxter's head disappear into a tub full of water as he tried to capture an apple for his son while a laughing group of parents and children urged him on.

"He's not used to being hurt like this, Mai," she said, her jaw tight. "He's used to the adults in his life keeping their promises."

"Maybe Nick couldn't get away," Mai said before bending to tie the flapping shoelace of a tiny pirate, who even wore an eye patch and wooden sword.

Cory waited until Jose Lopez ran off, then said in a low tone, "He could have called."

Mai flicked her a surprised look. "True," she said in a mild tone.

Cory tugged at the vivid purple scarf she'd twisted around her waist, cinching it tighter until the waistband of her flaring red skirt cut into her skin. She was dressed as a gypsy, complete with ruffled blouse and huge gold hoops in her ears. She'd even worn more makeup than usual to complete the costume. The kids had loved it. To her acute embarrassment, some of the fathers seemed to enjoy the outfit more than they should.

I should have dressed as a nun, she thought with a heavy sigh. "Hold the fort for five minutes," she told Mai. "I need to take some aspirin."

Mai adjusted the cat's ears she had made from fake fur to go with her leopard costume. "Another sore throat?" she asked solicitously. "Maybe you'd better go in for a checkup."

"I didn't sleep much last night," Cory muttered before she caught herself.

Mai's eyebrows rose. "Oh?"

"Stop looking so interested. I was finishing Timmy's costume," she said, turning away.

"Wait." Mai caught her arm. "Does Nick drive a black Corvette?"

"Yes, why?"

"See for yourself." Cory followed Mai's gaze toward the window. With a screech of tires, the Corvette rocked to a stop in the red zone in front of the school entrance. The door opened and Nick emerged, his hair a windblown tangle, his expression harried. With a quick jerk of his arm, he unclipped his revolver from his belt.

"What's he doing?" Mai asked, reminding Cory that she wasn't alone.

"Locking his gun in the glove compartment."

"I never thought of that."

But Nick had, Cory thought, watching him comb his hair with his fingers before he turned and jogged to the door. He was wearing his usual disreputable jeans, but his shirt was a new one she hadn't seen before. The pale yellow color gave his face a swarthy darkness she found intensely appealing.

"Whoa, that's what I call a well-packaged male," Mai whispered close to Cory's ear. "Look at those great thighs and...everything else. Some smart ad agency should use him to advertise jeans. Or X-rated movies."

"Mai, stop it!" Cory hissed, looking around quickly to see if anyone heard. No one had—but her. And the blatantly sexual images that Mai's teasing words had brought to mind refused to be dislodged.

The door opened suddenly and Nick stood there, chest heaving, his quick, sharp gaze sweeping the room. When he saw her, his chin came up and his restless searching ceased. Cory felt the look he gave her all the way to her yellow espadrilles.

"Momma, Momma!" Timmy called over the din. "Uncle Nick is here." He took off running toward the door.

Nick caught the excited little boy on the fly and swung him into his arms. "Hey, who're you? I don't know any clowns."

Timmy giggled. "It's me, Timmy! Momma did my face."

Nick's gaze flickered to Cory's face and stayed there. "Sorry, I couldn't get away sooner," he said as he walked toward her. It took every scrap of discipline he'd managed to exert over himself to keep from taking her mouth again.

"Bad day?" she asked, worried about the look of exhaustion around his eyes.

He shrugged off her concern. "I would have been here sooner, but I had to talk my way out of a speeding ticket. Damn CHP."

He sounded hassled, but he looked sexy and virile, like a man who knew how to make a woman feel like a wanton, or a princess, depending on the look in his eyes. At the moment Cory was wondering why the blouse that had seemed so modest at home suddenly felt too tight and too skimpy.

"I . . . we're glad you made it, aren't we, Timmy?"

"Uh-huh." Timmy sucked on his thumb, beaming at everyone in sight.

Cory was aware of a movement at her elbow, but before she could introduce Mai, her friend was introducing herself. "Hi, I'm Mai."

Nick's smile flashed, erasing years from his lined face. "Nick Donatelli."

"I know. Welcome to the Sunshine School."

"Thanks. I've been looking forward to it."

Mai smiled, then flipped her braid over her shoulder and hurried off to help a harried-looking mother cope with four bickering little boys.

Nick took a tighter hold on Timmy's wiggling little body and tried not to stare at the wildly sexy gypsy with the flushed cheeks and irresistible eyes. He'd seen Cory in all kinds of attire, from her ratty bathrobe to a chic wedding gown, but he'd never felt an almost savage desire to tear those clothes from her and take her quickly and thoroughly the way he was feeling at the moment.

Conscious of the veiled and not so veiled looks directed her way by the other adults in the room, Cory tilted her chin a tad higher and tried not to notice the way Nick's eyes seemed to devour her.

"There are punch and pumpkin cookies, if you're hungry," she said.

One side of his mouth lifted in an ironic smile. "Uh, thanks. I think I'll pass."

Bemused by the sight of this big, tough man cradling her son as though he were the most precious thing in the world, Cory couldn't seem to look away from that very masculine face.

"Looks like you found yourself something to wear," he said after the silence stretched into tension.

"Yes."

Nick cleared his throat. "Very nice."

"Thank you."

"You're welcome."

Childish chatter and shrill laughter swirled around them. The pressure in Cory's chest increased until it was difficult to breathe.

"Nice place," he said, looking around. "Has a happy feeling."

"I hope to expand next year. Add another teacher—if...if everything goes well."

Nick knew she was thinking about the lawsuit and felt helpless to ease her worries. The last he'd heard, the suit was going forward. And if he knew that, so did Cory.

"I have some money," he said. "Not much, but it might help."

Cory smiled. "I can just see you investing in a nursery school."

"I'm not. I'm helping an old friend. Or is it a new friendship we have?"

Cory felt the impact of his lazy, sensuous look all the way to her bones. She began to feel warm from her hairline to her toes. "I...both, I guess," she answered in a husky tone.

They stared at each other, seemingly oblivious to the noise of the party, until Timmy became impatient and began jumping up and down in Nick's arms to get his attention.

"I'm gonna get *lots* of candy tonight," Timmy confided when he'd succeeded.

"Sounds good to me," Nick said. "Can I have some?"

"Sure, only you have to come trick-or-treating with me. Okay, Momma?"

"Of course, if—" She broke off as a pint-sized princess with a crooked tiara barreled into her legs. "Mrs. Kingston, Mrs. Kingston, Andy threw my licorice in the fish tank, and Lorenzo Lion Fish is trying to eat it!"

Seeing the tears welling in Amanda Wilson's eyes, Cory knelt down and hugged the thin little girl. "Calm down, Mandy," Cory said with a smile in her voice. "Lorenzo doesn't like licorice."

"Yes, he does," Mandy wailed in a shrill voice. "Andy *said*."

Watching Cory gentle the agitated little girl, Nick was aware of the creamy V of suntanned skin stretching above the frilly neckline of her gypsy blouse. Through the white material he could see the faint outline of a lace bra cupping her breasts.

He ran his free hand down his flank and jerked his gaze away. He was so tired he felt each ache and pain in his body, and yet he still wanted her with a need as raw and throbbing as his determination to win more than friendship from her.

"Uh, c'mon, Tim," he said, his voice as strained as his control. "Let's see if we can get us one of those apples."

"Mom, you talk to Uncle Nick for me. He'll listen to you."

Cory looked up from the candy she was dumping into a large wooden bowl for the trick-or-treaters to see the mutinous look on Joey's face.

"Joey, we've gone over this too many times already. Uncle Nick thinks you should stay in tonight, and that's it."

After the party, she'd come directly home, while Nick had taken Timmy for the promised ride in the Corvette. She expected them back any minute.

Jennifer unwrapped a miniature peanut bar and popped it into her mouth. "What's the matter, Joey?" she taunted. "You afraid Melissa will get tired of waiting for you to get off restriction and start going out with Toby Ramsay again?"

Joey rounded on his sister, his eyes blazing. "Shut up!"

"Mom!"

"Cut it out, both of you. You're going to spoil Halloween for your baby brother."

"He started it," Jen grumbled, chomping on another candy.

"Yeah, right," Joey retorted, his voice dripping with sarcasm. "Miss Piggy is too busy stuffing her fat face to do anything wrong."

Cory gasped, and Jennifer looked stricken. "Apologize to your sister, Joey," Cory ordered in an outraged tone. "I'm ashamed of you both."

Joey's face twisted. "Sorry," he muttered, but his green eyes blazed with defiance, and his fists were clenched at his sides.

"I hate you," Jen threw back at him, her words thick with emotion. "Marky Ramsay wanted to go with me to the dance tonight, but his mother wouldn't let him because you got Toby in trouble."

"No way! Marky didn't ask you because you're the biggest nerd in the whole school."

Before Cory could protest, Nick's deep voice cut through the frozen silence. "Upstairs, Joey."

Joey's head snapped around, surprise whitening his mouth. Nick stood by the back door, one hand still on the knob, the other holding Timmy's.

When Joey didn't move, Nick jerked his head toward the hall. "Now."

Joey muttered an expletive and sprinted out of the kitchen.

"I wish they would've kept him in jail," Jenny said in a choked voice before she spun around and started for the hall.

"Jenny, don't run away," Cory called after her. "We need to talk."

"I don't want to talk!" she shouted. "You're always on his side. You do everything for Joey or Timmy, never for me!" She slammed out, her sneakers pounding on the floor.

Cory realized her hand had stolen to her throat and slowly dropped it to her side. As the silence settled, she looked up to find Nick watching her.

"Are you all right?" he asked when she tried a smile and failed.

Cory nodded. "I'll give her a little time to compose herself, and then I'll talk to her, although, God help me, I don't know what I can say to make it right."

"Don't look at me," Nick said in a brusque tone. "I sure as hell don't have the answer."

He closed the door, then bent down until he and Timmy were eye to eye. "Do me a big favor and play in your room for a while, Tiger, so your mom and I can talk, okay?"

"But it's trick-or-treat time," Timmy protested, frowning.

"Not yet. Not until it starts to get dark outside. Okay?"

At the assertive note in Nick's voice, Timmy's frown cleared. "Okay."

Cheeks reddened by the brisk fall wind, the little boy ran to give his mother a hug, then trotted out of the kitchen, leaving Nick and Cory alone.

"See how smart you were not to want children?" she asked in a shaky voice.

"Not smart. Scared. I didn't want them to grow up hating me the way I hated my father."

She stared at him. "You never told me that."

"We wanted different things. It didn't matter why."

Because her legs felt as though they were about to buckle, she pulled out a chair and sat down. "Joey and Jen have had their share of arguments, but he's never been mean before," she said, more to herself than to Nick.

"He's running scared, Cory. Sometimes guys do things they regret when they feel trapped."

Cory's fingers began pleating the candy wrapper Jenny had discarded. "Theo called."

At the mention of the other man's name, Nick felt his gut tighten. The man had come around several times, to talk about the case, he'd said. To get into Cory's bed was more like it.

Nick prowled the kitchen, his long legs tense. "Did he say anything important?"

"The prosecutor is offering a deal. Six months in Juvenile Hall and two years probation, if Joey pleads guilty."

"What does Theo recommend?"

"He says it's up to me."

"Wrong. It's up to Joey. He's the one who has to do the time."

Cory's hand crushed the bright waxed paper into a ball. "I love him, Nick, and I believe in him. I don't know what I'd do if . . . if I found out he was lying to me. That he was capable of doing those terrible things."

"He's capable, Cory. What's important is whether he did them or not."

"He took Joe's death hard," she said as she picked up the jacket Joey had thrown on an empty chair and brushed a piece of lint from the collar. "I tried to be there for him, but more and more, he just seemed to shut me out."

"It's his age. All males feel the need to separate from their mothers during adolescence. It doesn't last."

"I hope not. It's about to drive all of us crazy." She hung Joey's jacket on the back of her chair, smoothing the material gently.

Nick remembered those small pretty hands sliding over his skin, tentatively at first, and then, as her confidence grew, with a boldness that had brought him to his knees. His body quickened, taunting him.

"Joey loves you, too, Cory. And, deep down, I'm sure he loves his sister."

As he spoke the words meant to reassure, Nick realized he rarely thought about love, but when he did, Cory always came to mind. He'd always envied Joe because he had been able to love her. And accept her love in return.

Cory glanced toward Timmy's truck, lying forgotten by the counter. Once it had been Joey's. "I know he has to grow up, but sometimes I miss the little boy he used to be. Sometimes I get so scared I'm doing all the wrong things with him."

Nick leaned against the counter and rolled his shoulders, trying to ease the knot at the back of his neck. "I don't think you could do the wrong thing if you tried."

Fatigue had put dark crescents under his eyes and lined his face. When did he sleep? she wondered, remembering the nights she'd heard his quiet tread on the stairs hours after she'd gone to bed.

He exuded a stark loneliness that made her want to reach out and touch him, to press against that warm chest and soothe the tension from his face.

She stood up and went to him. He looked startled, then wary, as her hand came up to touch him. "You're working too hard," she said.

"That's what you used to say to Joe," he said, his voice rough.

"Did I?"

He nodded. "I'm not Joe, Cory. I can't be what he was to you." It hurt to talk about Joe. It hurt worse to know that he would never be the man his partner had been.

"I know that."

Nick drew in a quick breath of air. "Then remember that no man wants to be a substitute for another, especially not me. You were mine first."

The doorbell rang, startling both of them. Cory dashed a hand over her hot cheeks and tried to smile. "Trick or treat," she said in a wan tone.

"Let me," Nick said, reaching for the bowl of candy. "You've had enough to handle today."

"No, it's okay," she said quickly. Too quickly. "I'll go."

Nick moved closer until his thigh was a scant inch from her shoulder. "As soon as you talk to Jenny, you and I are taking Timmy trick-or-treating. After that, I'm taking everyone out for dinner. You pick the place."

Before she could protest, he bent down to brush his mouth over hers. "For what it's worth, I wish I had been man enough to accept what you were offering twenty years ago. If I had been, it might have been my family I was taking out tonight."

"Oh, Nick," she cried softly, her eyes filling with tears.

His thumb rubbed a stray tear from her cheek, his eyes roaming her face like a starving man searching for a crumb to keep him alive.

The doorbell pealed again. "Hold that thought," he muttered, taking her mouth once more, this time with a fierce insistence, before he left her.

Chapter 11

The diner was decorated in a fifties motif, complete with a magnificent jukebox in one corner and the front end of a classic Thunderbird embedded in the far wall.

The food was also fifties fare, cheeseburgers and chili dogs, malts and fries. None of the songs on the jukebox had been recorded later than 1960.

The waitress wore a carhop's uniform, complete with red tam and saddle shoes. Her name was Cindy, and she was in Joey's class at school.

As soon as she'd seen them troop in, she'd done a doubletake, then begun whispering urgently to her fellow waitress. Joey had grumbled something rude under his breath and started to leave, until a glance from Nick had him thinking better of it.

"Would anyone like dessert?" Cindy asked after they had worked their way through a mound of burgers and fries.

"Ice cream," Timmy shouted, clapping his hands. "Chocolate."

Joey rolled his eyes. "He's not really my brother," he muttered in a long-suffering tone that drew a warning look from his mother.

Cindy laughed and wrote the order on her pad. "How come you're not at the dance tonight?" she asked Joey while Jenny was studying the dessert menu.

"It's kid stuff," Joey scoffed. "How come you didn't go?"

"I need the money for college."

"Good for you," Cory said with an encouraging smile.

"Thanks, Mrs. Kingston. With five brothers and sisters at home, I sometimes feel like I'll never get there."

"Sure you will. I put myself through school waiting tables in a campus dive. It's not easy, but it can be done."

Cindy beamed. "How about dessert?"

"Just coffee for me," Cory said, looking down at the half-eaten cheeseburger still on her plate. Dinner had been tense. Joey was sullen, Jenny uncommunicative. The girl had refused to go to the dance, and nothing Cory said had changed her mind. She'd even refused to accompany them to dinner—until Nick had had a private talk with her.

Cindy's gaze shifted to Nick, who sat with one arm stretched along the back of the booth, his fingers only inches from Cory's shoulder. "Sir?"

Nick ordered pumpkin pie and coffee. Joey ordered the same, without the coffee. Cindy scribbled in her book and started to turn away when Jenny spoke up. "Hey, you forgot me."

"Sorry, Jenny. What can I get you?"

Jenny closed the menu and handed it to the other girl. "A banana split with extra sprinkles," she said, her tone rushed, as though she could hardly wait.

Joey rolled his eyes again, and Jenny shot him a murderous look. "Mom! Make him stop," she hissed as soon as Cindy had gone.

"Just kidding. Don't be so sensitive."

"I'm not sensitive!"

"Oh yeah? How come you decided all of a sudden not to go to the dance?"

Jenny's face flamed. "None of your business, you jerk."

"Pardon me while I go to the men's room and cry," Joey muttered sarcastically before he left his seat and ambled toward the front of the diner.

Nick saw the tears standing in Jenny's eyes and wanted to follow Joey into the bathroom and turn the smart-mouth kid over his knee. Instead, he slid from the booth and extended his hand toward the miserable-looking girl. "C'mon. Jen. Dance with your old Uncle Nick."

Jenny looked toward the small dance floor in front of the jukebox, where several couples were dancing the fifties' version of the jitterbug.

"I don't know how."

Nick hid his surprise. He thought every girl of thirteen knew how to dance. They all seemed to in L.A.

"C'mon, I'll teach you. Besides, you'll be doing me a favor. I haven't danced to this kind of music since I was a kid. It'll make me feel young again."

Jenny shook her head, her expression so self-conscious that Cory felt like crying. "Go on, sweetie," Cory encouraged. "It's not hard."

"Especially when you have a terrific teacher," Nick said immodestly, drawing Cory's gaze. His grin flashed. "Right, Mom?"

Cory remembered the first time they'd danced. He'd been by far the better dancer, but it had hardly mattered, since they'd scarcely moved. By the time the song had ended, Nick had been fully aroused and she had been breathing hard.

"Right," she said, her voice abnormally husky.

"See," Nick told her daughter. His fingers closed around Jenny's arm, and he tugged her to her feet.

"Oh, all right," Jenny grumbled. "But I'm not going to be any good at it."

"Sure you will. You're a natural, just like your mom."

Cory watched as Nick dropped a strong arm over Jenny's shoulders and led her through the tables. He was so dark, and she was so fair. No one would ever mistake them for father and daughter.

It might have been my family I was taking out tonight.

What kind of daughter would Nick have given her? she wondered. A dark-haired, feminine version of himself? With those same expressive dark eyes and irresistible smile?

She remembered the way his eyes had slid over her belly the first time he'd seen her pregnant. For a split second he'd looked exactly like a man who'd been dealt a fatal wound, then his face had split into a grin.

"What do you know, a baby?" he'd said, thumping Joe on the back. "Didn't think you had it in you, partner."

Things had been different between the three of them after that. Nick had stopped coming around as much, and when he did, he seemed to avoid being alone with her. Once, when he'd stayed the night, he'd wandered bleary-eyed into the kitchen the next morning to find Joe's hand resting on her belly.

"Hey, Nick, come here and feel this kid kick," Joe had said with a proud grin. Nick had made some excuse and left. At the time, she'd been hurt. Now she wondered if Nick had been reluctant to touch her because he'd been imagining that it was his child growing inside her.

Her hand dipped beneath the table to press against her stomach. A baby. Nick's baby, she thought, her gaze drawn to the dance floor again.

Jenny's face was flushed, and she was laughing at something he had just said. Her movements were awkward and still very self-conscious, but Nick was so good he made her look good, too.

It was warm in the diner, and he'd rolled his sleeves above his elbows. His collar was open, revealing a V of olive skin that looked very dark against the pale material.

He was grinning, reminding her of the sexy young cop who could make her melt inside with a look. Light from the overhead fixtures emphasized the silver at his temples, reminding her that they were both twenty years older.

The music ended, and Jenny threw herself into Nick's arms for a hug. His gaze met Cory's across the tables, and she found herself smiling around the lump in her throat.

I could love this man, she thought, then gasped. No, she told herself in wild denial. It wasn't love he excited in her. That had ended years ago. What she felt now was lust, as hot as a fever in her system, but just as transitory.

She was still repeating that to herself when everyone arrived at the table at once—Nick and Jenny, Joey, the waitress. In his excitement, Timmy tipped over his milk glass. Fortunately it was plastic and didn't break, but milk spattered the table and his shirt, and got all over Nick's hands.

Cory grabbed a napkin and mopped up the mess, while Joey glowered and Jenny looked pained. Nick went off to wash his hands. By the time he returned, Cory had regained her equilibrium.

Head down, Jenny attacked her banana split, her cheeks still glowing. Nick and Joey ate in silence, while Cory gulped coffee and tried not to notice the speculative looks directed their way.

Timmy chattered nonstop, even as he was shoving one spoonful of ice cream after another into his mouth. Ordinarily Cory would have chided him for speaking with his mouth full, but his cheery nonsense helped diffuse the tension that still lingered in the booth.

"Did you see us, Mom?" Jenny interjected when Timmy finally paused.

"I sure did, sweetie," Cory said with genuine enthusiasm. "You were great!"

Jenny beamed, her eyes shining behind her glasses. "Uncle Nick said he'd teach me to slow dance, too." Her head turned toward Nick. "Didn't you?"

"Absolutely!" he confirmed, pushing his empty plate away. "Although I have to admit I'm pretty rusty."

"I doubt that," Cory said before she thought.

One thick black eyebrow arched, and a grin hovered at the corners of his mouth. "Looks like I'll have to prove it to you," he said in a deeper than normal voice.

"That's not necessary," Cory said before gulping down the rest of her coffee.

Nick leaned back and dug into the pocket of his tight jeans for a quarter. "Jen, do me a favor and play *Twilight Time* by the Platters."

"No!" Cory protested. "I can't."

"No fair, Mom," Jenny said with a grin. "You made me get out there. Now it's your turn." She took the money and left the booth.

A few seconds later the mellow sounds of the old song drifted over the buzz of conversation. Nick gave Joey a look, and the boy slid from the booth, allowing Nick to stand. When Cory didn't move, he turned and bowed. "May I have this dance, my lady?" he asked with a look of sensuous anticipation in his eyes.

"I'll get you for this," she grumbled, trying to look reluctant. But inside she was fighting a warm excitement.

His hand was tight around hers as he led her to the floor and swung her into his arms. His free hand came to rest on the small of her back, and he pulled her closer until her breasts were pressed against his chest.

"Relax," he whispered against her temple. "Jenny's watching."

"So is half the town," she muttered into his shoulder.

His laugh rumbled, close enough to her ear to tickle. "Shall I tell you what they're thinking?"

"No, thanks."

His fingers tightened around hers as he brought their entwined hands to his shoulder. "The women all wish they looked exactly like you. The men are jealous as hell because I'm the guy with a sexy gypsy temptress in his arms."

He increased the pressure until her thighs were welded to his. Before she could protest, he spun them around and around, making her breathless.

The music became slower, more seductive, and his sinuous body mirrored the tempo. More couples had joined them, and the floor was crowded, restricting their movements. Twice another couple jostled them, and Nick cursed under his breath.

"Maybe we should sit down before we're both black and blue," she said in a breathy tone. The pressure on her spine eased, and she edged backward.

Nick saw the laughter in her eyes and felt the reaction all the way to his groin. He savored the quick burst of pleasure it gave him, even as he willed his body to behave.

"I have a better idea." The hand on her back moved a few inches lower to the spot where her buttocks began to round, joined by his other hand. His arms tightened, drawing her closer to his body until she was forced to arch against him like a small warm cat.

He lowered his head until his cheek was resting against her temple. The heat of his body enveloped her in a heady scent of musk and soap, and his skin was slightly rough with the whiskers he hadn't had time to scrape off. His heart was beating wildly against her breasts.

She matched his slow movements exactly, her body fitting against his as though they'd been made for just this one purpose. Through the fullness of her skirt she felt his body swell and then harden. What had begun as a faint whisper of desire deep inside her quickly became a throbbing heat.

Nick hugged her against him, almost afraid to believe it was really Cory whose breasts were pressed against his chest. Or that it was her soft thighs rubbing his, her sweet-smelling hair tickling his throat.

He closed his eyes and pretended he didn't have to let her go when the song ended. His hand stroked her hair, moving slower and slower. He was mesmerized by the feeling of contentment that just touching her gave him.

The music ended on a swirl of violins. There was a smattering of applause and a murmur of comment. Nick opened his eyes and reluctantly drew back, his breath catching.

Cory's eyes were closed, and her lips were curved at the corners, giving her a drowsy, sensuous beauty that ripped through him in almost physical agony.

"It's been a long time," he said, his voice smoky.

Cory opened her eyes and smiled. "Yes," she whispered. "A long time."

Another song, a fast one this time, blared from the speakers, and those remaining on the floor began gyrating to a pounding rock and roll beat. Cory blinked, and the world settled again.

As though he had all the time in the world, Nick folded his hand over hers where it rested on his shoulder and lifted it to his lips.

"Tonight, you're mine," he murmured against her wrist. "No past, no ghosts, just you and me."

"Yes," she whispered, unable to refuse him. "Just you and me."

* * *

The old house was never completely quiet, but as Cory belted her robe and walked to the window, it seemed to sigh and creak with an especially agitated intensity.

A harvest moon was rising, plump and yellow against the matte black sky. Moonbeams streamed through the lace curtains to dust the thick rug with gold. Beyond the cool panes the graceful branches of the towering eucalyptus swayed in rhythm with the breeze.

It was just past twelve. Everyone was in bed. Everyone but her. Behind her, the sheets she'd abandoned gleamed white in the moonlight. For an hour she'd tried to convince herself that she was tied in knots because her long, hectic day had worn her to a frazzle.

But the tension that burned in her muscles was more than fatigue. It was sexual need, insistent and hot, the kind that only Nick had ever aroused in her.

She'd been so sure he would come to her. She'd been so sure that she wanted him to, and equally sure that she didn't. The turmoil had exhausted her.

"I'll get over it," she muttered to the accompaniment of the wind. "It's better this way." After a last lingering look at the silvery land beyond the trees, she slipped out of her robe and slid under the coverlet.

The sheets had cooled and felt crisp against her hot skin. She sighed, then froze as her door clicked open. For an instant Nick was silhouetted against the faint glow from the night light on the landing, his shoulders stretching almost the width of the doorway, his bare chest a ripple of muscle and sinew in the moonlight. And then he was closing the door behind him, bringing the clean scent of shaving soap and shampoo into her room.

"The door wasn't locked," he said in a low voice.

"I never lock my door," she whispered, her fingers folding tightly over the satin edge of the blanket. She heard the key scrape in the lock, sending tension running like wildfire through her body.

Nick moved toward her into the beam of light from the window. He was wearing white running shorts and nothing more.

"I thought Joey would never go to bed." His deep voice carried an edge of humor. "I nearly went crazy waiting."

"Maybe we shouldn't, Nick," she said, her voice coming out too soft and too breathless.

"No second thoughts, *cara*. Tonight is mine."

"It might not be safe. I stopped taking the pill when Joe died. I don't have anything." Who was she trying to convince? she wondered. Him, or herself?

"It's all right," he answered, his voice very deep. "I took care of that a long time ago."

Cory stared at him. "A vasectomy? You?"

"Yes. Does that make you feel better?"

"I . . . why?" she blurted out.

"You know why. I didn't want to bring a child of mine into the world."

No, he hadn't, she thought with a rush of disappointment, and yet she had a feeling he was coming to love hers. What a complex man he was. Was that why she found him so compelling? Because she never knew what he was thinking, or why?

Slowly, his eyes devouring her, he took off his shorts. In the pale light his body was a long stretch of burnished teak, his chest arrowed with crisp, dark hair, the musculature classically male, the sinews steely bold.

With one fluid movement he jerked the blanket from her and tossed it to the edge of the bed. She shivered, not from cold, but from the feverish look of hunger in his sky-black eyes.

He came to her swiftly, the heavy weight of his body rocking the mattress and making the springs protest.

"If I asked you to stop," she began, but he silenced her with two fingers against her lips.

"Don't ask, Cory," he ordered, his voice reflecting the savage restraint that was now close to breaking.

No, she thought. The time to stop him had been earlier, when he'd given her a fierce good-night kiss that had left them both breathing hard.

Nick realized he'd been waiting for the tension in her face to relax into the same drowsy look of desire that had been tormenting him since their dance. When it did, he knew that not even the devil himself could stop him from taking her.

Nick leaned toward her, his long arms and big hands bracketing her shoulders. Even though his broad chest was still inches above her breasts, they began to swell and burn, and the nipples began to tingle.

"It's been a long time since I've made love," she murmured before dampening her dry lips with her tongue.

"For me, too," he whispered before bending to wet those same lips with his own tongue. The pleasure was intense, taking her by surprise.

"Do you like that?" he murmured against her mouth. Taking her soft moan for assent, he repeated the slick exploration of her lips before gently insinuating the tip of his tongue between them. His tongue thrust, retreated, thrust again.

"And this?" he demanded.

"Yes," she gasped against his mouth.

His hands pushed into her hair to trace the curves of her ears, and she began to tremble. He shifted, bracing his body on one arm while he twined the other hand in her hair. His kiss became urgent, his mouth alternately persuading and demanding.

Her fingers ran over the hot flesh stretched over hard muscle, tearing a groan from his throat. His hand moved, down the sleek satin of her gown to the even sleeker skin beneath. His fingers stroked upward, raising the gown at the same time, until her thighs were fully exposed and gleaming in the moonlight.

Nick drew back, his breathing a hot rasp in his chest. Slowly, fighting the hunger urging him to bury himself deep and hard inside the lushness he knew waited for him, he gazed at the woman lying beneath him.

Her face was a luminous blur, her features softened into fragile beauty by passion, her eyes dark beneath her drowsy lashes. Her throat was creamy and slender above the low neck of her gown, and her breasts thrust against the thin material, begging to be caressed and molded by his palms. She looked young and sweet and so ripe for love that he wondered if he might burst before he could make her ready for him.

His mouth found hers again, pushing her deeper into the pillow. At the same time he used his hands to raise her gown higher until her breasts were exposed.

Braced on his palms, his mouth still welded to hers, he lowered himself over her until his chest just touched her nipples. He began to move in an exquisitely slow circle, massaging her breasts until she was breathless with pleasure.

"I want you too much to be gentle," he warned, hunger deepening his voice.

She had trouble hearing him over the thudding of her heart. Her senses were alive, her vision blurred by desire. "I'm not afraid," she answered, running her palms up his arms.

Nick saw the wild, desperate need darken her eyes. He slipped the gown from her between kisses. When she was lying naked, he eased back, reacquainting himself with the creamy curves and secret angles of her.

Beneath his hands her skin was damp, the undersides of her breasts pearling with sweat. He used his tongue to lap her dry, then began molding every inch of her with his hands.

She was soft, silky, her skin flowing under his fingers like warm sweet milk. His hand shook as his fingers explored the tender flesh inside her thighs. She was moist, demanding, as eager as he was.

Hunger spiked hot inside him, and he drew back, his expression tortured. "I thought I remembered... I've wanted this so much, and now..." His words ended in a hoarse groan that seemed ripped from him.

Whispering his name, she pressed trembling lips to his throat, inhaling deeply the musky, provocative scent of his skin. Nick felt her twist under him, and his mouth had to have hers again.

Her response was fiery, sending all thought of restraint out of his head. He followed her lead, kissing her where she kissed him, touching her as she touched him, until his body was throbbing and aching, his skin on fire, his muscles shuddering with the need to thrust inside her.

Cory was mindless, caught in a maelstrom, whirling, needing, hungering. She heard him groaning out her name over and over, his breath hot against her skin. He used his tongue and his hands to take her higher, higher, until she buried her face in the pillow to muffle the cry of release exploding from her.

Again and again he took her to climax until she was exhausted but hungering for more. Hands tangled in his hair, she clung to him, urging his body into hers, her skin damp with his sweat as his was damp with hers.

Nick felt the tiny tremors take her again. His breath was coming in gasps, and his teeth were clenched to keep his groans inside.

He nudged her thighs aside, testing her readiness with a hand that shook. She was hot and ready, as ready as he was. "Yes, oh yes," she whispered on a sob of need. "Now."

With a groan, he thrust into her, his body shuddering in a shock of the greatest pleasure he'd ever felt. Somehow he hung on until he felt her convulse against him. Arching his back, he pushed into her, hard, fast, as deeply as he could, fusing them together.

Cory felt the shock take him, her body absorbing the shuddering of his. He collapsed against her, his face buried in the curve of her shoulder.

He couldn't stop the shudders. He crushed his arms around her, needing to feel her warmth and love. "Don't ask me to go," he whispered against the breast his sweat had dampened. "Not yet."

"No," she whispered, her fingers stroking his hair. "Not yet."

Nick heard the throb in her voice and let his eyes drift closed. It had been so long since he'd felt this drowsy sense of security, so long since the barbed emotions driving him had relented long enough for him to feel good inside.

He rubbed his cheek against the satiny skin beneath him. His arms tightened, and he held her close, afraid to let her go.

He wasn't a man who believed in second chances, especially for someone who had sinned as much as he had, but making love to Cory again was as close as he would ever get.

He felt good—terrific, in fact—and, for the first time in years, sleepy as hell. With a deep sigh he let himself relax against the warm, yielding woman in his arms.

Feeling the bunched muscles of Nick's arms gradually relax, Cory smiled into the darkness. She was floating, her body sated and quiescent, her heartbeat slowly settling into a normal rhythm again.

Slowly, she turned her head, her gaze searching the shadows for the wedding photograph on the bureau. Moonlight glinted off the silver frame, but the faces remained dark. In her mind she saw Joe's self-conscious grin and her own loving smile.

She had been faithful to Joe, and she had no doubt that he'd been entirely faithful to her. Their love had been special, a bond forged of their mutual devotion to each other and to their children, and a shared desire to make a stable home.

Never once, in all the years they'd had together, had she wished that she had married Nick instead of Joe. Never once had she doubted that her love for Nick was dead and buried. And it had been, just as that idealistic young cop was buried somewhere in the cynical, battle-weary man Nick had become. What she felt now was new, different. But it was still love.

Chapter 12

At eight the next morning Cory was just coming out of the boys' bedroom when Nick caught her around the waist and kissed her.

"Hey, gorgeous lady, how about spending the day at the beach?" he whispered as he nuzzled her ear. "No kids, no school, no LAPD. Just you and me." His hands bracketed her waist, his fingers warm and possessive.

"Sounds wonderful," she murmured, feeling excitement course through her. "But I can't."

"Why not? Jen can baby-sit Tim. I'll even make the lunch." He had been out running, and he smelled like autumn leaves and sunshine. Sweat burnished his skin to bronze.

"It's not that," she said, casting a worried look over her shoulder. "It's Joey. There's a bug going around, and I'm afraid he's caught it."

A frown replaced the seductive glint in his eyes. "He's sick?"

She nodded, her eyes dark with worry. "When Timmy came down for breakfast, he was complaining because Joey was making funny noises in the bathroom and wouldn't let him in to use the toilet.''

"Funny noises, huh?" His eyebrows slid upward over a devilish glint in his eyes. "With a sixteen-year-old male that doesn't necessarily mean he's sick. Come to think of it, some forty-year-old guys make the same noises when the lady of their choice is, uh, reluctant." His eyes crinkled beguilingly, and Cory felt a blush spread over her cheeks.

"Hush," she said, glancing over her shoulder.

Masking his disappointment, Nick dropped an arm over her shoulder and led her to the door of her bedroom. "How about a quickie, then?"

"Nick, be serious. Joey needs me."

He pulled her close and let her feel him. "So do I. I woke up wanting to be inside you again."

Cory's blush deepened, delighting him. He laid his fingers along the curve of her cheek. "Why, Mrs. Kingston. I think you're the one with the fever," he murmured, his voice dipping seductively.

After backing her up against the door, he braced both arms against the panel and leaned forward to brush tiny kisses over her mouth. His tenderness warmed her, and love welled inside her. When Nick was like this, she couldn't resist him. But she had to. For both their sakes.

"You're crazy, you know that?" she said with laughter catching in her voice.

"Crazy about a sexy green-eyed gypsy, you mean." His tongue traced the whorls of her ear, sending little shivers running through her. His mouth grew hungry. His arms pulled her tighter. Her breasts yielded to the solid width of his chest.

Nick felt himself coming to life again, numbness giving way to a fevered excitement, pain receding into a tidal wash of sensation. Her hips hugged his, enticingly soft, her warmth invading the places that had been so cold for so long.

Yes, baby, he wanted to beg. Come back to me. I won't hurt you, I promise. But the feeling between them was so fragile, so newly changed from the harsh anger he'd lived with for so long, that he was terrified he would do something to spoil it.

They needed time together, time to turn friendship and sexual attraction into something more lasting, something that would make them both happy.

Nick felt her body begin to shake and knew a moment of primitive agony. He was pushing too hard, too fast. But, God, she felt good in his arms.

On a groan, he raised his head and kissed the tip of her nose. He wanted her so badly he felt a shuddering begin inside him.

"When this is all over, you and I are going away, someplace with a beach and lots of sun, where I can have you all to myself." Nick kept his tone light, but inside, his belly was twisted with tension at the memory of the blazing, shattering pleasure she'd given him only a few hours ago. He wanted that again.

But more than sexual satisfaction, he wanted her to trust him again. One step at a time, he told himself. Now that he was back in her bed, he would find a way to be patient.

He hugged her fiercely, then released her. "I'll check on Joey, and then I need to grab a shower before I head into the city."

"Into the city?" she said, trying to get her heartbeat to calm down. Every time he touched her, he unsettled her more.

"Paperwork. The cop's curse. It's been piling up. As long as I can't play, I might as well work." He kissed her again, as though he hated to leave her, and then walked across the landing to Joey's door. He knocked once, then entered and closed the door behind him.

Oh, Nick, she thought as she headed down the stairs to get juice for her son. Don't you understand? It isn't just the two of us. It can't be. And she was so desperately afraid that was the one thing that would drive him away.

Nick let the Corvette idle at the deserted intersection, a frown tightening his face. One road led to the freeway and L.A., the other to the park where he and Joey had played a pickup game of basketball with the boy's friends last weekend.

He muttered a terse oath over the rumble of the engine. Joey wasn't sick. The kid was hung over. He ought to know, he thought. He'd seen that same gray face and bloodshot eyes in his own mirror often enough to recognize the telltale signs.

He would bet his pension the kid had snuck out last night. Ordinarily a mouse couldn't have moved in that house without his hearing it. But he'd been so wrapped up in making love to Cory, he wouldn't have heard an elephant tramping through the place.

Damn the kid, he thought. His instincts had been telling him all along that Joey wasn't telling the whole truth about that night at the high school, but he hadn't wanted to believe them. Now he had a choice. He could ignore the whole thing, or he could do some checking.

And then what? What if he found out Joey had slipped out to party? Did that mean he'd also beaten up an old man?

Nick rubbed the scar over his temple. His head was beginning to ache, and his gut was almost as tight as it had been a month ago when he'd walked into Cory's house.

Would Cory understand? he wondered. If he went to her and told her that her son was lying, would she hate him for forcing her to see the truth? Probably, he thought with a mental shudder. He couldn't handle that again. Not again.

Don't be an idiot, he told himself. Let it go. She's forgiven you. She's even let you make love to her. But you have a long way to go before you can be sure she's forgotten why she was alone in that bed for so long. Don't do anything to make her resent you again.

After all, he wasn't Joey's father. He wasn't responsible for the kid's future. If he'd wanted kids, he would have found someone to marry to give them to him. But he didn't. Not ever. Not his own. Not anyone else's. He had vowed a long time ago never to be responsible for anyone but himself, and that was the way he wanted it. Frown deepening to a scowl, he threw the car into gear and tromped on the gas.

Miles later, with the freeway on-ramp in sight, he stepped on the brake and swerved the 'Vette to the shoulder. After checking the mirror, he made a quick *U*-turn and headed back to town.

His gut told him that Joey was in more trouble than he knew, the same kind of trouble he'd been in at the kid's age. He'd started out with petty stuff, too, boosting candy bars first, and then beer and cigarettes. Stealing the Cadillac had been easy. Too easy. His conscience hadn't even bothered him—until Judge Clarence L. Brown had forced him to think about the road he'd put himself on, the road that led sooner or later to prison or death.

Years later, after he'd been accepted to the Police Academy, he'd gone back to Judge Brown to thank him. "Pass it on, Dominic, someday when you see another boy like yourself heading for trouble," the old man had said with a smile on his kindly black face. "It isn't easy to care. Some folks will hate you, but the ones you help won't."

Judge Brown was long dead now, but Nick had never forgotten his words. Since that time, he'd tried to live up to them. "I hope you're right, Judge," he muttered as he parked in the lot by the courts. "You can't imagine how much."

There was a spirited game in progress between three black boys and three white ones. The teams seemed evenly matched, both lousy. Nick leaned against a post supporting the chainlink fence and watched.

He knew they were aware of him by the quick sidelong glances they slanted his way, but they gave no greeting. Let 'em wonder, he thought, lifting his face to the sun. A person who was nervous talked more than he intended to.

Finally, twenty minutes or so into the game, the ball bounced off the knee of one of the boys and rocketed his way. He scooped it up, but instead of tossing it back, he held it loosely between his palms and walked toward them.

"Hi, guys. How's it going?" he asked when he was within a few feet of one of the baskets.

"Hey, give us the ball, man," one of the black boys said with a scowl. With a flick of his powerful wrists, Nick shot the basketball toward the boy who'd spoken. The others eyed Nick nervously, their expressions ranging from sullen to curious.

"I was supposed to meet Joey Kingston here, but after the night he had, I have a feeling he just might be hung over. Guess he can't hold his booze the way you guys can."

That brought grins all around. "Man shouldn't party if he can't hold his liquor, know what I mean?" one said, glancing at the others for support.

Even as he grinned amiably, Nick felt a hole open up in his stomach. "I hear you," he said in a man-to-man tone. "How about Toby Ramsay? Does he hold his liquor, too?"

The boy with the ball bounced it a few times before grumbling. "Not him. Dude's from San Diego. Guys down there are wimps."

"San Diego? I thought he was raised here."

"Naw, been here two, three years. Thinks he's hot stuff 'cause he was a surfer."

"Girls think so, too," another grumbled, and the others joined in.

"Even after what happened with that old man?" Nick asked, shoving one hand in the pocket of his jeans. The movement moved his jacket just enough to reveal the butt of his revolver. A visible tension ran through the group, and most of the faces closed up tight.

"Hey, I know you," a stocky boy with dark hair and glasses said with a warning look at the boy next to him. "You're the cop who busted Joey."

"Is he a friend of yours?" Nick asked.

The teenager scowled. "No way, man. He's one crazy dude, know what I mean?" He flicked a glance at the smallest of the six, a Latino with intelligent eyes and a wicked looking bruise on his jaw. "Tell the man, Manny."

The boy called Manny ducked his head. "Forget it, Lawrence," he said to the bigger boy. "I don't want no more trouble."

"See that bruise on Manny's head?" Lawrence said, ignoring his friend's protest. "Joey did that last night, just 'cause Manny was talking to Melissa."

"Has this kind of thing happened before?"

The boys exchanged looks before Lawrence said pointedly, "Some guys get real mean when they drink, know what I mean?"

"Yes," Nick said with a sigh. "I know exactly what you mean."

Nick sat at his desk, staring at the half-completed arrest report on the computer screen. But all he saw was the growing look of trust in Cory's eyes.

Not even the darkest hours in intensive care, when he'd wondered if he could find a reason to live another day, had he dared to hope he would see that look again.

He'd worked like hell to deserve that trust, fighting instincts that were imprinted deeply in his psyche. For weeks he'd wrestled with the restlessness that had him eager to change her routine to his instead of the reverse. Every night, when he'd left the office, he'd struggled with an almost compulsive urge to take a different road, leading to a different destination. Not forever. Just for a few hours. Just for a change.

So far he'd resisted. So far he'd been able to stand the restrictions. Because of Cory, because of his need to be with her, to hear that quick little laugh that came to her throat when he made a joke, to watch her smile grow warm just for him, to lie quietly and at peace with her after making love. Being able to do those things was a miracle, and he was terrified he was going to blow it.

Without realizing it, he began to rub the rough patch of skin on the back of one hand where the tattoo had been. He'd told her it was a gang insignia, when, in fact, he'd had it done on a dare from the girl who'd taken his virginity. One tattoo and a lot of pain had gotten him one night of sex. He'd been ashamed to tell Cory the truth, and so he'd lied to her, the only lie he'd ever told her. She'd believed him without question, and the guilt he'd felt had made him swear privately never to lie to her again.

Son of a bitch, he was tired, he thought, closing his eyes and wincing. Withholding information wasn't really a lie, was it?

Damn it, Donatelli, you have to tell her. She has to know.

Tell her what? he argued with himself. That her son is a liar and likes to party? That maybe, just maybe, he's also a punk who likes to beat up old men when he gets drunk?

For one solid week he'd been wrestling with himself, trying to find reasons to keep the information from her long enough for their relationship to find some solid ground. But he was running out of time.

"It's your roll, Uncle Nick," Jenny said with an impatient glance at his bowed head. It was Sunday afternoon, the fourth Sunday Nick had spent with them, and the family had gathered in the den.

Nick looked up, a preoccupied look on his face. "What? Oh, sorry."

He leaned forward to take the dice from her hands. As he began to shake them, he was conscious of Cory's gaze on him. She was seated at the desk, helping Joey with his homework, and the desk lamp cast a golden glow on her face.

All day he'd been acutely aware of the ripe curves under the fuzzy blue sweater and tight jeans. All day he'd been trying to find a time to hold her against him, to taste her again, to bury his face in the perfume of her hair. But she'd been kept busy, handling one domestic crisis after another. It was driving him crazy.

He threw the dice and began moving his marker. Because his mind wasn't on the game, he lost count and had to start over again.

"You act just like Joey acted last Saturday," Jenny complained, straightening her already straight piles of Monopoly money. "Maybe you've got what he had."

"Not for a long time," he said, and Joey looked up from the Spanish composition Cory was helping him write, alarm written on his face. He caught Nick's eyes on him and quickly looked down at his book.

"Boardwalk!" Jenny exclaimed. "With two hotels, you owe me—"

"More than I have," Nick said with a grin that didn't quite erase the lines that seemed to have deepened at each side of his mouth. "You win, Squirt."

"That makes three in a row. I'm the grand champion of the world."

She stood and raised both arms in triumph, and Cory laughed. "How about making popcorn for all of us, champ? There's a Disney movie on in twenty minutes."

"Okay," Jenny said, bending to put away the game.

Nick unfolded his legs and got to his feet, wincing at the tightness in his neck and back. "I think I'll pass on the movie and take a walk instead," he said with a smile for Cory that made her warm all over.

"I'll come with you," she said, rising, an expectant look in her eyes. With all the hustle and bustle caused by three active children, it was difficult to find time to be alone with him.

"No, it's a rotten day," he said, moving toward the door. "You stay in and keep warm. I won't be long. I just need some fresh air."

Jenny followed him out, chattering as she headed for the kitchen and the popcorn. Joey's gaze met Cory's for an instant before he looked away.

"I'll keep you company, Momma," Timmy said, leaving his fleet of trucks and climbing into her lap, his thumb immediately poking into his mouth as soon as he was settled. As she hugged him close, she realized she was shivering.

It was starting, she thought, her blood going icy with fear. Actually it had started the morning Joey had been sick and she couldn't go with Nick to the beach.

He'd been brooding and quiet that evening, even though he'd done his best to hide it. And he'd been quiet all week. Sometimes she'd surprised him looking at her with an expression like pain in his eyes before his grin had wiped it away.

Probably no one else would notice the changes in him, but she did, because she'd lived through this before. Nick was acting exactly the same way he'd acted twenty years ago, withdrawing from her more every day. The only time they talked was in bed.

Even then, she sensed a distance in him whenever she tried to get him involved in the children's little dramas. Just last night, when she'd tried to tell him how well Joey was doing in school, how much his attitude had improved since Nick had come to live with them, she'd sensed his reluctance to discuss the boy with her.

And not once, not even in the heat of the most incredible passion, had he said he loved her. She knew now that he never would. Nick wanted one thing from her, the same thing he'd always wanted—an affair. With no promises, no happily-ever-after.

Face it, Cory, she told herself, resting her cheek on Timmy's silky head and closing her eyes. He was preparing himself to leave, just as he'd been preparing himself to tell her years ago that he wouldn't marry her.

"I need a break," Joey mumbled, throwing down his pencil. "Okay if I go upstairs and crank some tunes while Timmy is down here with you?"

Cory nodded. "But keep it down, okay? The plaster in this place is old, remember?"

"Aw, Mom," he groaned as he walked out, leaving Timmy and her alone in the den.

Timmy stirred against her breast. "Momma?"

"What, sweetie?"

He lifted his head and looked up at her with solemn eyes. "Is Uncle Nick going to be my daddy now?"

Cory tried to conceal her surprise behind a noncommittal smile. "Why would you ask that?"

"'Cause Ryan Pancake's mommy and daddy are always kissing, and Mrs. Pancake said that's what mommies and daddies do best. And I saw you kissing Uncle Nick."

"Would you like him to be your daddy?" she asked, her voice low and thick.

Timmy nodded vigorously. "He's fun, and he takes me for rides in his car."

"That's what uncles do, sweetie. But they're not the same as daddies." Her eyes misted with tears, but she blinked them back. Struggling to keep her voice calm and reassuring, she added brightly, "Uncle Nick will visit us lots and lots when he has to go back to the city, but he's not going to stay here and be your daddy. Do you understand what I'm telling you?"

Timmy nodded. The sad droop to his little lashes made her weep inside, and she pressed a kiss to his slightly damp forehead, poignantly aware of the familiar scent that was uniquely his. Blindfolded, in a room full of little boys, she would be able to tell Timmy by his smell alone. It was an instinct most mothers possessed, along with a fierce need to protect their children from hurt.

Oh, Nick, she thought. I wanted to believe. I wanted to believe so very much.

It had been too easy to love him again, too easy to believe that he had changed, that he could handle the day after day tedium of a home and family without feeling trapped.

Easy. And foolish. Nothing had changed.

Yes, he cared about her and the children. Yes, he wanted to sleep with her. Maybe he even wanted to try to fit himself into their lives. But sooner or later he would leave. He was too driven, too restless, to be content with her kind of life for long.

If things were different, if she had only herself to think about, she would be willing to live with him in his world for as long as he wanted her. But things weren't different, and she couldn't bear to put the children through the same kind of pain she'd felt when their relationship fell apart the last time.

Face it, Cory, she thought. You can't let this go on.

"Sweetie, why don't you go help Jen with the popcorn?" she whispered in Timmy's ear. "Momma has a phone call to make."

"Can I have soda?" he asked, his face brightening.

"Yes, tell Jen I said to give you a glass," she said, lifting him from her lap.

"'Kay, Momma," he said as he ran from the room. A second later she heard him call his sister's name.

Cory reached for the photo on the desk and ran her finger over the two faces. Nick's was as dear to her now as Joe's. The only two men she'd ever loved. And she'd lost them both.

After opening the desk drawer, she carefully placed the photo inside, face down, before closing the drawer again. Tears flooded her eyes, and she buried her face in her hands.

So close, she thought, swallowing her sobs so that no one could hear. They'd come so close. But it was too late. Maybe it had always been too late.

On a strangled sigh she dashed the tears from her cheeks, cleared her throat and picked up the phone to punch out Theo's number.

"It's Cory," she said when he answered. "I'm glad I caught you."

"Me too," he said, his voice warming into what sounded like a smile. "I wish you wanted to catch me more often."

Cory managed a laugh. "I'm calling because I, uh, want you to do something for me."

"Anything for you, Cory. But before you tell me what it is, I have some information for you. Buster Arnett—you know, the alleged victim in Joey's case—has disappeared."

"When? How?"

"Who knows? Slovik himself called to tell me. Seems Mr. Arnett is wanted in Kentucky for passing bad checks. Guess he figured it wasn't worth risking extradition just to collect on a lawsuit."

Cory closed her eyes and breathed a quiet prayer of thanks.

"Cory? Are you there?"

"Yes, I'm here. I want to say I'm glad because he left town, but I feel sorry for him, too. Poor homeless man. No matter what he's done, he didn't deserve to be beaten up."

"I agree," Theo said after a pause. "But that's life these days." He cleared his throat. "Now, what may I do for you, my dear?"

As she took a tighter grip on the phone, she realized her heart was racing and her mouth was dry. She cleared her throat. "I want you to find a way to convince the judge to release Joey from Nick's custody."

"Problems?"

Cory ran her tongue over her lower lip. A sweet heaviness still lingered deep in her body from last night's lovemaking.

"It's just not working out, that's all. Nick has to drive an hour and a half each way, sometimes more. He has to go into the city every weekend to catch up on paperwork, and he . . . he looks so tired. It's not fair to him."

"I see."

Cory heard a speculative note in his voice and rushed on. "Joey's doing really well, Theo. He got three B's on his report card, and there hasn't been one single problem since we brought him home. I'm sure if you explained all that to the judge, he would understand. Don't you?"

Instead of answering, Theo asked a question of his own. "What did Donatelli say about this? Or was this his idea?"

"Oh, no, I . . . it was my idea. He's taking his responsibility very seriously, but . . . you know how it is. He's not used to three kids and . . . and all that."

She stared blindly at the wall, tears wetting the receiver. She had to make Nick go now, while she could. Otherwise it would hurt too much, too terribly much.

"If that's what you want, I'll try," Theo said.

Cory clamped her lower lip between her teeth to stop the trembling before she said softly, "It's what I want."

Chapter 13

Theo called on Saturday. Cory was just walking into the kitchen to start dinner when the phone rang.

"I talked to Macias," he said without preamble. "No go. He's standing firm."

Cory leaned against the kitchen counter and watched Timmy chase the neighbor's cat around the fenced yard. "There has to be something you can do."

"Not without more ammunition. Either Nick stays put or Joey goes back to Juvenile Hall."

She cleared her throat against a growing scratchiness. "Did you tell him about Joey's improved grades? His good behavior?"

"Yes, everything you told me I told him. Macias was gratified, but immovable. The man's reputation as a hard-nose is well deserved."

Silence hummed along the line. "Cory, is there something you're not telling me? Another reason why you want Donatelli out? Something I can hang a better argument on?"

Tell the judge I don't want him to break my heart, she almost said before she caught herself.

She bit off a sigh. "I . . . it's difficult to explain, actually. It has to do with Joe's death," she said slowly. "Nick . . . Nick . . ."

She broke off as the sound of the Corvette's engine rumbled through the kitchen. "I can't talk now, Theo. Nick is home."

"Have dinner with me tonight. We can talk then."

Cory watched Timmy streak across the backyard to the gate, a happy grin on his face. "Uncle Nick!" he shouted. "Take me for another ride, okay?"

Turning away, she said hurriedly into the receiver, "I'll meet you at The Fish Place at seven."

"No, I'll pick you up at your house."

Cory heard Nick's key in the lock and stiffened. "This is business, Theo, not a date. I expect you to charge me for your time."

"All right, condition noted. But I'm still going to pick you up. See you at seven."

He hung up before Cory could protest.

Timmy and Nick came in together, Timmy chattering away as usual. "Hi," Nick said when he saw her standing by the phone. He had a garment bag slung over one shoulder and a stack of file folders under one arm. He'd taken to doing some work in the evenings while she prepared activities for the next day at school. Just like an old married couple, she thought with a wave of sadness. But not for long.

"Hi." She told herself her voice was suddenly husky because of the rotten cold she'd been fighting all week, not because he looked so sexy with his face burnished by the wind and his hair tousled over his forehead.

"Momma, guess what?" Timmy said, his eyes swimming with excitement. "Uncle Nick says I can have a kitten of my own, if it's okay with you."

"Whoa, tiger," Nick chided gently. "I said we would talk about it."

"You said you like kittens," Timmy protested.

"I do, but maybe your mom doesn't."

"She will if you tell her to," Timmy said in a confident tone. "Won't you, Momma?"

Nick saw the fire kindle in Cory's eyes and knew he was in trouble. "Say, tiger, do me a favor and take this bag to my room," he said.

"Okay," Timmy said amiably, crushing the long plastic bag against his pudgy middle. It folded in half, the hanger dangling only inches from the floor as the little boy struggled toward the door.

Nick waited until Tim was gone before directing a cautious smile in Cory's direction. "Are you mad at me for promising him a kitten?"

"No, I know you're a softie when it comes to Timmy," she said, feeling the counter press into her spine. Her skin felt hot, but she couldn't seem to stop shivering.

"You look tired, *cara*. Hard day?"

"I think I'm catching a cold. It's an occupational hazard in my line of work. All those little ones with runny noses."

Nick dropped the folders onto the table and walked toward her, wanting her with a hunger that threatened to push everything else aside. Without makeup she looked surprisingly young and fragile. Their late nights together had put faint shadows under her eyes, and his kisses had swollen her mouth into a sultry fullness.

"You work too hard. I never knew kids took so much time and energy. It's like you have two full-time jobs."

Although his words sounded more rueful than complaining, Cory felt the sadness inside her deepen. "They're worth it. I wish you believed that."

"Who says I don't? I like kids, as long as they're someone else's responsibility." He fingered a strand of soft, shimmering hair that had escaped from her chignon. It felt like cool silk.

"You're more restless now than when you first came to stay," she said, looking up at him. "I know it's been hard on you, driving all this way, giving up your time at the beach and . . . and other things. But it's almost over."

His hand, in the process of smoothing back her hair, stilled, and a wary look came into his eyes. "Are you thinking about throwing me out? Is that why you keep looking at me like you're trying to figure out something important?" His voice was silky, almost teasing, but the tension around his mouth warned her that he was deadly serious.

"Our lives are so different. Mine is here, with the kids and my school. Yours in the city, where you can always find someone to talk to in the middle of the night when you can't sleep."

His fingers began a sensuous massage of her neck, sending flutters of pleasure down her spine. "I slept last night—until I had to leave you."

"But that's just it. You'll always have to leave. That's the way it is with . . . with illicit lovers."

Humor flashed in his eyes. "You've got your centuries mixed, *cara*. What we do together isn't illicit. It's special, and all the way right for both of us."

"If it's so right, why do you leave in the middle of the night to go back to your own bed?"

"You know why. It isn't just the two of us in this house."

"Exactly," she said with as much sadness as firmness.

"But that doesn't mean we can't work it out." He began pulling the pins from her hair until the heavy chignon fell against her neck.

"Nick, don't."

"I love your hair. It's always so soft and shiny. And it smells so good. What do you do to keep it that way?"

"I have good genes," she said, unable to keep from leaning into his hand.

"Mmm, I'll say. Sexy ones, too." His hand stroked through the thickness, his fingers brushing the sensitive spot between her neck and shoulder. But his gaze was on her mouth. Instinctively, Cory wet her lips. The betraying gesture sent Nick's blood pressure soaring.

"All day I've been waiting for this moment, when I could kiss you again." A tremor went through him, and his expression was suddenly serious. "I can't stop thinking about you, and that scares the hell out of me. But I can't seem to walk away."

"But you will, someday," she said. "You know it, and I know it, and when that happens, it'll be the children who'll be hurt."

"Are you asking me to stay?"

She took a deep breath and tried to ignore the heated look in his eyes. "Would you, if I asked?"

Nick hadn't expected the question, but he should have. Tension rode his shoulders, reminding him that he had some hard choices to make. And soon. First, however, they had to get past the problem with Joey.

"You know better than to ask a cop a hypothetical question," he said with a slow, sexy smile. "We deal in the facts, ma'am. Just the facts. And here's one for you. Tonight I'm taking you to a special place I found overlooking the ocean. We'll have dinner, and then afterward, we can be alone at my apartment."

"Oh, Nick—"

"Shh," he ordered in a rough purr before capturing her mouth. "I've spent every lunch hour for a week cleaning the place, and I've even changed the sheets for my sweet, fastidious Cory."

Even as her mind screamed a warning, her hands were circling his neck and her mouth was clinging to his. His lower body molded against hers, trapping her against the counter.

He moved against her, tantalizing her body with his. She felt his arousal, restrained only by his jeans. His eyes were closed, his breathing rapid.

The hunger in Nick was a living thing, pushing him, taunting him. He'd had his share of women in the past twenty years, but far fewer than Cory imagined. None had satisfied more than his immediate physical needs; none had come close to bringing him to his knees emotionally, the way Cory could do with just a kiss.

He'd never wanted a woman the way he wanted her, with a hot ache that tormented him until he would sell his soul to lose himself in her pliant, moist body. Until he could think of nothing but her smile and her warmth and her laughter. Until all he wanted was Cory.

With a harsh groan he raised his mouth from hers and opened his eyes. Hers were still closed, her feathery lashes making dainty crescents on her cheeks, and her face was soft with passion.

When Nick's grip loosened, Cory swayed and would have fallen if he hadn't tightened his arms around her.

"I've taken care of everything," he said when she opened her eyes and looked up at him. "Jenny's agreed to baby-sit Tim, the reservations have been made, the champagne's chilling." A wickedly sexy grin slanted crookedly into his hard cheeks. "I've even brought my best suit to wear so I won't embarrass my elegant lady."

"I can't," she whispered, her voice thick.

His thumb slowly wiped the sheen of moisture from her lower lip. "No excuses," he said with the intense look of a man who was barely restraining himself. "You need a night out without kids, and God knows, so do I. But if you're worried, I promise I'll have you home before the sun comes up."

Cory felt the dizzying passion slowly drain away. "No, you don't understand," she began, but her voice broke.

"Tell me," he said, the corners of his mouth soft and indulgent. "I promise I'll understand."

Cory's fingers loosened, and her hands slid from his neck to his shoulders and then fell to her sides. "I'm having dinner with Theo tonight."

Anger came swiftly, surging through him like an electric shock. His fingers started to clench against her before he controlled his fury.

"Cancel," he ordered, his voice changing from warm to cool, his eyes turning darker than she'd ever seen them.

"It's business. About Joey."

She hated it when his face went so still. It meant he was pulling in tight, withdrawing from her.

"Who suggested dinner. You?"

"No, he did. And it really is business."

The back of Nick's neck began to seize up. He believed her, and yet, something wasn't right. But he couldn't give his misgivings a name, and that made him uneasy. If a feeling had no name, he couldn't control it. "Do you want me to come along?"

Cory experienced a moment of raw panic. "I . . . no. I'd rather you took the kids out, just the four of you. It'll be a real treat for them."

"If that's what you want."

That was the second time a man had asked her that question in recent days. She nearly laughed, but her laughter would have been without humor. "Please," she said, looking up at him with her feelings for him shining in her eyes.

Nick felt something tearing inside him, exposing emotions that had been buried for a long time. Along with the hunger came a different need. Softer, and yet, in a way, more punishing.

"Don't look at me like that, or, God help me, neither of us will get any dinner tonight."

This time when he kissed her, Cory wanted to cry, so tenderly did his mouth take hers.

By the time Theo returned her to the house a little before eleven, Cory was beginning to feel very strange. Her eyes burned, and her throat was raw. Not even three cups of hot tea spiked with lemon had relieved the painful scratchiness.

"Looks like someone is still up," Theo said as he made a U-turn across the wide tree-lined street in order to park in front of the brick walk.

Light from the parlor's bay window spilled through the faint mist onto the grass, giving the yard an aura of ghostly loneliness. A halo surrounded the porch light, adding to the eerie feeling.

"Jen's very careful to leave the lights on when I'm gone."

Her gaze rose to the window above the living room. Nick's bedroom was dark. Slowly she released the air in her lungs and tried to relax.

Theo killed the engine and turned off the lights before pulling the keys from the ignition.

"Good night, Theo, and thank you," Cory told him with a quick smile.

"I was hoping you were planning to ask me in for coffee," he said, his tone coaxing.

"Of course," she returned politely before she thought. Coffee meant another hour of conversation, at least, and her head was already swimming. She was definitely coming down with something.

She waited for Theo to open the car door for her, then took the arm he crooked toward her. "Do you have your key?" he asked when they reached the porch.

"Oh, sure," she said, fumbling in her purse for her key ring. Light glinted off Theo's glasses and burnished his fair hair to gold. He looked handsome and suave in a well-fitting suit, and his hair looked freshly styled. Had he gone to all that trouble for her? she wondered, and then suffered a pang of guilt when she decided that he had.

He'd been kind and considerate and more tactful than she deserved. She'd given him most of the details of Joe's death, carefully excluding the part that Nick had played, and he had agreed that having Nick around was a painful reminder to her children of the father they had lost. He had also agreed to take that argument to the judge.

The foyer was quiet, but as she closed the door behind Theo, she heard the crackle of flames coming from the parlor. Someone must have lighted the fire she'd laid in the grate.

Pausing at the wide double doors, she felt her body contract in shock. Nick was stretched out on his back in front of the flickering fire, his dark head resting on a throw pillow from the sofa. One brawny arm was flung over his face, the other was curved protectively around the little boy curled up next to him, his blond head pillowed on Nick's shoulder.

Timmy was dressed in pajamas, his hair brushed, his cheeks shiny clean. Nick looked rumpled and boyishly sexy in worn corduroys and an old Police Academy T-shirt. Both were asleep.

"Looks like Tim wore him out," Theo whispered at her side.

"Or vice versa," she whispered back, her throat clogged with tears she didn't dare shed.

Storybooks littered the floor. An elaborate structure of building blocks had somehow grown out of the coffee table. From the looks of it, the intricate edifice had been designed as a garage for some of Timmy's favorite trucks.

Was she making a terrible mistake? she thought. Would Nick really be content to spend his nights entertaining a four-year-old?

Yes, for a while, came the answer. But his first choice had been a night on the town with her—without the children. Just as he'd wanted to take her to the beach, just the two of them. That would always be his first choice, but it couldn't be hers.

"I'll make coffee," she said, leading the way toward the kitchen. She flipped on the light and started to remove her coat. Theo hurried to help her.

"Just put it anywhere," she murmured, brushing a stray lock of hair away from her hot cheeks.

Theo folded the coat with careful precision before laying it over the back of a chair. "Sit down," he said, pulling out another of the chairs. "I'll make the coffee. Just tell me where to find the grounds."

"In the cupboard to your left," Cory said, sinking into the chair with a grateful sigh.

Five minutes later they were sipping freshly brewed coffee, talking quietly. After one sip Cory realized that the coffee was a mistake, but she made herself take a few more, just to be polite.

"Too strong?" Theo asked, watching her. He was slightly myopic, and the lens of his glasses made his blue eyes appear smaller.

"No, just hot." She managed another tiny sip without grimacing at the galling taste.

He visibly relaxed, drawing another pang of guilt from her. "It's a help, knowing you understand," she said, touching his sleeve. "It means a lot to me to know I have you to depend on."

He covered her hand with his and squeezed gently. Hoping she wasn't being too obvious, Cory pulled her hand from beneath his and wrapped it around her mug.

"Don't worry if you don't hear from me right away," he said, seemingly unperturbed. "I have to figure out the best way to approach Macias. If I go in again without sufficient cause, he'll have my head."

"I...hope I'm doing the right thing," she said, her voice so low he had to lean forward to hear her. "It's just that, well, I don't want Nick to be hurt."

Theo's eyes narrowed behind the gleaming lenses. "It might come down to that, Cory. A choice between hurting Nick or hurting your children, I mean."

Cory blinked in the bright light that seemed to be growing more painful by the second. "What exactly are you saying?"

"Just this," Theo said with quiet force. "We already know Macias will reject all but the most compelling reason for granting your petition. I'll need facts to convince him Nick's continued presence may be injurious to Joey."

"But surely the fact that Nick was...that Joe died because Nick was hung over..." Cory stopped abruptly, startled by the suddenly alert look on Theo's face. Had she told him that before? She couldn't seem to remember.

"Don't look so stricken, Cory. I figured there was more than you've told me."

Cory was feeling more and more shaky. "Theo, listen—"

"No, it's okay. Just give me your bottom line. Which is more important to you, protecting Nick's feelings or preventing further hurt to Joey?"

She tried to make sense of Theo's words. Concentrate, she ordered silently. Was he asking her to choose between Nick and Joey?

"My children have to come first," she whispered. She was responsible for bringing them into this world. She had a duty to protect them.

Theo leaned forward until his shadow fell over hers. "Cory, are you absolutely certain you want me to make this happen for you?"

Was she? Could she live with herself if she was making a terrible mistake?

Momma, is Uncle Nick going to be my new daddy?

I like kids, as long as they're someone else's responsibility.

"Yes," she whispered. "Make it happen, please."

Her gaze slid from his. Her eyelids were heavy, her head buzzing. She could trust Theo, couldn't she?

"So be it." Theo said, biting off his words. "You have my word I'll do everything in my power to get you what you want."

Cory drew a long breath. "I meant what I said, Theo. I want you to bill me for tonight, and for the conversations we've had on the phone."

"Naturally," he said with a teasing grin that took some of the stiffness from his handsome features. "One of these days."

"No, I mean it. I don't want any favors. That's not my way."

His grin faded. "I know that, Cory. If it makes you happy, I'll send you a whopper of a bill. But I'm also serving fair notice that when Joey's trial is over, I intend to come courting."

Cory felt a vague depression settle inside her. "Theo—"

"No, don't say anything. Just walk me to the door, okay?" Before she could say more, he rose from his chair and extended his hand. Smiling her gratitude, she laid her hand in his.

When they reached the foyer, she found that Nick and Timmy were still asleep. Only the crackling of the flames broke the silence as she unlatched the door and clicked it open.

"Good night," she murmured, raising her gaze to Theo's. "The dinner was wonderful."

"You hardly touched yours," he chided in a low voice.

"I didn't think you noticed."

"I notice everything about you, Cory Kingston," he said, pulling her into his arms. His kiss was pleasant, his lips firm and warm, but Cory felt nothing more than affection for the man kissing her.

"I'll call you," he said, brushing his fingertips across her cheek.

"Thank you," she said, not really knowing whether she was thanking him for his professional help or for his understanding. Probably both, she decided as she closed the door and locked it.

She watched through the window by the door until he drove away. Then, with an exhausted sigh, she turned toward the parlor, intending to carry Timmy up to his bed.

"Man kisses like a wimp," Nick said, his eyes open and focused intently on her face.

Cory jumped, her heart speeding. "How long have you been awake?" she demanded, her voice coming out strangely weak.

"Who says I've been asleep?"

He tucked his free arm under his head and drew up one knee. Firelight shadowed his face, transforming the arrogant angles into a beguiling sensuality.

Cory's head began to throb. "Timmy should have been in bed hours ago."

"He was enjoying the fire." His voice seemed as hypnotically soft as the hiss of the flames, and his face began to go in and out of focus.

"Will you carry him up, or shall I?" she asked in a tired voice.

"I will. You look beat." He stood, then carefully hoisted Timmy to his shoulder. Timmy mumbled in his sleep, his brow knotting in a frown.

"It's okay, tiger. I've got you," Nick said, and the little boy immediately put his arms around Nick's neck and snuggled closer.

A feeling like a smothered sob went through her. Timmy would be devastated when Nick was gone—and so would she.

Damn him, she thought, turning away. Why couldn't he want the same things she wanted? Because he needs excitement to feel alive, she told herself as she walked back to the kitchen, intending to tidy up the coffee things, but a wave of weakness overtook her at the door.

"Tomorrow," she muttered, snapping off the light.

The parlor was shrouded in darkness when she passed. Firelight cast a circle into the blackness, filling her with a longing she was too numb to fight. With each step she climbed, she began to feel more woozy.

You are not going to get sick, she told herself over and over. The kids need you. The school needs you. Mothers don't get sick.

Nick was closing Timmy's door behind him when she reached the landing and paused for breath. "Is Joey asleep?" she asked, her words coming out oddly slurred.

He nodded, then gave her a piercing look. "Cory? Are you all right?"

"Yes, fine. I'm fine."

Moving closer, Nick saw the pallor in her face and the glazed look in her eyes. "I don't think so," he said, putting a hand to her forehead. She flinched, and he muttered a low oath. "You're burning up."

Cory looked at the strong shoulder in front of her and had an overpowering urge to lean her cheek against that strength for just a moment. Just long enough to regroup, but not long enough to get used to the feel of Nick's arms closing around her.

"I'm fighting a cold," she said, trying to move past him.

"Like hell! You're about out on your feet."

"Don't—" she warned, but it was too late. Nick had already swept her into his arms and was striding toward her bedroom. With a sigh Cory buried her face in the curve of his neck. He smelled woodsy, like the fire, and felt so dear.

Her eyes were closed, but she had a sense of security and warmth as he leaned down and, with one hand, pulled back the covers before laying her on the cool sheets.

After turning on the light, he sat next to her and began unbuttoning her blouse. "I can manage," she croaked, grabbing his hands in hers. "Really."

"For a smart woman, you can be incredibly stupid," he said, his jaw tight, his eyes as black as pitch.

"Thanks a lot," she mumbled.

"Don't push me, *cara*. I don't know who I want to punch, that idiot Kennedy or you." He pushed her hands aside and began working the tiny buttons, swearing under his breath as his blunt fingers had trouble with the slippery silk.

Her thigh rested against the rigid line of his broad back. His forearm rested on her belly. He looked fiercely angry and determined.

"It's not Theo's fault," she said, her throat pinching with pain at each word she forced past the tender membranes.

"The hell it isn't. Doesn't the man have eyes? Couldn't he see you were sick?" He finished with the second button and started with the third. His knuckles brushed against the soft fullness of her breasts, and she winced. He froze, his gaze flickering up to her face.

"Are your breasts sore?" he asked.

"A little." She wasn't about to tell him the nipples were still swollen from the hot, eager kisses he'd impressed on them in this bed last night.

His jaw tightened. "Sorry."

An ominous frown of concentration knitted his brow as he tried to work the button without touching her. Cory felt an urgent need to cry. Closing her eyes, she tried to ignore the whirling pinwheels in her head. She began to float. Whatever happened, she was safe. The man she loved was with her. For now.

"C-cold," Cory murmured, curling into a ball against the warmth at her back. Her skin was damp, and her eyelids felt so heavy she had trouble lifting them.

"Shh," came the rumble of a deep voice.

Cory tried to swallow. Her throat was raw and felt swollen. "Nick?" she managed to whisper hoarsely.

"Here, baby. Go back to sleep."

A corded arm tightened around her, supporting her until she was able to raise her head. Gradually, as her burning eyes focused, she saw a strong bronzed throat and a stubbled chin.

Nick was stretched out on her bed, his back to the headboard, his arms cradling her against him. One of her legs rested between his. The other was stretched along his body. One hand lay on his thigh. Sweat poured from her, wetting the T-shirt and corduroys he was wearing.

Her cheek rubbed his chest as she tried to lift her head far enough to see his face. "How do you feel?" he asked, his voice sounding like the rasp of silk on steel.

"C-cold," she repeated, trying to burrow into his warm chest. His shirt smelled like him, bringing the hot sting of tears to her eyes.

"Here, drink this," he ordered, holding a glass to her lips. The water was cool, but it hurt to swallow.

"Can you manage some aspirin now?" he asked, removing the glass.

Cory nodded, the dimly lit room wavering in and out of focus. She lifted her hand from his thigh and held it out, noticing with great detachment that it was shaking very badly. Somehow, though, she managed to get the three aspirin into her mouth.

"Drink," he said, holding the glass for her again. Cory managed a few swallows before it hurt too much for more.

She drifted, feeling the cool pressure of a damp cloth against her forehead. "Nice," she said, or maybe she only thought she did. The effort to decide exhausted her.

"Rest, *carisima*," Nick's deep voice crooned.

Carisima. My dearest one. If only that were true, she thought, sinking into the waiting darkness.

"Good morning."

Cory blinked her eyes in disbelief. "Dr. Ibarra?" she managed to croak out. The sheet had been pulled to her chin, but underneath she was naked.

"None other," said the rotund, kindly-faced man standing by the bed.

Before she could say another word, he popped a thermometer into her mouth and reached for her wrist. Sunlight streamed through the window, but the clock showed that it was only a little past seven.

Nick stood at the foot of the bed, his arms crossed, his expression controlled, his brows drawn. Black stubble darkened his jaw, giving him a ruggedly masculine panache, but his face was lined with weariness, and his eyes were shadowed.

Their eyes met and held. "How are you feeling?" he asked, his voice oddly hoarse. He had pulled on jeans and changed his shirt, but the feel of that hard body cradling hers all through the long restless hours remained imprinted on her skin.

"Great," she lied as soon as Ibarra pulled the thermometer from her mouth. "I'm sure I can get up," she added, trying not to show how much pain each word was costing her.

"We'll see about that," the doctor murmured as he unwrapped a sterile tongue depressor. "Open wide."

An hour later Cory made her way back to the bed, leaning heavily on Jenny's arm. Outside, she heard the muffled sound of church bells.

"I feel so silly," she muttered as her daughter helped her climb back between the sheets. A shower had cooled her hot skin and washed off the salty sweat. The aspirin Nick had forced down her every four hours had helped her headache, but her throat was still agonizingly sore.

"How's that?" Jenny asked anxiously, plumping her mother's pillow.

Cory smiled her thanks. "Tonsillitis at my age," she said with a disgusted squeak.

"At least Dr. Ibarra doesn't plan to put you in the hospital and rip out your tonsils."

Cory grimaced. "I didn't know doctors even made house calls anymore."

A wide grin split Jenny's plump face. "They do when Uncle Nick calls."

Cory drew a long breath. "Was he, uh, rude?"

Jenny poked the bridge of her glasses, sliding them more securely on her nose. "More like insistent. He was really worried about you."

Cory nodded, a small, sad feeling settling in the pit of her stomach. She turned her head, needing a moment of privacy. She saw a small bouquet of orange and white mums on the nightstand and knew that Nick had put them there for her.

"Jen, where's the phone? I need to call Mai."

"Uncle Nick took the phone out so you wouldn't be bothered. But he said to tell you that he's already called Mai, and she's arranged for Mrs. Bradshaw to sub for you next week."

Cory groaned. Irma Bradshaw was a retired kindergarten teacher and a dear. But the kids ran roughshod over her every time she substituted. "I hate to think what the kids will be like when I get back," she muttered.

"Uncle Nick's taking the week off, too. Said they owed him time."

Cory nodded. "Where is everyone?" It hurt to talk, but the thought of remaining mute was worse.

"Joey's watching videos. Uncle Nick took Timmy to Sunday school. I'm in charge of taking care of you till he gets back."

Cory's fingers tightened on the embroidered edge of the sheet. "Sunday school?"

"Don't you remember?" Jen said, pouring water from an insulated pitcher into Cory's glass. "This is your Sunday to teach Timmy's class."

Cory closed her eyes on a wince. "I forgot."

"Uncle Nick said he would take your place. He said it would be a new experience for the kids to have Presbyterian lessons taught by a Catholic who was the worst altar boy in history."

Cory's laughter came out on a wince, and she closed her eyes, trying to picture Nick coping with twenty preschoolers by himself. He would probably yell a lot, the way he sometimes did with Timmy when his limited patience was used up, but he would also be affectionate and kind and dear. The kids would love him.

"Mom?"

Cory slowly opened her eyes to find Jenny watching her with a hopeful look on her face. "Hmm?"

"Wouldn't it be great if Uncle Nick could live here all the time?"

Stalling for time, Cory swallowed half the water in the glass. "Uncle Nick wouldn't be happy here," she said after she had safely returned the glass to the nightstand.

"Sure he would. He loves us."

You, but not me. "That's not enough, Jen." She swallowed against the pain. Her head was beginning to ache again, and her body felt hot and heavy. "Uncle Nick needs to be free. He would hate coming home to the same place every night, doing the same things over and over. It's not that he doesn't care, but he's like . . . like a wild animal that needs to be free in order to be happy."

Jenny frowned, as though she were trying hard to understand. "Are you still mad at him?" she asked after a moment's silence.

Cory shook her head, her fingers clenching and unclenching around the sheet. "No, sweetie, I'm not."

"One night I was sad and missing Daddy a lot, and Uncle Nick said Daddy used to talk about me all the time. About how smart I was and how p-pretty. He said Daddy was very lucky to have a daughter like me." Jenny sat down on the bed, tears in her eyes.

"He was," Cory choked out. "Very."

Jenny snuggled into her mother's arms, her arms tightly wound around Cory's back.

"Momma, if I can't have my own daddy back, I want Uncle Nick."

The pain started somewhere close to her heart and spread outward with sharp claws until Cory hurt all over. "I know, baby," she whispered. Silently she added, So do I.

The shakes came near dawn. Nick jerked from a doze, his arms tightening around Cory's huddled body even before he realized that she was shivering violently again.

The light he'd left burning hurt his eyes, and he winced. A quick glance at the clock told him it was more than an hour before her next dose of antibiotics was due.

The doctor had warned him that her fever would probably spike higher at night. "Keep her cool," Ibarra had ordered. "Any way you can."

Flinching at the stiffness in his neck and shoulders, Nick eased her shuddering body to one side and slid from the bed. Cory's eyelashes fluttered like small wings against her too-pale skin, and a low moan came from her dry lips.

Nick's hand shook as he brushed her tousled hair away from her face. He needed to touch her, to reassure himself that the frightening heat searing her skin hadn't returned in full force. Her skin was dangerously warm, but not nearly as hot as it had been twenty-four hours earlier.

Every time he touched her, he experienced the same raw terror he'd felt when he'd first realized how very sick she was. He'd always accepted the sexual feelings he'd had for her and learned to live with them, but he'd never realized how fiercely he would want to take care of her. Or how terrified he would be at the thought of losing her again.

When he withdrew his hand, Cory moaned again and tried to burrow her cheek into the pillow like a restless child caught in a bad dream.

"Easy, Cory," he whispered. "I'll be right back."

The water in the basin by the bed had gotten warm, and he replaced it with cool from the tap in the bathroom that was part of the master suite. Yawning, he returned to the bed, set the water on the table and wrung the washcloth nearly dry.

Her gown was soaked, and Nick cursed silently as he eased it up her body. "Nick?" she murmured, her eyes fluttering open.

"Relax, *cara*. I just need to cool you off."

"C-cool?" she whispered, touching her lower lip with her tongue. "Already c-cold." Her brows drew together drunkenly, and she struggled to focus.

"I know," he said, his voice deeply strained. "Trust me, okay?"

Her hand came up to touch his face. "Don't leave," she murmured before letting her lashes close again. "Please don't leave me again."

Nick felt pain rip his gut. His arms tightened, and he crushed her against him, his face buried in the silky waves covering her shoulder.

"Don't give up on me, *cara*," he whispered. "Just give me some time."

Chapter 14

"See, it's normal, isn't it?" Cory said with a hopeful smile. "Isn't it?" she repeated when Nick took his time reading the thermometer he held up to the light.

It was twilight of the fifth day since she'd all but collapsed in his arms. Her throat had stopped aching, and her head felt clear and focused for the first time since the fever had taken her.

"Close enough," he said, sliding the thermometer into its case before putting it down next to the almost empty pill bottle on the nightstand.

"That means I can get up," Cory said, grinning up at him. Above the pink blanket, the ivory lace covering her breasts shimmered seductively in the lamplight.

Too conscious of the creamy skin above the gown, Nick kept his gaze on her face. When she'd been so sick, his thoughts had been focused on relieving her suffering. Now that she was better, his hunger for her was returning, stronger than ever.

"You've been up," Nick said, sitting down beside her to block her exit.

"But only for a few hours before you bullied me back to bed."

"If you hadn't been so stubborn, we would have gotten along a lot better."

One of his thick black eyebrows slowly lifted until Cory found herself smiling. "If you hadn't insisted on having everything your way, you mean."

"If I had things the way I really wanted them, I'd be in that bed with you."

Cory's pulse leaped at the deep vibration of desire in his voice. "If I remember correctly, you were," she said, her own voice shivering with emotion.

"Yeah, and you had a temperature of one hundred and three."

Cory laughed at the look of frustration tightening his jaw. For days he had watched over her, rarely leaving her room for more than a few minutes, and then only when one of the children needed him.

For the first two nights he'd even slept with her, holding her close when she was restless, cooling her skin when the fever went higher. She'd never felt more cherished or more loved, not even with Joe.

She knew now that she'd just been kidding herself when she'd believed she could push him out of her life without feeling as though she'd cut away a part of herself.

"Where are the kids?" she asked, glancing toward the closed door.

"Watching a Disney video."

"Joey, too?"

"Yeah, for once. I threatened him with grievous bodily harm if he didn't cooperate."

"Poor Nick," she said, running her finger along the clean line of his mouth.

"It'll be poor Cory if you don't stop that." His dry tone was irresistible, and she laughed. He captured her hand with his before turning to kiss her wrist. "Laughing at a man in pain, are you?"

"Maybe I'm in the same pain," she said in a rush, her heart tumbling and racing at the same time. If Macias granted her petition, Nick would soon be free to go. This might be the last time they had together.

Her hands twined around his neck, and her tongue touched his lower lip. A visible tremor went through him, and his face tightened until he looked as though he were in agony.

"Don't, *cara,*" he said, his voice as pained as a groan as he pulled her hands from his neck. "You're still weak."

"Lock the door," she urged, her voice husky and filled with a yearning Nick would have sold his soul to hear. His heart raced, and his skin felt hot. He wanted her so much he was burning inside, but her health was more important than his need.

"Be sensible, baby. You've been sick."

She felt his body tense and knew he intended to leave her. Unable to bear the thought, she slipped her arms around his waist and rested her head on his shoulder. Such a complicated man, she thought with a sigh of pleasure. Fun-loving, arrogant, and yet compassionate and kind at the same time.

At nineteen she'd been both frightened and enchanted by his recklessness, but it was the deep compassion she'd sensed in him that had drawn her to him. That and the stark loneliness that always seemed a part of him, even when he was in a crowd.

"Lock the door," she repeated, sliding her lips down the thick muscle on the side of his neck. "Please, Nick."

He fought to control the instant response of his body to the purr of invitation in her voice. He'd gone without women for long periods at other times in his life without raising a sweat. But holding Cory without being able to have her had twisted him into knots.

"Are you sure? We can wait."

"No more waiting," she said, thinking about the petition Theo was filing.

"I'll be careful," he said, hugging her with a restraint that cost him dearly.

"No, I don't want you to be careful." She ran her knuckles along the raspy edge of his strong jaw. "I've been careful too many times in my life."

Nick saw the drowsy look of anticipation in her sea-green eyes, and his stomach gave a slow rolling lurch. He wanted to make it good for her, but more than that, he wanted to be a part of her again. He needed that more than he'd ever needed anything, he realized as he left the bed and crossed to the door.

Unbuttoning his shirt with one hand, he locked the door with the other. "Last chance," he said, his gaze devouring her as he returned to the bed.

"For you, too."

In the fading light, his body seemed larger, more powerful, a lean composite of steely sinew and rangy muscle. In other times he would have been the man picked by the tribe to fight the hardest battles, to lead the most arduous hunts, to take the greatest risks. In other times he would have died young, with a fierce cry of rage on his lips, and she would have been left to mourn, just as she would be left to mourn now when he was gone again.

Cory threw off the blanket and moved over to give him room. Nick felt a tug of emotion at the obvious gesture of welcome. Was that the way it was with married couples, small moments of intimacy mingled with the highs of passion and the lows of tedium? He didn't know. He'd never lived that kind of life with a woman, not even Cory.

"You've lost weight," Cory said, watching him shed his boots. "You're doing too much."

"I like it when you fuss over me," he said with a grin, his fingers working the buttons of his jeans. "It's a new experience."

Yes, she thought, smoothing her palm over the cool sheet. Nick had the look of a man who'd never been pampered, never been indulged. His parents must have been cold, perhaps even neglectful, people.

Impatience tightened his face and hastened his movements as he stripped off his shirt and shucked his jeans. His torso was scarred where the torn flesh had been stitched together to heal into a long puckered line. His stomach was corded, flat, bisected by a provocative arrow of jet black hair that disappeared into the elastic band of his dark red briefs. Below the band the cotton was stretched taut and straining.

"Oh my," she whispered softly, and then turned pink when his gaze shot to hers.

"See what you do to me, *cara?*" His breathing was hoarse, his eyes glittering, as he bent to remove his briefs. Cory held her breath, her gaze devouring the powerful lines of his naked body.

A warm, melting tension gripped her own body, making it difficult for her to control her breathing. She tried to smile, but her lips trembled, ready to be claimed by his.

The mattress dipped under his weight, and a shiver of anticipation ran through her. "Did I ever tell you how beautiful you've become?" Nick said, sliding his hand along her cheek. She leaned into his palm, loving the rough texture of his skin.

"No," she whispered. "You didn't."

His thick black lashes lowered as his gaze rested on her mouth. "Beautiful and sweet and crazy." His voice was deep and not quite steady.

"I'm not crazy," she managed to protest with a smile, and he traced the curve of her lips with his thumb.

"Crazy and adorable." His mouth hovered over hers, his coffee-scented breath warming her skin. Her eyes drifted closed, and she held her breath. "Your mouth is so sexy I have trouble concentrating on anything else."

His mouth touched hers, then retreated. Cory felt the impact shudder through her. "And I love your smile," she whispered, before leaning forward to touch the corner of his mouth with her tongue.

His hand hooked around her neck, holding her as he kissed her again and again, each kiss probing deeper until his tongue began tasting the hot sweet moistness behind her lips. Cory reached for him, trying to pull him closer.

"Not yet," he murmured, his voice raspy. Cory felt the tension running through him as his hand palmed her breast for a long moment before his fingers began stroking her through the iridescent satin.

Sliding her hands over his chest, she felt the small shudders beneath the skin wherever she touched. Her fingers shook as they burrowed through the crisp black hair to find the tiny nub of his nipple.

As soon as she touched him, the small bud whitened, and the muscle beneath involuntarily hardened into a rigid slab against her stroking fingertips. Slowly she bent to kiss the rounded hardness of his shoulder, her senses filling with the musky scent of his skin.

Expecting him to take control, she was amazed to feel his restraint, his patient acceptance of her lead. The contrast between his openly naked body and her modest covering was deliciously erotic, sending wild pulses of desire stabbing deep. Drunk with the power he was giving her over him, she bent further to touch her tongue to his hard nipple.

His control nearly at its limit, Nick shuddered, his muscles clenching with the effort to remain passive. But the pressure in his loins tipped over into a driving need for relief.

Struggling for control, he grasped Cory's arms and eased her back against the pillow scented with the perfume of her hair. Her mouth parted, and her breath began coming in urgent little gasps.

Her fingers tangled in his hair, urging him closer, but he refused to be rushed. Instead, heart crashing wildly in his chest, he began easing the silky gown up her thighs, anointing each slow inch with kisses.

His fingers encountered skin as smooth and warm as sunwashed honey. Discovering the faint silvery lines angling along the rounded curve of her belly, he bent his head to reverently trace each one with his lips.

Tension rippled under his mouth, and he raised his head to find a drowsy look of uncertainty clouding her passion-dark eyes. "*Bellisima.* Beautiful," he whispered, kissing her again.

His head moved up until he found her breasts. Taking his time, he kissed each erect peak through the satin, his mouth moistening the material until the nipples were wet and distinctly outlined.

Cory writhed, sensations building inside her. The fever of sickness had left her, but the fever of need was far more powerful, elevating the temperature of her skin to a delicious, almost unbearable heat.

He touched, tasted, his hands gentle yet arousing, his fingers finding all the places he had been the first to sensitize.

Cool air ran over her body and shivered her damp nipples as he removed her gown. Her hair cascaded over her shoulders, and he buried his face in its thickness.

Cory felt the long, hard length of his arousal press her thigh, and she twisted toward him, trying to absorb his throbbing flesh.

At the first contact of hot shaft to moist sheath his body shuddered, and he groaned out her name. He shifted until he was poised over her.

Needing to feel him closer, Cory writhed, her hands running up and down the muscle-thickened arms bracketing her body. Slowly he lowered his upper body until his mouth found one breast. His tongue swirled around the nipple until the soft tissues beneath swelled into a hot ache.

Cory moaned and thrust upward. His teeth gently nipped before he released her and turned his attention to the other breast.

Nick raised his head, savoring the look of passion softening the fragile contours of her face into a loveliness so exquisite he had trouble breathing.

The urgent little moans, the desperate pressure of her fingertips, the involuntary fluttering of those feathered lashes, all for him. Because of him.

Feelings for this woman he'd refused to accept pressed against his control. His physical needs, so powerful he felt as though he were about to explode, were swamped by an emotional yearning so violent he was shaking with it.

"God, Cory," he cried out, his voice hoarse. "I can't...I need..."

"Yes," she whispered on a moan. "Please. Now."

Nick's breath escaped in a ragged groan, as though he had been waiting to hear that one plea. Bracing himself, he slowly began to ease into her, his body swelling, throbbing, craving hot sweet release deep within her.

Cory shuddered as his flesh slid deeper into hers. Needing to see him, she opened her eyes to find herself looking into eyes so dark with longing she nearly flinched. His face was tortured as he held himself back, putting her pleasure above his. His arms were corded with restraint, his skin beaded with sweat.

She whispered his name, words of love so deeply felt they were nearly incoherent. Nick felt his control slip as the need built in him, clawing deeper and deeper into his groin.

Unable to wait, he began to move, his movements merging with hers until neither knew who was giving and who was receiving the most pleasure.

Cory writhed, the heat building, building. Her hands clutched the pillow, and she rolled her upper body from side to side, mindless now with the ecstasy he was arousing in her. His name was forced from her lips, a broken whisper of sound.

His body taxed to the point of excruciating pain, he held off until he felt the small shudders of her climax pulse against him. Control gone, he poured himself into her, crying out as hot indescribable pleasure surged through him.

They lay tightly bound together, kissing and stroking as small aftershocks took them both. With Nick's head pillowed on her shoulder and his sweat drying on her skin, Cory reveled in the sense of completeness spreading through her.

Gradually, as his heartbeat began to slow, Nick became aware of a deep peace stealing through him, gentling the restless need to be on the move that had been with him for as long as he could remember.

Somehow, with Cory nestled in his arms, the freedom he'd fought so hard to preserve didn't seem quite as vital. With her legs entwined with his, he had no urge ever to leave this bed. This woman. This family.

Maybe, just maybe, they might make it this time. If he could find a way to make these feelings last. If he could allow himself to trust her enough to let the love he wanted to feel for her take root in his cynical soul.

Opening his eyes, he saw the angelic smile of satisfaction on her lips and felt something hard and hurting give way inside him. Throat too tight for words to escape, he contented himself instead with a long tender kiss.

Cory smiled and cuddled more closely against him. They lay quietly, their hands lightly touching, until the muted bonging of the clock downstairs drew a reluctant sigh from him.

"Time to go," he murmured, kissing her shoulder. "The movie will be over soon, and I promised Timmy a story."

"Isn't tomorrow Friday?" she asked in a drowsy voice, her finger tracing lazy circles in the hair on his chest.

"Yes," he managed to answer.

"And Mrs. Bradshaw is subbing for me tomorrow?"

"Yes."

"Good," she said with a long contented sigh. "Then you and I can be alone all morning."

Nick gave a groan of pure male frustration and sat up. "Don't tempt me," he said in a raw tone.

"You don't want me?" Cory asked with a playful pout, running the flat of her palm up and down his arm.

"I think that's damn obvious," he said with a growl deepening his voice.

"Then what's stopping you?"

"Not me. Both of us. When I got home from taking the kids to the video store, there was a message from Theo on the machine. Judge Macias wants to see us at ten o'clock tomorrow."

Theo arrived at the courthouse only a few minutes after Cory and Nick. "Good morning. Rotten day, isn't it?"

"We need the rain," Cory said, her voice edged with tension.

"True enough," Theo said, shaking the raindrops from his coat before glancing at his watch. "We still have fifteen minutes. How about coffee? Unfortunately it's from a machine in the basement, but it's hot."

Cory nodded. "It might help," she said, turning to Nick. "Would you mind?"

His eyes narrowed as they shifted from her face to Theo's. Cory realized she was holding her breath and let it out slowly. "Please?" she added, laying a hand on Nick's arm.

One corner of his mouth softened while the other remained hard and forbidding. "*Cara,* if you want to be alone with Kennedy here, just say so."

"It's not that, exactly." The guilt that had been festering all night had her nerves pinched tight, and lack of sleep was making her light-headed.

"Lawyer-client privilege," Theo said with a taut smile. "You understand, don't you, Donatelli?"

"More than you think, Kennedy."

Cory gritted her teeth. "Forget it. I'll get the coffee myself," she muttered, turning away. But Nick stopped her, his eyes clouded with an expression she didn't recognize.

"Stay here and have your talk. I'll be right back."

He walked away, his stride long and controlled, his back straight. He was wearing the suit he'd brought for their night on the town, a dark gray wool that snugged his shoulders perfectly and emphasized the magnificent breadth of his chest.

Cory's gaze followed him hungrily, her heart thudding a slow funeral beat in her chest.

"Come, sit down," Theo urged, his hand cupping her elbow. He chose the same bench where they'd sat before. This time, however, they were to meet the judge in his chambers, instead of the courtroom.

As soon as the elevator doors closed, she turned to Theo and said in a rush, "I've changed my mind, Theo. I don't want to do this."

He studied her expression in silence for a long moment. "I can see that," he said with precision clipping his words. "What I can't understand is why."

"I've decided to fight for what I want."

"What is it you want?"

"I don't have time to explain. I . . . please, just talk to the judge. Blame me. Say I'm neurotic. Maybe I am, who knows?"

"Are you sure about this? Really sure?"

Cory hesitated. All night long she'd been battling the part of herself that still had doubts. Nick had been forced into a different life-style by a court order. Once that restriction was lifted, would he be content to come home every night? Would he be happy making love to just one woman? She still didn't know, but she loved him enough to risk the pain if she was wrong.

"Can we ever be sure of anything, Theo?" she asked, her voice low.

Theo rubbed his hands on his bent knees, then slowly got to his feet. "If you'll excuse me, I'll go see Judge Macias. I hope I come back with everything intact." A smile hovered around his mouth. "Only for you, Cory," he said, a deep note of regret in his voice. "Only for you."

He picked up his briefcase and headed down an intersecting corridor leading to Macias's chambers.

Seconds ticked past, agonizingly slow, as Cory sat alone, listening to her heart thud. Outside, the storm turned the streets into treacherous, oil-slick obstacle courses. Wind blew the rain against the windowpanes so violently that the drops sounded like hail.

The elevator doors swished open, and Nick walked toward her, a plastic cup of coffee in each hand. "Where's Kennedy?" he asked, handing her one of the cups.

"He went to see the judge." Her voice echoed in the deserted corridor.

"What's going on, Cory?"

"Nick, there's something you should know. Theo...that is, I asked Theo..."

Her voice faltered, and she took a quick sip of the coffee. It was scalding, burning her tongue, and she winced. "Hot," she said with a smile he didn't return. Instead, he took her cup and his and placed them on the floor before sitting down next to her and taking her hand.

"Talk to me, Cory. Haven't I shown you that you can trust me?" His hands sandwiched hers in warm strength. His expression was sober and concerned, his eyes radiating tenderness. "If something's bothering you, I want to help."

Tears filled her eyes, brimming like raindrops on her long lashes. "I do trust you, Nick. I do." Her fingers curled over his.

"Then, what—"

Footsteps echoed off the high ceiling, and Nick broke off, his gaze zeroing in on the direction of the sound. A second later Theo appeared, a drawn look on his face.

"It's out of my hands, Cory," he said, before adding, "The judge is ready for us. All three of us."

Twenty minutes later Cory had all but destroyed the strap of her purse, twisting it between nervous hands. To her right Nick sat in stony silence, his jaw thrust forward, his gaze riveted on the stern man behind the big desk. Theo sat to her left, and he wasn't looking at her, either. A court reporter sat unobtrusively to one side of the desk, recording every word.

Cory couldn't believe what she'd been hearing. Theo, or someone he'd hired, had done his homework, digging up everything in Nick's past that could in any way be used to impugn him.

In a cold monotone the judge had read a long, detailed list of allegations about his lack of responsibility, characterizing him as an immature hell-raiser and a careless cop who was more concerned with preserving his self-indulgent lifestyle than with following the rules.

The attorney had done a thorough job, taking statements from some of Nick's fellow cops, a bartender or two, even a neighbor who had described a party that Nick had thrown one New Year's Eve at his apartment.

A young woman, the date of one of his friends, had nearly drowned when some of the men had thrown her into the pool while she'd been dead drunk. It didn't seem to matter to the judge that Nick had been the one to pull her out and administer CPR while waiting for the paramedics.

"If these things are true, Sergeant," Macias said when he finished reading, "I can understand why Mrs. Kingston has reservations about you as a role model for an impressionable sixteen-year-old."

"So I hear," Nick said in a clipped, hard voice. Sitting so close, Cory saw a muscle tighten along his jaw. She had a feeling he knew she was watching him, but he kept his gaze straight ahead. He hadn't looked at her once since Macias had told him why they were there. But the look he'd given her at that moment was indelibly imprinted on her mind. Deep hurt had flashed in his dark eyes before he'd wiped it away.

"My concern is not just for the law in this matter, Sergeant," Macias continued, leaning forward to emphasize the seriousness of his words. "It's also for the well-being of the juvenile in question, and, I must say, I have some serious doubts."

"Yes, sir."

"Do you dispute the information Mr. Kennedy has included in his petition to reorder custody?"

"No, sir. It's all true."

"I admit that I was disappointed when I received this petition. The officer described here is a disgrace to the badge he wears and a very poor example of a man."

"I agree," Nick said, his voice as cold and reproving as the judge's. Cory bit her lip to keep from crying.

"I thought you might."

Macias took a folder from one of the baskets on his desk and opened it. Inside was a lone page from a yellow tablet, the lines covered with handwriting. "Yesterday, I had another private, on-the-record chat with Lieutenant Frazier about these allegations. He told me about your partner's funeral, and the battle you've had to redeem yourself in the eyes of your fellow officers—which he says you're winning, by the way. He also suggested that I speak with Captain Anthony Donatelli about your personal life."

Nick frowned. "Tony?"

"Yes. The man doesn't mince words. I like that. He corroborated what Frazier said and also told me he hasn't seen you take a drink in years. Nor has he seen you at a party or in any of your usual, er, watering places. Is that true?"

Dusky color began climbing Nick's neck. "Yes, sir."

"When was the last time you had a drink, Sergeant Donatelli?"

Nick's fingers tightened around the leather padding on the arms of his chair. "Five days after my partner's funeral."

"When was the last time you went to a party?"

"The night before Joe died."

Cory began to shake. All she wanted right now was for this to end, so that she and Nick could talk, so that she could explain.

"Your Honor, may I say something?" she asked, her voice unsteady. Beside her, she felt Nick stiffen.

"Of course, Mrs. Kingston."

She had to blink aside the tears before she could see the judge's face clearly. "I didn't intend . . . Sergeant Donatelli has done so much for us, but I could see it was taking its toll. The driving, the extra hours on the weekends that he had to put in, I thought it was unfair to ask so much of him. But I never meant to suggest that he was . . . was unfit." She gave Theo a frozen look of fury.

The judge noted the look and Theo's stiff frown but said nothing. Taking a deep breath, Cory made herself continue. "Sergeant Donatelli has been as good to my children as their own father would have been. For Timmy, my four-year-old, he's the only male role model he's ever had, and Timmy loves him very much. It will be . . . difficult when he leaves."

Macias cleared his throat. "I understand you wish to withdraw this petition."

"Yes, I do. I never should have asked Mr. Kennedy to file it."

Macias redirected his attention to Nick. "I have no objection, but I think the final decision should be up to you, Sergeant. Do you wish to continue as Joseph's temporary guardian?"

Cory waited for the hard tension in Nick's face to ease. It didn't. "If I don't, will he be allowed to remain with his mother?"

"No. He'll be returned to Juvenile Hall."

Nick looked down at his fist resting on the arm of the chair. When he'd first realized what Cory had set in motion, he'd wanted to strangle her. But now the rage he'd felt was directed at his own head.

He'd let himself hope, let himself believe, that he could start over. That, with Cory's help, he could someday put the remorse he felt behind him. But he knew now that he'd only been reaching for a dream that didn't exist.

Get out now, he told himself. Walk away and forget she ever existed.

But she did exist, she and the children he'd come to love, and he owed them all a debt he could never fully repay.

"I'll stay," he said, his gaze meeting the judge's head-on.

Macias's stern countenance softened into a brief smile. "Good," he said briskly, tucking his notes into the folder again before intoning, "The court will allow the petition to be withdrawn."

He nodded to the court reporter, who lifted her fingers from the steno machine and sat back, her expression distant.

Nick stood. "If that's all, sir, I'd like to get out of here. I've taken enough time off this week. More than enough."

"That's all, Sergeant. Thank you for coming."

Nick returned his nod, then turned to give Cory an impersonal look. "Don't wait dinner for me. I have work to catch up on." He was gone before she could answer.

The twisting country road was deserted. Weeds grew right to the ragged edges, and the tarmac was sun-bleached and crumbling. The Corvette rocked violently from one side to the other as it screamed around the corkscrew turns.

Nick drove with one hand, a rock and roll song turned to full volume on the tape deck. Behind his aviator sunglasses, his eyes were stormy. His mouth was clamped into a hard white line. Wind coming through the open windows drove his hair back from his forehead and blunted the metallic whine of the engine.

Gritting his teeth, he floored the accelerator, and the powerful car shot forward into the next turn. Gravel flew and the back fishtailed violently, but he held the heavy car on the road.

The next turn was even more treacherous, but he didn't slow. The Corvette careened out of the curve on two wheels, dust flying. Ahead, the tarmac ended abruptly, giving way to gravel for a hundred yards or so before running up against a heavy pipe gate. Barbed wire stretched to each side, blocking his way. He would die instantly if he hit the gate at this speed.

He braked hard, and the old car shuddered, the big mahogany steering wheel bucking and threatening to jerk from his hands. Cords stood out on his arms as he held on. At the last minute, just as the slowing vehicle was about to slam into the gate, he spun the wheel, and the Corvette rocketed around in a circle. It tipped to one side, nearly overturning, but the weight of Nick's body kept it upright.

Dust rose in a cloud, clogging his throat and stinging his eyes. Slowly he relaxed his grip on the wheel and wiped his sweating hands on his trousers. His heart was beating so violently he felt light-headed, and his vision was blurred.

He sat motionless, listening to the rasp of his breathing over the rumble of the idling engine. Damn, he hurt, he thought. Inside, where no one could see. As much as he'd hurt at Joe's funeral. More.

Slowly Nick folded his arms over the steering wheel and rested his forehead on the back of one wrist. Day by day, year by year, he'd tried so hard to change, to be the kind of man Cory could respect.

He'd turned himself inside out, fought battles that had left him bleeding inside, trying to make up for the pain he'd caused her. Hardest of all the things he'd done had been to ask her to forgive him. He'd been so damn sure she had—until today, when he'd walked into the ambush arranged by that bastard Kennedy.

Maybe she hadn't put the words on the paper, but she'd turned Kennedy loose on him. Maybe she'd really believed she was doing it for his sake, but he knew enough about human nature to know what was really going on. She'd wanted him gone, out of her life again—because she still didn't trust him not to hurt her.

He'd given her everything he had to give. Every damn thing. But it hadn't been enough. Nothing would ever be enough to wipe Joe's blood from his hands.

It would always be there, between them, no matter how hard they both tried to wipe it away. He'd made one mistake too many, and he would pay for that mistake for the rest of his life.

Chapter 15

Joey's trial was less than two weeks away when Theo called Cory and suggested that he meet with Nick and her to discuss the case. They settled on four o'clock on the Monday before Thanksgiving in his office, located in one of the newer buildings near the Spanish-style arcade.

"Your cheeks are pink," Theo commented as he helped her off with her coat.

"There's a wind," she said, her tone distant.

Theo hung her coat on a rack in the corner, then returned to his desk. "Thank you for coming. From the things you said to me after we left the judge's chambers, I was sure you were going to find another attorney."

"Theo, let's not go over this again, okay?" she said, settling into one of two armchairs reserved for visitors. The other was still empty. Nick was coming directly from work. "If you weren't the best attorney in town, I wouldn't be here."

"At least we agree on one thing," he said, one side of his mouth pulling into a rueful grin as he settled into his throne-like chair. "I *am* the best."

"You went too far, Theo."

"It was all true, every word."

"It was slanted, just like that newspaper article you quoted."

He looked away, then back at her face, his eyes clouding behind the clear lenses. "Donatelli is no good for you. He's responsible for your husband's death, for God's sake. What I can't understand is why you're defending him."

"I have my reasons."

Theo's fingers worried a slim gold pen back and forth on the blotter, his expression troubled. "You're in love with him, aren't you?"

"Yes."

Theo picked up the pen, looked at it, put it back down again. "Does he love you?"

"Would you, if you were him? After what I put him through?"

"Not you. Me. I'm the one who dug up the information in the brief. You just gave me a place to start, that's all."

"He doesn't believe that, and I don't blame him." Her gaze shifted again to the empty chair. She and Nick hadn't been alone since that day in Judge Macias's chambers. By his choice, not hers.

A dozen times she'd walked to his door, which was usually closed now, intending to explain. A dozen times she'd talked herself out of it. What could she say? I love you, but I was so certain you would hurt me again that I tried to send you away before it was too late? Admitting that would only deepen the wounds she'd already inflicted.

Theo cleared his throat. "Do you want me to talk to him, to explain my part in all this? I will, if you think it will help."

Cory considered his offer, but what good would it do? The basic problem hadn't changed. Nick couldn't fit into her world, and she couldn't handle his. It was better this way.

She shook her head. "It's too late. Maybe it always was. I don't know. I'm tired of trying to figure it all out."

"What about him?"

"You remember what Mount Saint Helens was like before it blew?"

"That bad, huh?" Theo asked with a self-conscious smile.

"Worse."

"Funny, I would have thought Donatelli was more like an iceberg than a volcano."

Cory felt herself beginning to smile, but it took too much effort. Everything did, these days. Even her usual excitement over the holidays was missing. In fact, she'd almost forgotten to buy the Thanksgiving turkey, until Jenny had reminded her.

"He's not the one who's ready to explode. I am."

The tension around Theo's mouth increased. "Men deal with hurt in a different way, Cory. Right now, I imagine he's still trying to deal with a feeling of betrayal. Once he works that through, who knows?"

"Who knows?" she echoed to be polite. But she already knew. Whatever feelings Nick had begun to have for her had been too fragile to withstand another slap in the face.

Theo's chair creaked as he shifted. "Hey, don't look so glum. The holidays are almost here. Peace on earth. Brotherly love. The time of miracles."

"I'm just trying to get through the Thanksgiving play at school," she said with a halfhearted grin. "After that—"

A sudden rap on the door interrupted her. It opened, and Theo's secretary entered.

"Sorry to interrupt, Mr. Kennedy, but Sergeant Donatelli is here."

Theo gave Cory a reassuring smile before turning to his secretary to say, "Send him in please, Gladys."

The prim middle-aged woman bobbed her head. "Right away," she said before disappearing.

Theo stood, tense, waiting. Cory sat up straighter, her mouth suddenly dry.

Nick brought the scent of the outdoors with him when he entered. His shoulders were rain-spotted, and his hair looked as though he'd given it a hasty brushing with his hand. It was too long, curling erratically behind his ears and over his collar. It seemed to Cory that there was now more gray mixed with the black.

His gaze swept the room, assessing everything, resting for an instant on her face. She started to smile, but he was already looking away to nod a cool greeting to Theo. Neither man seemed inclined to shake hands.

"Semi jackknifed on the Ventura," Nick said. "CHP had all but one lane blocked."

"Sounds bad," Theo said, waiting for Nick to sit first.

"Bad enough," Nick said, giving Cory the same impersonal nod he'd given Theo before shrugging out of his shabby leather jacket. He slung it carelessly over the back of the chair before settling into the seat and stretching out his legs.

He looked tired, and a perpetual frown seemed to have settled between his brows. Lack of sleep had lined his face, and his eyes were bloodshot. With the exception of the faint scar that had replaced the bullet crease, he looked worse than he'd looked that first morning when he'd just come off a stakeout.

The fact that she was responsible added fuel to the guilt burning inside her. Uncomfortable in his presence, she shifted in her chair, wondering with black humor if she dared ask Theo to turn up the thermostat to counter the chill Nick had brought with him into the room.

"One important thing first," Theo said as he sat down and reached for a thick folder. "Slovik's come up with two new witnesses." He opened the folder and took out a typewritten list. "Someone named Lawrence Evans, and a boy in Joey's class named Manuel Rodriguez."

"Manny," Nick muttered, sitting up and crossing one ankle over his knee.

"You know him?" Cory asked, looking at him directly for the first time in days.

"I've met him."

"When?"

Nick flicked dried mud from his boot, then turned to meet her gaze. There was no lazy smile, no softening around his mouth, no raw masculine hunger. His face was closed, the look of a stranger in his eyes. At that moment Cory felt the full force of all she'd lost.

"When I went out one day to ask some questions. It's what I do when I get a nagging feeling in my belly that someone's lying to me."

Cory felt heat surge to her cheeks. "Lying? Who?"

"Joey."

"No," she said, her voice unsteady. "He wouldn't."

Seeing the disbelief and hurt flood her eyes, Nick needed all of his considerable control to keep his gaze steady on hers. "He would, to keep from being punished."

"Exactly what did these boys tell you?" Theo asked, his voice now brisk and businesslike.

Shifting his attention to the man behind the desk, Nick recounted the conversation with nearly perfect recall. As he spoke, Cory got colder and colder, until she needed to hug herself to keep from shivering.

When Nick finished, Theo let out his breath in a long low whistle.

"What does that mean?" Cory asked, her expression mirroring the anxiety in her voice.

"It means we might be in big trouble," Theo told her with a calm that wasn't reflected in the quick look he and Nick shared.

Cory's chin angled into a stubborn line. "You don't believe them, do you, Theo?"

"I've never seen Joey drunk," he hedged. "Have you?"

She shook her head. "Of course not! I don't even have anything in the house. Ask Nick, if you don't believe me."

"I believe you," Theo said in a soothing tone. "But I also believe that those boys know something we don't."

Cory turned to Nick. "Is that what you think, too?"

"Far as I could tell, they had no reason to lie."

The last remnant of hope in her eyes died. "This isn't happening. I won't let it."

For days now Nick had kept himself angry enough inside so that he wouldn't feel anything else. Anger had kept him safe, distant. But now he was close enough to touch her, close enough to catch a whiff of her perfume when she moved, the same perfume that had lingered on his hands after they'd made love, and the need he always felt for her was returning, overriding the anger.

He wanted her, he would probably always want her, but he didn't need another lesson in pain to accept the fact that he and Cory would always be poles apart.

"There's something else you should know," he said to Theo instead of Cory. He stood up and pulled a small notebook from his back pocket. Still standing, he flipped to the last page.

He'd memorized the information as he'd taken it over the phone, but he needed something to keep his hands occupied and his mind off the woman next to him.

"Joey wasn't the only kid I checked on." He kept his mind focused on the facts and his gaze on Kennedy. "Before he and his family moved here a little over three years ago, Tobias Ramsay was arrested in San Diego for vandalism and malicious mischief."

"Well, well, well," Theo said, a wide grin breaking over his face. "That from a reliable source?"

Nick tore the pages from the book and dropped them in front of Theo. "The name of the kiddie cop in San Diego who handled the case is on the bottom of the last page, along with Toby's probation officer. You should be able to subpoena the records."

Cory blinked, her stomach clenching. "How come Davila didn't know all this?"

Nick took his time returning his notebook to his pocket. "Why should he? He had his case. Toby looked like a saint on paper. He probably looks great in person, as well."

"But . . . but that's not fair."

"It's the system." Nick sat down and tried to get comfortable in a chair that was too narrow and too soft. He felt trapped, caged, unable to escape. Next to him Cory was fighting a different battle, one she would have to fight alone, just as he was fighting his.

"This changes things a good one-hundred-eighty degrees." Theo said, sending a congratulatory look toward Nick. "With this I should be able to put enough doubt in Macias's mind to draw an acquittal."

"That's wonderful!" Cory exclaimed, her eyes brightening and her grin curving. "Isn't that wonderful, Nick? An acquittal!"

Relief erased the faint lines around her mouth, but the purple shadows beneath her eyes remained. He reminded himself that he couldn't afford to care.

"If that's what you want," he said without inflection.

"If... of course it's what I want. I'd want anything that kept Joey out of jail."

"Even if he's guilty?"

Cory shot to her feet and turned to face him. "Will you stop saying that? *He's not guilty!*"

Nick braced one foot against the massive desk and pushed the chair back onto two legs. "I think he is," he told her in a voice that was quiet but rasped with steel. "I think everything Davila said is true."

Cory saw the hard light of truth in his brown eyes, and her anger stuttered into raw fear. "You think he should go to jail?"

"I think he should admit responsibility for what he did and accept the consequences, no matter what they are. Joe would have felt the same way."

"But *jail!* That would kill a sensitive boy like Joey."

"It didn't kill me."

"You're stronger than he is."

"With you as his mother and Joe as his father?" he scoffed. "The kid has to have something inside him." He let the chair fall and stood up. "If he were my son, I'd tell him to plead guilty and do the six months without complaining."

He hooked the collar of his jacket with one finger and threw it over his shoulder. "I'm sorry, Cory. I didn't want to tell you these things. But I care too much for Joey to lie, even to keep from hurting you any more than I already have."

For an instant his hand came out, and she held her breath, certain that he would touch her face in the sensuous, possessive way she'd come to love. But his hand dropped before it reached her.

"I'm sorry, too," she said, her voice low and tinged with sadness.

One side of his mouth moved in what might have been a smile before he controlled it. "I'll see you at the house," he said before he walked out, leaving her standing there feeling as cold as ice.

Cory woke suddenly, her heart pounding. Her bedroom was bathed in moonlight, but the moon was no longer visible from her window. A quick glance at the clock told her it was still an hour before dawn.

Friday, she thought. No school because of the Thanksgiving holiday. She could sleep in for a few hours before she tried to figure out what to do with the leftover turkey no one had been particularly interested in eating.

Both she and Nick had tried to keep their rift from hurting the children, but they had sensed the tension. No one but Timmy had seemed to enjoy Thanksgiving.

Four more days, she told herself, and then life would get back to normal. No, not exactly normal. Life would go on, but there would be an empty place in the family where Nick had been.

Closing her eyes, she turned over and tried to sink into the heavy lethargy gripping her, but her body refused to relax. She was turning again when, suddenly, she heard a sound, like something heavy falling, followed by a muffled cry.

She shot up, her hand going to her throat. One of the children, she thought, throwing off the covers and scrambling into her robe.

She went from one room to the other. Jen was sleeping soundly. So was Timmy. Joey's bed was empty. Cory quickly tucked the covers closer to Timmy's curled body, then checked the bathroom. It, too, was empty.

Frowning, she hastened down the stairs. At the bottom the rumble of raised voices coming from the den caught her ear.

At the door, she froze. Joey was sitting on the floor, the shattered remnants of her ginger jar desk lamp surrounding him. The window over the desk had been opened wide, and the curtains fluttered in the brisk wind.

Nick, dressed only in half-buttoned jeans, stood with his bare feet spread wide, his fists anchored on his hips. ''Give me one good reason why I shouldn't haul you down to Juvenile Hall and leave you there to rot," he demanded in a tightly controlled tone.

Joey blinked with exaggerated slowness, as though he was having difficulty concentrating. "Just wanted to have a li'l fun," he muttered, his voice slurred.

"You're drunk."

Joey's grin was woozy, and he was having trouble focusing his eyes. "No way, man. Only had two beers."

"Don't try to run that bull on me, kid. I know drunk when I see it. And smell it."

Cory's hand crept to her mouth, and she slumped against the doorjamb. Neither of the two saw her, so intently were they staring at each other.

"Don't preach, man. I've seen you drunk lots of times," Joey said with a sloppy attempt to get up. He fell over, then righted himself and used the edge of the desk to pull himself to his feet.

Nick looked into the boy's drunken face and saw himself. Shame ran through him like a hot blade. Theo was right about him. He was one rotten example.

"This isn't about me," he said quietly. "This is about you."

"Right," Joey sneered, squinting against the glare from the overhead light. "Do what I say, not what I do. Isn't that the way it is with adults these days?"

"Have you seen me coming in drunk since I've been here?"

Confusion crossed Joey's face. "That's only 'cause Mom would kill you if you did."

A muscle stretched along Nick's shadowed jaw. "Wrong. I don't get drunk anymore because the last time I partied, I ended up killing the best friend I ever had."

Joey's face went white. "You're lying. I . . . Jen said . . . it wasn't your fault."

"Oh, yes, it was. If your dad had gone into that liquor store first, we'd both be alive. But I went first, splitting headache, queasy belly and all. No hangover was going to stop me, no way! Nick Donatelli could drink anyone under the table and work a double shift the next day, no sweat."

Cory's eyes misted, and her heart thudded heavily. Oh, Nick, she thought. I love you for what you're doing for my son. I wish it didn't hurt you so much to do it.

Nick had to take a deep breath before he could continue. He'd never told anyone but his brother the things he was telling Joey. But he was fighting for the kid's future the way he'd tried to fight for his own with Cory. Tried and failed. But maybe it wasn't too late for Joey.

"I was still congratulating myself on being such a hell of a man when that kid pulled a gun. Any other day and he would have been dead before he could get off a shot. But my reflexes were off, and your dad died because of it."

Joey's throat worked, but he couldn't seem to get out any words. Nick's own throat felt as though he had swallowed something barbed.

"Let me tell you what it's like living with guilt, kid. Every day when I open my eyes it's the first thing I think about. When I see you or Jen or Timmy, I remember why I'm here and your dad isn't. At work, a lot of the men who used to be my friends go out of their way to shun me, and I don't blame them. But there's nothing I can do to change the past, Joey. I can only try to change the man who made the mistake."

"But if that's true, Mom...you...I mean, she's not mad anymore."

"No, but she can't forget either."

Cory closed her eyes against a wave of pain. The sadness in his voice was tearing her apart, and yet she knew now that he was right. No matter how much she wanted to forgive Nick, a part of her was waiting for him to let her down again.

Nick drew in a slow, ragged breath. "For the rest of my life I'll have to live with what I did. And so will you. That's the way it is with mistakes. But you have what I don't, a chance to make things right before it's too late. Admit what you did, take whatever punishment the judge gives you, like the man your dad would want you to be, and then put it behind you."

Joey was beginning to look sick. His brows were drawn, his mouth white. "I can't go back to that place, Uncle Nick. Guys on dope...damn guards always staring, it'll kill me."

"No, it won't. But the things you're doing now might. Or, worse, make you wish you *were* dead."

Joey shook his head drunkenly from side to side. "Mom . . . Mom will never forgive me."

"Yes, she will, son. She loves you very much."

"I don't feel so good," Joey muttered, his voice slurring again. He took a step forward, then swayed and would have fallen if Nick hadn't caught him.

Cory gasped, her hand pressing her mouth. Both Joey and Nick swung around to stare at her. Nick's expression was tight, Joey's slack as his gaze dropped from his mother's white face to the floor beneath his sneakers.

"Is he all right?" she asked Nick, her voice thin with strain.

"He will be, after he sleeps it off."

Cory tried to swallow the sick feeling in her throat, but it only seemed to get worse. Pressing her hands tightly together, she crossed the room slowly until she and her son were only a few feet apart.

"Sweetie, Uncle Nick is right. I do love you. We can get through this together, I promise."

Joey's head bobbed drunkenly, and tears swam in his reddened eyes. "It was just a joke," he mumbled, his words nearly incoherent. "But that old guy, he went psycho on us, yelling, waving this broken bottle. It was an accident, Mom. I . . . honest."

"Baby," she said, her voice breaking. "We'll make it right. Somehow."

She started to put her arms around him, but Joey stumbled backward until he fell against the desk. "Don't hate me," he pleaded. "Please, Mom. Not like the way you hated Uncle Nick."

Before Cory could reach him, Joey suddenly turned sheet white. Clapping his hand over his mouth, he bolted from the room. Seconds later she heard the pounding of his feet on the stairs, followed by the slamming of the bathroom door.

Cory stared at the broken lamp, wind from the open window chilling her face. "My baby, my little boy, why didn't I know what was happening? Why didn't I see it?" She looked up at Nick's shadowed eyes, her own eyes brimming, her mouth shaking.

"You wanted to believe in your son. There's nothing wrong with that. I wanted to believe him, too."

He'd also wanted to spare her this. But maybe it was a good thing it had happened. Maybe now Joey would be forced to deal with his faults instead of running away from them, the way he'd done for too long.

"I . . . I have to do something, talk to him, get him some help." But Cory couldn't seem to move. Her feet felt rooted to the floor, and her body had gone strangely numb, as though all the blood had drained away. "I love him. I do."

The trembling of her mouth nearly undid his vow never to touch her again. "I know you do. He will, too, when he thinks about it."

"It's a parent's job to protect her child, to keep him safe and happy. But I didn't."

"If anyone's to blame, it's me. If I hadn't screwed up, Joey would still have the kind of father he needs."

Cory wanted to touch him, but she knew that would only lead to pain for both of them. "I don't blame you, Nick. Not for any of this. Please don't blame yourself."

Next to her, Nick muttered a low curse. "Come on, Cory. Let's get you to bed. I'll take care of Joey."

It was such a small thing, a light touch of his hand against her shoulder. But something told her he would never touch her again. She began to tremble, tears filling her eyes. "I . . . please hold me. Please."

His face tightened, but he turned her into his arms, holding her loosely. She buried her face against his chest and wrapped her arms around his waist.

"I thought I was so strong," she said, her tears dampening his skin. "So many things, Joe's death, Timmy's birth, moving here. I thought I was handling everything beautifully, piece of cake. Everyone said how brave I was, how . . . oh God. I made a mess of everything."

"No you didn't Cory. You gave your kids a great home, laughter, a whole lot of love. Some kids never have any of that."

Cory raised her head to look at him. The anguish she saw there made her breathing falter. "I never wanted to hurt you."

He released her and stepped back, as though he could no longer bear to touch her. "It'll always be there, the pain I caused you. That's what hurts."

Nick inhaled slowly, his big chest shuddering with the effort to keep his emotions under control. "I care about you and the kids, more than I've ever cared about anyone. I'm just sorry I can't be the man you deserve."

Before she could say anything, his hand cupped her chin, and he kissed her, without passion, without hunger. "You get some rest and try not to worry. I'll get Joey cleaned up and put him to bed. I've had a lot of practice with drunks."

And then he was walking away, his back straight, his shoulders braced. It was a long time before she could make herself leave the den.

"Mom?"

Cory looked up from the check she was writing to see Joey hovering at the door to the den. His face was pale, and his eyes were bloodshot. He was dressed in sweatpants and a T-shirt.

"How do you feel?" she asked without smiling.

"Lousy," he muttered. "I'm never going to drink again."

She allowed herself a small smile. "Can I get that notarized?"

It was nearly noon. Timmy was playing outside. Jen was at a friend's house. Nick had been gone when she'd dragged herself out of bed. A note on the refrigerator said he'd gone into the city to get his mail.

"I was really wiped out, wasn't I?"

"Yes, you were. Where was the party?"

"At Melissa's place. Her folks are out of town for the weekend." With one hand steadying his head, he walked to the sofa and carefully lowered his body until he was sitting on the edge of the cushion. Slowly he turned his head toward his mother. "I guess you're pretty mad at me."

"I think I have a right to be, don't you?"

"I guess," he said in a dispirited tone. "Is Uncle Nick mad, too?"

"I don't know. You'll have to ask him."

"Where is he?"

"In the city."

Joey's chest heaved in a deep sigh. "He's gonna kill me," he muttered. "I know he is."

Cory put down her pen and twisted in her chair until she was facing him directly. "Do you remember coming home?"

"Some. Sorry about the lamp."

"Do you remember the things Uncle Nick said to you?"

"Most of it, yeah. The man has a real burr up his—"

"Joey!"

"Sorry," he mumbled, his mouth taking on a sullen slant. "He didn't have any right to say those things. He's not my dad."

"That doesn't make him wrong."

"You weren't saying that four years ago!" he exclaimed. "What's changed? Is he that good in bed?"

Cory sucked in her breath, her pupils flaring with anger. "Don't you *ever* talk to me like that, Joseph Kingston. I don't deserve it, and you don't have the right."

Joey's mouth twitched, but his eyes blazed with defiance. "Then don't tell me what to do!"

"I'm not." Cory rose from her chair and crossed to the sofa. Bending her knees, she balanced on her haunches and took her son's hands in hers. "Joey, I would spend every cent I have, do everything within my power, to help you if you were innocent," she declared with quiet vehemence, her gaze holding his. "But I believe with all my heart that Uncle Nick is right. If you don't admit responsibility for the mistakes you've made, sooner or later, the guilt will destroy you."

His eyes flickered, but remained steady on hers. "You want me to go to jail, is that it?"

Cory swallowed hard. "If that's what has to happen, yes."

"No way! I'll do anything else, but that. You can't make me!"

Cory stood up and gave her son a sad smile. "I love you, Joey. And Uncle Nick loves you. We always will. But neither of us is very proud of you right now. Perhaps that doesn't bother you, but if it does, remember this. Only you can change that."

Nick parked the van in the usual spot. His own car was parked on the street. His suitcases were already in the trunk. He'd put them there this morning, before they'd left for court.

"Funny," Cory said, staring through the windshield. "Everything looks the same. The house, the yard, the...the wood that Joey was going to chop."

Nick pulled the key from the ignition and put the ring in her purse. "Six months isn't such a long time, Cory. He'll be back home before you know it."

But you won't, she thought. A holiday now and then, maybe a birthday, but not to stay. "I'm so proud of him. It must have been hard for him to stand up there and take the blame."

"Harder than you know," Nick said in a low tone. "But he's a good kid, Cory. As long as he knows you haven't given up on him, he'll be okay."

"You were there for him, too."

"But I didn't make the decision for him. He did." He pulled the knot of his tie free of the tight collar and undid the button.

Cory smiled. "At least you won't have to wear a tie for a while."

"Not until the next time I have to testify," Nick agreed, feeling the tension across his shoulders twist tighter. He opened the door and started to get out.

"Wait," Cory said in a soft voice. "Before you go, I want you to know that no one could have been a better father to Joey than you were while you were here. I want you to believe that, because it's true." She tried to smile. "I heard what you told him, and I know how hard it was to say those things, but you did it because you love him."

Nick felt as though he were strangling. "I tried, Cory. Harder than I've ever tried in my life," he said, taking her hand in his. His long fingers entwined with hers, holding her captive. She drew a shaky breath, loving the feel of her hand in his. And the smell of his skin. And the sheen of his silvered hair.

"I know you did," she said, her voice shaky. "So did I."

"I've been scared a lot in my life. Of my father when I was too scrawny to fight back, of dying in a rice paddy halfway across the world before my life had barely gotten started, of getting gut shot in the line of duty. But I could handle those things."

There was an air of steely control about him, and Cory realized he was reaching deep inside himself for the words he was saying, because he cared, because he wanted her to understand. She made herself smile in encouragement, but inside she was slowly being shredded by the pain.

"What I couldn't handle was the thought of being trapped, of being locked into someone else's life so tightly I would strangle on it. I don't know why I felt that way, but I did. I still do."

He raised her hand to his cheek for a long moment before releasing her and climbing from the van. Cory sat staring straight ahead as he came around to open her door.

He extended his hand, and she slipped hers into it. His fingers tightened as he helped her out. A cold wind from the north flattened her skirt against her legs and tore at the neat coil of her hair.

Nick moved to his right, blocking the worst of the wind's fury. "I'll keep a close check on Joey's progress," he said, his fingers coming up to brush away the wisps of hair loosened by the wind.

"Thank you." She was so tense it was difficult saying the words.

Nick, too, seemed to be having trouble speaking. He stood in silence, looking down at the ground. Finally he shifted his shoulders with military precision and raised his head to look at her. "Cory, there's a lot I could say, but it wouldn't help either one of us."

"No, you're right. Besides, we've played this scene before."

Nick smiled, despite the loneliness gnawing at him already. "Take care of yourself, okay? And the kids."

"Sure. You too."

He nodded. "Sorry I didn't get to build Tim the playhouse I promised him. I explained about the rains coming too soon, but I'm not sure he understood."

Cory drew a deep breath, twining both hands in the strap of her purse. Why didn't he just go? Dragging it out was pulling her apart inside. "Maybe this summer."

"Maybe." Nick glanced toward the Corvette. "Guess I'd better go."

"Yes, the traffic shouldn't be too bad this time of day."

The shiver of pain in her voice nearly did him in. "Goodbye, Cory."

"Take care." Slowly she bent forward to press her mouth to his. "I love you." She was fighting, even though she knew she had no chance to win.

A shudder passed through him, and his fingers closed around her arms. "Don't," he whispered hoarsely. "I can't stay."

Try as he might, he couldn't keep the pain out of his voice, and that gave Cory hope. She snatched at it, making her own voice soft and inviting. "Come at Christmas. Families should be together then."

His face twisted, and she saw the sheen of tears in his eyes. "I know the promises you want, and I want to give them to you. It's just..." He shrugged, his eyebrows pulling together. "I wouldn't be able to keep them."

Cory touched the triangle of tension at the corner of his mouth, her fingers shaking. "It doesn't matter anymore. I'll come to the city as often as I can. We'll find a way to make it work."

Nick felt the longing inside twist into raw pain. She would never know how touched he was by her caring. But it was time they both faced reality.

"My kind of life isn't for you, and I can't change. Sooner or later, you would come to hate me for forcing you into it." He trapped her hand and turned his head to kiss the pulse beating in her wrist. "It nearly killed me when you hated me. I couldn't go through that again."

He pulled her into his arms and kissed her, his mouth sliding over hers with a hungry longing that made her ache inside. His restraint was palpable, his pain even more so.

"Please, Nick," she whispered, tears streaming down her face. "Don't go."

"I have to. Otherwise, I would destroy us both."

He pulled her arms from his neck, turned, and walked away while he still had the will to leave her.

Chapter 16

Tony's fist plowed into Nick's gut, and Nick's breath exploded from his lungs. He fell back against the corner post and slid to the mat, his head spinning, his arms and legs leaden.

Tony shook the sweat from his face and spat out his mouthpiece. "Had enough, *fratello?*" he asked, his eyes pitying.

Nick removed his own mouthpiece. "Give me a minute," he said between gasps. He hung his head and fought a sickening dizziness.

"Forget it. If you want to kill yourself, you'll have to do it without my help."

Ignoring the stony glare Nick sent his way, Tony sat down next to him and rested his back against the ropes. "Settle this, Nicky. Either go back to her, or find a way to cut her out of that stubborn head of yours."

Nick wiped a soaked tangle of hair from his forehead with the back of his sweat-slick boxing glove. "What makes you think this has anything to do with Cory?"

"Because you've been strung tight ever since you got back from Ojai. You're almost as bad as you were after Joe died.

I'm half afraid to answer my phone at night for fear it'll be you on the other end, stupid drunk and ready to pick a fight."

Nick closed his eyes. "I'm not drinking."

"You're thinking about it, though, aren't you?" Tony pulled up one long, muscular leg and rested his crooked arm on his knee.

Nick opened one eye and looked at his brother. "What makes you so damn smart?" Tony was right. He was beginning to think he would resort to almost anything to get her out of his mind for a day, even a few hours.

Tony's mouth drooped. He looked older, tired. The divorce was taking its toll. "Because I've been in the same hell as you for months now—only I want to go back and Stacy won't have me."

"That's because you love her. I don't love Cory."

Tony grimaced. "The hell you don't! I've never seen a man have it so bad."

Nick stared at him, the midnight silence of the gym turning tense. "It's not love, it's sex."

Tony muttered a crude and succinct rebuttal. "If it's sex you want, how come you're not out right now with a willing lady?"

"Too busy."

"Tell me another one, little brother. You're so sick with wanting that woman, I would be doing you a favor if I *did* punch your lights out."

Nick rapped the back of his head against the post, his need for Cory as alive and twisting as the stinging ache in his gut. "I wish you would," he said in a gritty voice. "I wish the hell you would."

Nick sifted through the mail in his hands without much interest. Bills, circulars, a few Christmas cards, nothing very interesting, he decided, until he came to a large red envelope addressed in Jenny's handwriting.

God, he missed her, he thought. He missed all of them, but most of all, he missed Cory and the peace she'd given him. He hadn't slept worth a damn since he'd gotten home.

Most nights he spent more time on the beach than he spent in his bed, and as for all that freedom he'd wanted, he didn't seem to have the inclination to use it much.

Now and then he filled in at poker when one of the other detectives couldn't make the regular Wednesday night game, but that was mostly because he was so damn glad to be included again. Last Sunday Bill Frazier had talked him into going to the Raiders' game, where he'd spent the afternoon looking for Cory's face in the crowd. Not that he'd expected to see her. It was just that he was always looking for her, everywhere he went.

In the three weeks since he'd left, he'd seen her only once, when they'd coincidentally visited Joey at the same time. She'd looked good. Maybe a little pale, but her smile was just as sweet and her eyes just as soft. Too soft. They still haunted him.

"Damn," he muttered, walking toward his apartment. When did the wanting stop?

"Hi, stranger. Long time no see." He looked up to find the tall blond divorcée from the next apartment standing in front of her door. Coconut-scented lotion gleamed on the lush tanned breasts threatening to spill from the top of her bikini, and her sunglasses had been pushed to the top of her head, revealing eyes that were a sultry gray, smiling at him. From the paperback in her hand and the faint sunburn on her skin, he guessed that his neighbor had spent the day enjoying the unseasonably warm weather.

Her name was Ms. Deborah Granville to her clients, Deb to her friends and lovers, of whom Nick could be the next. She'd made that plain enough the few times they'd seen each other.

California sleek, with a perfect smile and expensive streaks in her upscale hairdo, she sold computer hardware to corporations in the Southwest, earning more in a week than he made in a month.

She was also persistent. He'd been dodging her subtle and not-so-subtle invitations for weeks. "How's it going?" he managed with a decent amount of civility.

"Couldn't be better! As soon as I change, I'm heading for my travel agent's office to pick up my tickets to Cancun for Christmas."

"Sounds nice," Nick said, fishing in his jacket pocket for his keys. "The computer business must be booming."

Deb laughed, then edged closer, her exotic face upturned toward his. "How about you? What are you doing for Christmas?"

"Nothing much," he said, catching a whiff of expensive perfume. "Thought I might do some skiing at Tahoe, if I can scrounge a reservation. Or I might head over to Hawaii for the sun. Haven't decided yet."

After all, he was free to go where he wanted, when he wanted, wasn't he? Damn straight he was! So why wasn't he doing it?

He thought about his brother's words. In his own finely tuned male assessment, the lady was attractive, sexy, intelligent—with a hell of a body, and a look in her eyes that said she would be just as wild as he wanted her to be. Best of all, having a good time was the most important thing in her life—next to her job. They were two of a kind. A perfect match.

"Are you thinking of going alone?" she asked.

Alone was relative. These days he was alone in the middle of a crowd. "Yeah, alone."

Deb smiled, sexual invitation shimmering in her eyes. "I reserved a king-size bed," she said, her voice a suggestive purr. "How about sharing it with me?"

"Momma, the angel's crooked."

Cory glanced down from the ladder at Timmy's frowning face. He'd been impossible since Nick had left. Nothing pleased him, not even the adorable tabby kitten she'd bought him, and he'd started having temper tantrums, something he'd never done before.

She herself had felt the same urge to scream and stamp her feet—between bouts of the worst depression she'd ever had.

"How's this?" she asked, straightening the angel's gilt wings.

"Looks dumb," Timmy grumbled. "I hate this old tree, and I hate Christmas."

Struggling with a need to cry, Cory climbed down from the ladder and sat beside him on the floor. "Santa will be here tonight, Timmy," she said, animating her voice. "Better not let him hear you."

Timmy pulled apart a leftover tangle of silvery icicles. "I'd rather have Uncle Nick come," he mumbled, his mouth drooping.

So would I, Cory thought. But in the real world we don't always get what we want most.

"He's busy, Timmy. I've explained that a dozen times. He has other responsibilities. And he did send you a present." She leaned forward to pluck a heavy red and green package from beneath the tree. It rattled like a toy truck. "Would it help you to like Christmas better if you opened it now?"

Timmy shook his head. "I want Uncle Nick."

"Well, he's not coming," Jenny said as she marched into the room and flopped down on the sofa. "I called his office to wish him Merry Christmas, and they said he was on vacation until after the first. But when I called his apartment, all I got was a stupid machine."

Cory returned the package to the place of honor under the tree and pulled Timmy into her lap. The little boy slumped against her and began sucking his thumb.

"Uncle Nick didn't like Christmas much," Cory told her daughter over her son's head. "He told me once his mother and father hated each other so much they spoiled every holiday with their fights."

"Is that why he isn't here? 'Cause you and him were fighting?"

Cory shook her head. "We weren't fighting, Jen."

Jenny rested her head against the sofa back. "I know. I heard him come out of your room one night."

Cory kept her face blank. "Does that bother you?"

Jenny grimaced. "I know the facts of life, Mom," she said in a disgusted tone. "I thought it was neat. Uncle Nick is awfully good-looking. I bet he's great in bed."

Cory felt her face flame. "Don't talk like that," she chided, but her heart wasn't in it. With Joey in Juvenile Hall and Nick gone for good, the holidays were turning into a series of dreary gray days, in spite of the bright winter sky outside.

The clock began to bong, and she sighed. "C'mon, Jen. Help me get Timmy ready for church."

Christmas Eve services were at seven and eleven. For Timmy's sake, they were going to the earlier one. Later, when he was asleep, she would put out Santa's presents and be asleep herself by eleven, even if she had to drink the entire bottle of vintage wine one of the parents at school had given her.

"Mom, look!" Jenny's voice came out in a swoop of excitement.

"I see, Jen." Nick's Corvette was parked directly under the streetlight in front of the house. So she would see it as soon as she came home? she wondered, excitement slamming her heart against her ribs.

"Wake up, Timmy," Jenny called in a happy tone over her shoulder. "Uncle Nick's at our house."

Timmy's eyes opened, and he looked around in confusion. "Are we home?" he murmured with a sleepy yawn.

"Yes," Jenny said with a wide grin. "And Uncle Nick is here."

Cory pulled into the driveway, her hands shaking so violently she had trouble controlling the steering wheel. Jenny had her seat belt off and the door opened before Cory had time to turn off the engine. Her orange parka was a blur as she ran toward the porch.

Cory extricated Timmy from his safety seat, laughing through her galloping nerves as he chattered about Christmas, about Santa. And, most of all, about Uncle Nick.

"Hurry, Momma," he urged. "Uncle Nick is here."

Cory stepped back, and Timmy scrambled out, then took off running, calling Nick's name. Such a simple thing, she thought. A man comes home and all's right with the world. Or is it?

Just because he'd come for Christmas didn't mean he'd come for good. Remember that, Cory, before you start spinning dreams again, she told herself as she closed the van door and walked slowly toward the house.

Nick was sitting on the steps with Timmy nestled on one knee and his arm around Jenny, who was leaning against him like a small animal seeking shelter.

"Well, well, well," she said, keeping her tone teasing and a smile plastered on her face. "Saint Nick."

He looked startled before his mouth curved into a wicked grin. "I'm no saint."

"No," she said, her voice suddenly husky. He wasn't a saint, but she loved him dearly. She knew now that she always would.

Cory walked past him to unlock the door, then stood and watched while first Timmy and then Jenny claimed his attention, their voices sometimes tumbling over each other. He listened and laughed and asked questions, his deep voice husky with affection.

Finally he called a halt. "You two scoot inside while I talk to your mom, okay?" he said to the children, his gaze going to Cory's face.

Timmy started to protest, but Jenny scooped him from Nick's knee. "C'mon, Timmy. Let's go turn on the tree lights." As her daughter walked past Cory into the house, she grinned. Cory attempted to grin back, but her lips were too stiff.

"So, how are you?" Nick asked as he stood up and came closer. Soap and sandalwood, she thought, and a look of loneliness around his eyes—those things hadn't changed.

"I'm doing fine," she lied. "How about you?"

"Do you want the truth?" The raw note in his voice shivered through her.

She nodded, too nervous to trust her voice.

He shifted, and the porch light caught a look of pain on his face. "My gut can't take any more of my brother's left jabs, I've lost half a month's pay in poker, and I passed up a hell of a trip to Cancun, all because I'm about to go crazy if I don't kiss you soon."

Her lips curved—soft and willing, as he'd been praying they would be—and Nick felt some of the knots begin to unravel in his tight muscles.

"Feel free," she murmured, laughter and tears mingling together in her voice.

He pulled her to him, one hand at her waist, the other hooked around the back of her neck. Her purse fell to the porch floor with a thud, and she rose on tiptoe, winding her arms around his neck so that she could pull herself closer.

His mouth was warm, seeking. Hers was eager, welcoming. Their lips clung, hearts pounding, bodies crushing together. When he dragged his mouth from hers, they were both breathing hard.

With the impatient, quick movements that she now associated only with him, his hands were busy removing the pins from her hair and dropping them to the floor. When they were all lying around their feet, he began combing her hair over her shoulders with his fingers. "There, that's better," he said with a heartfelt sigh.

Cory smiled. "Why do I always end up disheveled around you?"

His hands stilled. "I was afraid I'd lost you." The words seemed to shudder from him. "All the way up here I was rehearsing this great speech, all the reasons why you should let me back into your life."

For the first time in weeks her body felt buoyant and her smile felt natural on her lips. "Actually, I only need to hear one thing," she said.

His dark eyebrows drew together. "What?"

"That you want me."

His fingers tightened into a fist in her hair. "Want you, need you, adore you," he said in a voice deepened by emotion. "God, how I want you."

He kissed her with such gentleness that she felt the last lingering doubt sink away from her. Now they would both begin to heal, really heal.

Nick drew away but kept his hands on her shoulders. He was afraid to let go, afraid to hope. "Did you mean what you said the day I left?"

Cory frowned. "The day you left?"

"Yes." Nick swallowed hard. This was a thousand times more difficult than he'd imagined. "You said you loved me."

"Oh, that."

Nick felt panic begin to churn in his stomach. It couldn't be too late. He wouldn't let it be. Not even if he had to get down on his knees and beg.

"Yes, that, damn it. I spent a lot of energy telling myself it couldn't be true. That you were grateful because of Joey. That you were a hopeless romantic. That you would always hold Joe's death against me. Half the guys at work think I've gone deaf because they have to repeat things to me three and four times before they can penetrate the damn fog you've put me in."

He looked fiercely angry and, for the first time since they'd met, intensely unsure of himself.

She touched his face, her eyes shimmering and steady on his. "I meant it. I love you, Nick. Just the way you are."

His eyes grew dark, and his mouth took on an uncharacteristic vulnerability. "I know it's a gamble, Cory. Your life is here, I work in L.A. Even if the Ojai P.D. would have me, I'd lose seniority and probably have to take a pay cut. I'm not what my mother used to call a great catch."

Cory held her breath. What was he saying? That he was moving in?

"Living here isn't as expensive as the city," she said with just a hint of humor in her tone. But inside, she was shaking.

"Is that right?"

Cory nodded. "That's right."

Nick drew a long slow breath. "I've been on my own so long I'll probably make a lousy husband, but I'm willing to fight to make it work. If you'll have me."

Her chin angled, charming him and terrifying him at the same time. "Under one condition."

Dread thudded in his gut. He wasn't a man to accept restrictions, but if that was what she wanted, he would try. Because he didn't have a choice. Because he was only half alive without her.

"What condition is that?" He kept his hands easy on her shoulders, his head up.

"That we start over, from this moment. Just the two of us. No past, no ghosts."

Nick's face stilled. In his eyes, illuminated by the glow of the light, she saw the shadows deepen before they slowly faded into a look of wonder.

"I don't deserve you," he whispered, his voice unsteady, his thick lashes blinking raggedly. "But, God, I can't make it without you, Cory. Not anymore."

"I need you, too."

"Does that mean you'll marry me?"

"I don't know. Marriage. That sounds serious." She moved closer, needing to feel his hard strength.

Desire uncoiled inside him, making it difficult for him to concentrate on anything but the soft mouth smiling just for him. "You're enjoying this," he accused, his voice deep with frustration.

"Promise me you'll accept my condition. We've both cried for Joe, but he wouldn't want us to grieve forever."

Nick closed his eyes and pulled her against him. There was a catch in his voice as he whispered, "I accept. Now, tell me you'll marry me before I go completely crazy."

Cory felt laughter bubble. "I'll marry you," she whispered, feeling his body shudder.

It took a great deal of effort to control the wild rush of relief that ran through him. Maybe God didn't hate him after all.

His arms tightened until she couldn't breathe. His own breathing came hard. When he finally drew back, his mouth slanted into a self-conscious smile. "Can an engaged man sleep with his fiancée openly in front of her children, or do I have to sneak out before dawn again?"

"No more sneaking," she said, happiness radiating from her smile.

"Thank God," he murmured, his smile crooked. "I haven't had a decent night's sleep since I left here."

"Neither have I," she said through a sudden swelling of tears in her throat.

"Tonight, *carisima*. And for the rest of our lives."

* * *

"Timmy's gotten taller," Nick murmured against Cory's hair. It was Christmas night, and they were alone in Cory's bed. The children were asleep, and the house was quiet.

"He's growing out of everything, just like Joey did at his age," Cory said, snuggling deeper into Nick's arms. They tightened immediately, and he brushed a kiss over her temple.

"Jen looks terrific, almost as great as her mom. How much weight has she lost?"

She ran her finger along the corded arm holding her close. "Eleven pounds. She's given up desserts and second helpings. Speaking of which, there's more pie."

Nick shook his head. "I'm glad I don't have to wear a uniform anymore," he said with an exaggerated sigh. "Otherwise, I'd never get it buttoned after all that turkey you forced down me."

"Me?" Cory turned her head to kiss his wrist. "You're the one who kept asking for seconds and thirds and..."

Nick turned her toward him and silenced her with a kiss before tucking her into the curve of his shoulder again.

"Nick?"

"Hmm?" His eyes were closed, and his features were relaxed. But there was a look of tension around his mouth that made her uneasy.

"Don't you think Joey looked good today?" she asked. "I mean, really good. Like he's glad we're getting married?"

His blunt black lashes lifted, revealing a look of drowsy contentment in his brown eyes. "Seems to be," he said with a slow smile. "He called me 'Dad' when I hugged him goodbye."

"He did? I didn't hear him."

"Does that bother you?" An alert look replaced the contented heaviness around his eyes.

"No, I think it's wonderful. He needs a father. All the kids do. They love you."

"I love them, too," he said, feeling his throat constrict. Talking about feelings always made him edgy. He balanced Cory's hand on his palm. It was the left, the one that would soon wear his ring. Raising her hand to his lips, he kissed the ring finger.

"How would you feel about me adopting your children? If that's what they want, I mean."

"I'd love it." Even as she smiled, she wondered what was bothering him. The restless look was back in his eyes.

She withdrew her hand and sat up, her body twisting at the waist so that they were face to face. "But most of all I want what you want. I want to make you happy, really happy, the way you make me."

He dropped his gaze. "I, uh, was reading this article the other day. About vasectomies and how they can be reversed in some cases."

Cory felt her breath stop. "Are you saying you want to try for a child?" she asked, not daring to hope.

His eyes slowly rose to meet hers. "I'd like that, yes. If you would."

She threw her arms around his neck and hugged him. "I'd love it! When can you have it done?"

His laugh rumbled in his throat. "Well, not before the honeymoon, and maybe not for a long time afterward."

She drew back. "Okay, but this year. I'm not getting any younger, and neither are you."

Nick frowned, but inside, the hard edges of his loneliness were melting, making him feel warm and safe for the first time in his adult life. "Speak for yourself, woman. I'll have you know I can do more pushups than any of the rookies down at the station."

Cory reveled in the teasing glint in his eyes as she ran her hands over the heavy muscles of his chest. "My hero."

"Hero?" he grumbled. "I was horny as hell without you. I had to do something to get my mind off this sexy little body you keep pressing up next to me." He skimmed his palm over the creamy skin of her belly, his fingers ruffling the soft mound of hair between her legs.

Desire kindling, Cory pretended to pout. "You weren't complaining last night."

"I was half-crazed last night. You damn near wore me out."

"I beg your pardon? Who was doing the wearing out at six o'clock this morning?"

Nick blushed, and Cory laughed. "See."

Nick felt himself drowning in the loving light in her eyes. Slowly he raised his hand to touch her face. "It's more than sex, Cory. I never knew why I couldn't get you out of my head," he said, his voice rough with feeling. "Other women came and went, becoming blurs in my mind. But you..." He sighed. "You were my partner's wife, and I would wake up in the middle of the night, in his house, wanting you so much I knew I was going to burn in hell because of it. But I couldn't seem to stop."

Cory saw the anxiety in his face and wondered why these words were costing him so much to say. "Did Joe know?"

He shook his head. "No one knew but me. I was re-signed to taking my feelings to the grave."

Her pulse hammered. "You almost did," she said with a small shiver of memory. "I came to the hospital to tell you that I had forgiven you. But you passed out before I could get out the words."

Painful memories clouded his eyes. "I was awake. I felt your hands on my face. I knew when you kissed me."

Cory stared at him. "You were faking?"

He looked embarrassed. "I was afraid you'd leave if you knew I was awake. I had been hurting for so long, I needed you to be there, for as long as you would stay."

Cory shook her head. "You're impossible, you know that? I can see life is going to be very interesting around here from now on."

Nick tried to smile at the pleased-as-punch grin spreading over her glowing face. But suddenly he knew he was close to losing it. It was the closest he'd come to falling apart since Joe's death. But it wasn't grief that was tearing at him; it was another emotion, almost too strong to handle.

He took her mouth over and over, trying to tell her without words how much she meant to him. How much she would always mean to him. But the feelings inside him were too strong, too elemental, to control. His arms crushed her to him, and he buried his face in the fragrant warmth of her neck.

"Nick, what's wrong?" Cory asked in alarm, her arms tightening around his neck. "You're shaking. What is it? Tell me."

When he felt strong enough to face her, he drew back. His eyes were embarrassingly moist, his smile unsteady. Her green eyes searched hers, her mouth slightly parted, worry and love mingling on her face.

"I love you, Cory. I think I always have. That's why I could never forget you." He pulled her close and pressed a kiss to her throat. "Without you, I'm just a guy with a past and a big hole in his life."

Cory felt his lashes tickle her throat and then a faint dampness on her skin. Her fingers threaded into the familiar thickness of his hair, and a smile warmed her face. "And with me, Nick? What are you then?"

He lifted his head and looked into the eyes that had haunted him so long, the eyes that shone now with love—for him. "Happy," he said with the lopsided, sexy smile she loved. "For the first time in my life."

*   *   *   *   *

SILHOUETTE·INTIMATE·MOMENTS®

COMING
NEXT MONTH

#401 DESERT SHADOWS—Emilie Richards
Private investigator Felice Christy's latest assignment was driving her crazy! Stuck in a convent pretending to be a nun in order to protect a *real* sister, she had to deal with new handyman Josiah Gallagher, too. His drifter act didn't fool her for a moment. But did he spell trouble for her mission . . . or her heart?

#402 STEVIE'S CHASE—Justine Davis
Chase Sullivan's shadowed past made him a loner by necessity, *not* by choice. Then sweet Stevie Holt stepped into his life, and he dared to dream that things could be different. Suddenly he realized that he'd placed Stevie's life in danger, and unless he did something—quickly— they would *both* be dead.

#403 FORBIDDEN—Catherine Palmer
Federal narcotics agent Ridge Gordon's cover as a college football player didn't stop him from making a pass at sexy English professor Adair Reade. But when new evidence pointed to her involvement in the very drug ring he'd been sent to bust, he fumbled. Was he falling in love with a drug runner?

#404 SIR FLYNN AND LADY CONSTANCE—
Maura Seger
When Constance Lehane's brush with date rape ended in tragedy, she hired criminal lawyer Flynn Corbett to defend her against a possible murder charge. Instinctively she knew that his passion for the law would save her, yet the flames that burned between them hinted at a different sort of passion altogether. . . .

AVAILABLE THIS MONTH:

Take 4 bestselling love stories FREE

Plus get a FREE surprise gift!

SILHOUETTE®
OFFICIAL SWEEPSTAKES
RULES

NO PURCHASE NECESSARY

1. To enter, complete an Official Entry Form or 3" × 5" index card by hand-printing, in plain block letters, your complete name, address, phone number and age, and mailing it to: Silhouette Fashion A Whole New You Sweepstakes, P.O. Box 9056, Buffalo, NY 14269-9056.

   No responsibility is assumed for lost, late or misdirected mail. Entries must be sent separately with first class postage affixed, and be received no later than December 31, 1991 for eligibility.

2. Winners will be selected by D.L. Blair, Inc., an independent judging organization whose decisions are final, in random drawings to be held on January 30, 1992 in Blair, NE at 10:00 a.m. from among all eligible entries received.

3. The prizes to be awarded and their approximate retail values are as follows: Grand Prize — A brand-new Ford Explorer 4×4 plus a trip for two (2) to Hawaii, including round-trip air transportation, six (6) nights hotel accommodation, a $1,400 meal/spending money stipend and $2,000 cash toward a new fashion wardrobe (approximate value: $28,000) or $15,000 cash; two (2) Second Prizes — A trip to Hawaii, including round-trip air transportation, six (6) nights hotel accommodation, a $1,400 meal/spending money stipend and $2,000 cash toward a new fashion wardrobe (approximate value: $11,000) or $5,000 cash; three (3) Third Prizes — $2,000 cash toward a new fashion wardrobe. All prizes are valued in U.S. currency. Travel award air transportation is from the commercial airport nearest winner's home. Travel is subject to space and accommodation availability, and must be completed by June 30, 1993. Sweepstakes offer is open to residents of the U.S. and Canada who are 21 years of age or older as of December 31, 1991, except residents of Puerto Rico, employees and immediate family members of Torstar Corp., its affiliates, subsidiaries, and all agencies, entities and persons connected with the use, marketing, or conduct of this sweepstakes. All federal, state, provincial, municipal and local laws apply. Offer void wherever prohibited by law. Taxes and/or duties, applicable registration and licensing fees, are the sole responsibility of the winners. Any litigation within the province of Quebec respecting the conduct and awarding of a prize may be submitted to the Régie des loteries et courses du Québec. All prizes will be awarded; winners will be notified by mail. No substitution of prizes is permitted.

4. Potential winners must sign and return any required Affidavit of Eligibility/Release of Liability within 30 days of notification. In the event of noncompliance within this time period, the prize may be awarded to an alternate winner. Any prize or prize notification returned as undeliverable may result in the awarding of that prize to an alternate winner. By acceptance of their prize, winners consent to use of their names, photographs or their likenesses for purposes of advertising, trade and promotion on behalf of Torstar Corp. without further compensation. Canadian winners must correctly answer a time-limited arithmetical question in order to be awarded a prize.

5. For a list of winners (available after 3/31/92), send a separate stamped, self-addressed envelope to: Silhouette Fashion A Whole New You Sweepstakes, P.O. Box 4665, Blair, NE 68009.

PREMIUM OFFER TERMS
To receive your gift, complete the Offer Certificate according to directions. Be certain to enclose the required number of "Fashion A Whole New You" proofs of product purchase (which are found on the last page of every specially marked "Fashion A Whole New You" Silhouette or Harlequin romance novel). Requests must be received no later than December 31, 1991. Limit: four (4) gifts per name, family, group, organization or address. Items depicted are for illustrative purposes only and may not be exactly as shown. Please allow 6 to 8 weeks for receipt of order. Offer good while quantities of gifts last. In the event an ordered gift is no longer available, you will receive a free, previously unpublished Silhouette or Harlequin book for every proof of purchase you have submitted with your request, plus a refund of the postage and handling charge you have included. Offer good in the U.S. and Canada only.

SLFW-SWPR

SILHOUETTE® OFFICIAL SWEEPSTAKES ENTRY FORM

4-FWSIS-2

Complete and return this Entry Form immediately – the more entries you submit, the better your chances of winning!

- Entries must be received by **December 31, 1991**.
- A Random draw will take place on **January 30, 1992**.
- No purchase necessary.

Yes, I want to win a FASHION A WHOLE NEW YOU Sensuous and Adventurous prize from Silhouette:

Name _____ Telephone _____ Age _____

Address _____

City _____ State _____ Zip _____

Return Entries to: **Silhouette FASHION A WHOLE NEW YOU,**
P.O. Box 9056, Buffalo, NY 14269-9056   © 1991 Harlequin Enterprises Limited

PREMIUM OFFER

To receive your free gift, send us the required number of proofs-of-purchase from any specially marked FASHION A WHOLE NEW YOU Silhouette or Harlequin Book with the Offer Certificate properly completed, plus a check or money order (do not send cash) to cover postage and handling payable to Silhouette FASHION A WHOLE NEW YOU Offer. We will send you the specified gift.

OFFER CERTIFICATE

Item	A. SENSUAL DESIGNER VANITY BOX COLLECTION (set of 4) (Suggested Retail Price $60.00)	B. ADVENTUROUS TRAVEL COSMETIC CASE SET (set of 3) (Suggested Retail Price $25.00)
# of proofs-of-purchase	18	12
Postage and Handling	$3.50	$2.95
Check one	☐	☐

Name _____

Address _____

City _____ State _____ Zip _____

Mail this certificate, designated number of proofs-of-purchase and check or money order for postage and handling to: **Silhouette FASHION A WHOLE NEW YOU Gift Offer,** P.O. Box 9057, Buffalo, NY 14269-9057. Requests must be received by December 31, 1991.

ONE PROOF-OF-PURCHASE

4-FWSIP-2

To collect your fabulous free gift you must include the necessary number of proofs-of-purchase with a properly completed Offer Certificate.

© 1991 Harlequin Enterprises Limited

See previous page for details.